Edward Payson Roe

Poetic jewels

Edward Payson Roe

Poetic jewels

ISBN/EAN: 9783337137984

Printed in Europe, USA, Canada, Australia, Japan

Cover: Foto ©Andreas Hilbeck / pixelio.de

More available books at **www.hansebooks.com**

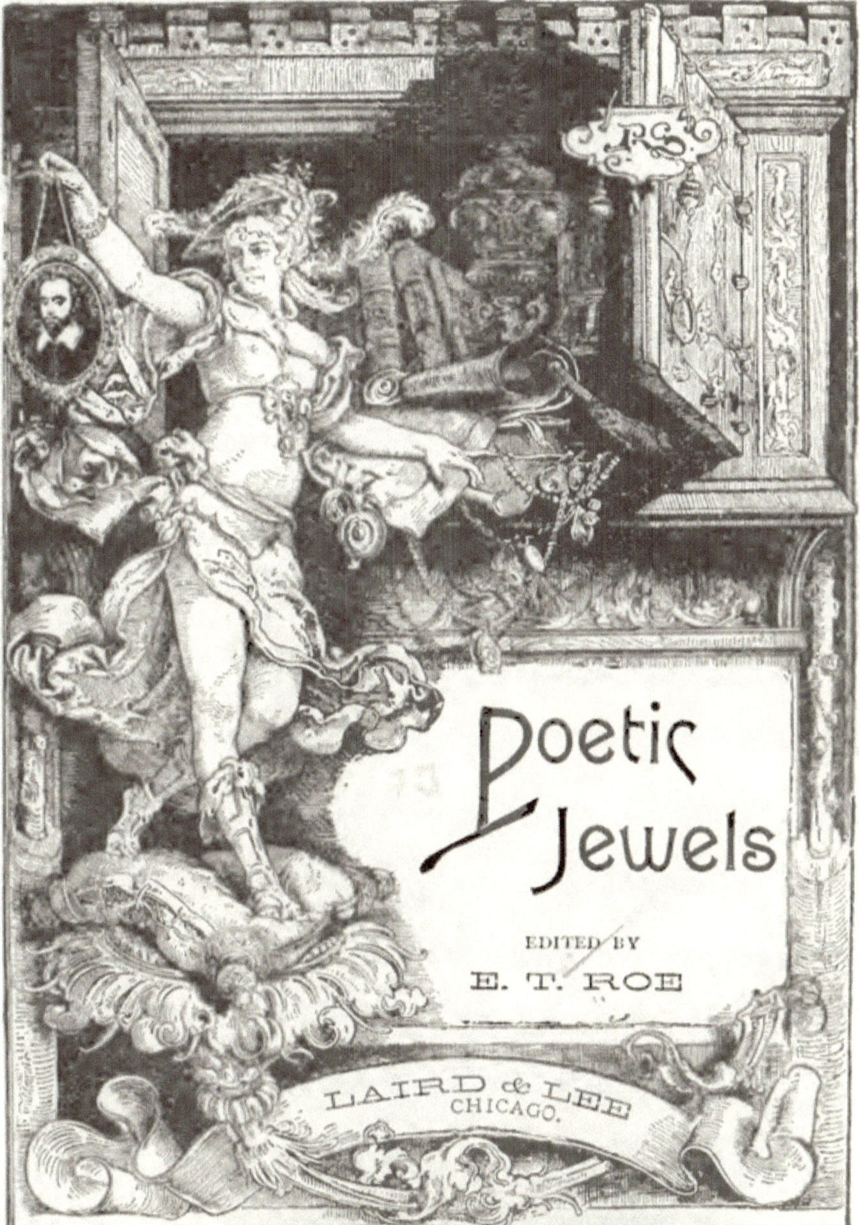

Poetic
Jewels
EDITED BY
E. T. ROE
LAIRD & LEE
CHICAGO.

PREFACE.

THE poems contained in this volume have not been gathered at random. They have been carefully sought after, and selected from amongst the most admired poetry in the English language. In many instances the authors themselves have been consulted as to the selections to be made from their poems, and some of the most eminent poets have themselves selected their favorite poems for this collection.

It has been the aim of the editor in making up this volume to place in an accessible form, the rarest gems of English poetry.

" For this end I have risen early and sat up late, have traveled far and near, ransacking the most famous libraries, and all to furnish you this magazine of the most excellent erudition."

E. T. R.

Poetic Jewels.

LIST OF AUTHORS.

LIST OF ENGRAVINGS.

Be thou the first true merit to befriend;
His praise is lost, who stays till all commend.
Short is the date, alas, of modern rhymes,
And 'tis but just to let them live betimes.

Pope.

WILLIAM CULLEN BRYANT.

Roslyn, Long Island N.Y.
June 29th 1877—

Dear Sir:

If any poem that I have written suits the purpose which you have in view you are welcome to take it for the Athenæum. You intimate that I might suggest some poem suitable for recitation. I will do so, but with this reservation, that you will not take it if you prefer another.

There is the poem entitled "Not Yet" which Mrs. Siddons recited with much effect giving the concluding "No" with different intonations — as there is the poem entitled "Italy", which might perhaps answer. For a more pathetic strain there is "Waiting at the Gate". But do not take either unless they suit you best.—

Yours truly,
W. C. Bryant

Mr. E. T. Roe.

P. S. Thanks for the Athenæum, which is well edited—
W. C. B.

NOT YET.

OH country, marvel of the earth!
　　Oh realm to sudden greatness grown!
The age that gloried in thy birth,
　　Shall it behold thee overthrown?
Shall traitors lay that greatness low?
　　No, land of Hope and Blessing, No!

And we, who wear thy glorious name,
　　Shall we, like cravens, stand apart,
When those whom thou hast trusted aim
　　The death-blow at thy generous heart?
Forth goes the battle-cry, and lo!
　　Hosts rise in harness, shouting, No.

And they who founded in our land,
　　The power that rules from sea to sea,
Bled they in vain, or vainly planned
　　To leave their country great or free?
Their sleeping ashes, from below,
　　Send up the thrilling murmur, No!

Knit they the gentle ties which long
　　These sister States were proud to wear,
And forged the kindly links so strong
　　For idle hands in sport to tear?
For scornful hands aside to throw?
　　No, by our fathers' memory, No!

Our humming marts, our iron ways,
  Our wind-tossed woods on mountain crest,
The hoarse Atlantic, with its bays,
  The calm, broad ocean of the West,
And Mississippi's torrent-flow,
  The loud Niagara, answer, No!

Not yet the hour is nigh when they
  Who deep in Eld's dim twilight sit,
Earth's ancient kings, shall rise and say,
  " Proud country, welcome to the pit!
So soon art thou, like us, brought low! "
  No, sullen group of shadows, No!

For now, behold the arm that gave
  The victory in our fathers' day,
Strong, as of old, to guard and save —
  That mighty arm which none can stay —
On clouds above and fields below,
  Writes, in men's sight, the answer, No!

                William Cullen Bryant.

ITALY.

VOICES from the mountains speak;
  Apennines to Alps reply;
Vale to vale and peak to peak
  Toss an old remembered cry;
        Italy
        Shall be free!
Such the mighty shout that fills
All the passes of her hills.

All the old Italian lakes
  Quiver at that quickening word;
Como with a thrill awakes;
  Garda to her depths is stirred;
        Mid the steeps
        Where he sleeps,
Dreaming of the elder years,
Startled Thrasymenus hears.

Sweeping Arno, swelling Po,
  Murmur freedom to their meads.
Tiber swift and Liris slow
Send strange whispers from their reeds.
        Italy
        Shall be free,
Sing the glittering brooks that slide.
Toward the sea, from Etna's side.

Monarchs! ye whose armies stand
   Harnessed for the battle-field!
Pause, and from the lifted hand
   Drop the bolts of war ye wield.
      Stand aloof
      While the proof
Of the people's might is given;
Leave their kings to them and Heaven

Long ago was Gracchus slain;
   Brutus perished long ago;
Yet the living roots remain
   Whence the shoots of greatness grow.
      Yet again,
      God-like men,
Sprung from that heroic stem,
Call the land to rise with them.

They who haunt the swarming street,
   They who chase the mountain boar,
Or where cliff and billow meet,
   Prune the vine or pull the oar,
      With a stroke
      Break their yoke;
Slaves but yestereve were they —
Freemen with the dawning day.

Looking in his children's eyes,
   While his own with gladness flash,
" These," the Umbrian father cries,
   " Ne'er shall crouch beneath the lash!
      These shall ne'er
      Brook to wear

Chains whose cruel links are twined
Round the crushed and withering mind."
Stand aloof, and see the oppressed
  Chase the oppressor, pale with fear,
As the fresh winds of the west
  Blow the misty valleys clear.
      Stand and see
      Italy
Cast the gyves she wears no more
To the gulfs that steep her shore.

Wm. Cullen Bryant.

HOW BABY CAME FROM HEAVEN.

ONE night, as old Saint Peter slept,
  He left the door of Heaven ajar
When through a little angel crept,
  And came down with a falling star.

One summer, as the blessed beams
  Of morn approached, my blushing bride
Awakened from some pleasing dreams,
  And found that angel by her side.

God grant but this — I ask no more —
  That when he leaves this world of sin,
He'll wing his way to that blest shore,
  And find the door of Heaven again.

David Barker.

WAITING BY THE GATE.

ESIDE a massive gateway, built up in years
    gone by,
Upon whose top the clouds in eternal shadow lie,
While streams the evening sunshine on quiet
    wood and lea,
I stand and calmly wait till the hinges turn for me.

The tree-tops faintly rustle beneath the breeze's flight,
A soft and soothing sound, yet it whispers of the night;
I hear the woodthrush piping one mellow descant more,
And scent the flowers that blow when the heat of day
    is o'er.

Behold the portals open, and o'er the threshold now
There steps a weary one with a pale and furrowed brow;
His count of years is full, his allotted task is wrought;
He passes to his rest from a place that needs him not.

In sadness then I ponder how quickly fleets the hour
Of human strength and action, man's courage and his
    power.
I muse while still the woodthrush sings down the golden
    day,
And as I look and listen the sadness wears away.

Again the hinges turn, and a youth, departing, throws
A longing look backward, and sorrowfully goes;
A blooming maid, unbinding the roses from her hair,
Moves mournfully away from amidst the young and fair.

Oh glory of our race that so suddenly decays!
Oh crimson flush of morning that darkens as we gaze!

WAITING AT THE GATE.

Oh breath of summer blossoms that on the restless air
Scatters a moment's sweetness and flies we know not where.

I grieve for life's bright promise, just shown and then
    withdrawn;
But still the sun shines round me: the evening birds sing
    on,
And I again am soothed, and, beside the ancient gate,
In this soft evening sunlight, I calmly stand and wait.

Once more the gates are opened; an infant group go out,
The sweet smile quenched forever, and stilled the sprightly
    shout.
Oh frail, frail tree of Life, that upon the greensward
    strows
Its fair young buds unopened, with every wind that blows!

So come from every region, so enter, side by side,
The strong and faint of spirit, the meek and men of pride.
Steps of earth's great and mighty, between those pillars
    gray,
And prints of little feet, mark the dust along the way.

And some approach the threshold whose looks are blank
    with fear,
And some whose temples brighten with joy in drawing
    near,
As if they saw dear faces, and caught the gracious eye
Of Him, the sinless Teacher, who came for us to die.

I mark the joy, the terror; yet these, within my heart,
Can neither wake the dread nor the longing to depart;
And, in the sunshine streaming on quiet wood and lea,
I stand and calmly wait till the hinges turn for me.

William Cullen Bryant.

SLEEP.

F all the thoughts of God that are
Borne inward unto souls afar,
Among the Psalmist's music deep,
Now tell me if that any is
For gift or grace surpassing this:
" He giveth his beloved sleep "?

What would we give to our beloved?
The hero's heart, to be unmoved;
The poet's star-tuned harp, to sweep;
The patriot's voice, to teach and rouse;
The monarch's crown, to light the brows?
" He giveth his beloved sleep."

What do we give to our beloved?
A little faith, all undisproved;
A little dust, to over weep;
And bitter memories, to make
The whole earth blasted for our sake. —
" He giveth his beloved sleep."

" Sleep soft, beloved ! " we sometimes say,
But have no tune to charm away
Sad dreams that through the eyelids creep;
But never doleful dream again
Shall break the happy slumber when
" He giveth his beloved sleep."

" More softly than the dew is shed,
  Or cloud is floated overhead."

O earth, so full of dreary noise!
O men, with wailing in your voice!
O delved gold the wailers heap!
O strife, O curse, that o'er it fall !
God strikes a silence through you all,

And " giveth his beloved sleep."
His dews drop mutely on the hill,
His cloud above it saileth still,
Though on its slope men sow and reap;
More softly than the dew is shed,
Or cloud is floated overhead,
" He giveth his beloved sleep. "

For me, my heart, that erst did go
Most like a tired child at a show,
That sees through tears the mummers leap, .
Would now its wearied vision close,
Would childlike on His love repose,
" Who giveth his beloved sleep."

Elizabeth Barrett Browning.

" GOD KNOWS."

[AN emigrant ship recently foundered in a storm, and of the 220 who went down, only one — a little child — drifted ashore. When the waif was laid at rest from her troubled baptism, somebody asked the question, " What name ? " and the reply was, " God knows." A gentleman present, touched by the words, caused a headstone to be erected bearing only this : " GOD KNOWS."]

I.

AN emigrant ship with a world aboard
 No tatter of bunting at half-mast lowered,
Went down by the head on the Kentish coast,
 No cannon to toll for the creatures lost.
Two hundred and twenty their souls let slip,
Two hundred and twenty, with speechless lip,
Went staggering down in the foundered ship!

II.

Nobody can tell it — not you nor I,
 The frenzy of fright when lightning thought
Wove like a shuttle the far and the nigh,
 Shot quivering gleams through the long forgot,
And lighted the years with a ghastly glare,
A second a year, and a second to spare!
'Mid surges of water and gasps of prayer.

III.

The heavens were doom, and the Lord was dumb,
 The cloud and the breaker were blent in one,
No angel in sight — not any to come!
 God pardon their sins for the Christ His Son!
The tempest died down as the tempest will,
The sea in a rivulet drowse lay still,

As tame as the moon on the window-sill,
The roses were red on the rugged hill —
The roses that blow in the early light,
And die into gray in the mists of night.

IV.

Then drifted ashore, in a night-gown dressed,
   A waif of a girl with her sanded hair,
And hands like a prayer on her cold blue breast,
   And a smile on her mouth that was not despair.
No stitch on the garment ever to tell
Who bore her, who lost her, who loved her well,
·Unnamed as a rose — was it Norah or Nell?

V.

The coasters and wreckers around her stood
   And gazed on the treasure-trove upward cast,
As round a dead robin the sturdy wood,
   Its plumage all rent and the whirlwind past.
They laid a white cross on her home-made vest,
The coffin was rude as a red-breast's nest,
And poor was the shroud, but a perfect rest
Fell down on the child like dew on the West.

VI.

A ripple of sod just covered her over,
   Nobody to bid her " Good-night, my bird!"
Spring waited to weave a quilt of red clover,
   Nobody alive had her pet name heard.
" What name?" asked the preacher.   " GOD KNOWS!"
   they said,
Nor waited nor wept as they made her bed,
But sculptured " GOD KNOWS!" on the slate at her
   head.

VII.

The legend be ours when the night runs wild,
  The road out of sight and the stars gone home,
Lost hope or lost heart, lost Pleiad or child,
  Remember the words at the nameless tomb!
Bewildered and blind the soul finds repose,
Whether cypress or laurel blossoms and blows,
Whatever betides, for the good " God Knows! "
" God knows" all the while, our blindness His sight,
Our darkness His day, our weakness His might!

Benjamin F. Taylor.

PARTING LOVERS.

LOVE thee, love thee, Giulio!
 Some call me cold, and some demure,
And if thou hast ever guessed that so
 I love thee — well; the proof was poor,
 And no one could be sure.

My mother, listening to my sleep,
 Heard nothing but a sigh at night —
The short sigh rippling on the deep —
 When hearts run out of breath and sight
 Of men, to God's clear light.

When others named thee — thought thy brows
 Were straight, thy smile was tender — " Here
He comes between the vineyard-rows?"
 I said not " Ay,"— nor waited, dear,
 To feel thee step too near.

I left such things to bolder girls,
 Olivia or Clotilda.   Nay,
When that Clotilda, through her curls,
 Held both thine eyes in hers one day,
 I marveled, let me say.

I could not try the woman's trick:
 Between us straightway fell the blush
Which kept me separate, blind and sick.
 A wind came with thee in a flush,
 As blown through Horeb's bush.

3

But now that Italy invokes
  Her young men to go forth and chase
The foe or perish — nothing chokes
  My voice, or drives me from the place:
  I look thee in the face.

I love thee! it is understood,
  Confest: I do not shrink or start;
No blushes: all my body's blood
  Has gone to greaten this poor heart,
  That, loving, we may part.

Our Italy invokes the youth
  To die if need be.　Still there's room,
Though earth is strained with dead, in truth.
  Since twice the lilies were in bloom
They have not grudged a tomb.

And many a plighted maid and wife
  And mother, who can say since then
" My country," cannot say through life
  " My son," " my spouse," " my flower of men,"
  And not weep dumb again.

Heroic males the country bears,
  But daughters give up more than sons.
Flags wave, drums beat, and unawares
  .You flash your souls out with the guns,
  And take your heaven at once!

But *we* — we empty heart and home
  Of life's life, love! we bear to think
You're gone — to feel you may not come ---
  To hear the door-latch stir and clink
  Yet no more you — — nor sink.

Dear God! when Italy is one,
  And perfected from bound to bound —
Suppose (for my share) earth's undone
  By one grave in't! as one small wound
  May kill a man, 'tis found.

What then?   If love's delight must end,
  At least we'll clear its truth from flaws.
I love thee, love thee, sweetest friend!
  Now take my sweetest without pause,
  To help the nation's cause.

And thus of noble Italy
  We'll both be worthy.   Let her show
The future how we made her free,
  Not sparing life, nor Giulio,
  Nor this — this heart-break.   Go!

        Elizabeth Barrett Browning

THE LADY'S DREAM.

THE lady lay in her bed,
  Her couch so warm and soft,
But her sleep was restless and broken still ;
  For, turning often and oft
From side to side, she muttered and moaned,
  And tossed her arms aloft.

At last she started up,
  And gazed on the vacant air,
With a look of awe, as if she saw
  Some dreadful phantom there —
And then in the pillow she buried her face
  From visions ill to bear.

The very curtain shook,
    Her terror was so extreme;
And the light that fell on the broidered quilt
    Kept a tremulous gleam;
And her voice was hollow, and shook as she cried :
    " O, me! that awful dream!

" That weary, weary walk,
    In the church-yard's dismal ground!
And those horrible things, with shady wings;
    That came and flitted round —
Death, death, and nothing but death,
    In every sight and sound!

" And, O! those maidens young
    Who wrought in that dreary room,
With figures drooping and specters thin,
    And cheeks without a bloom —
And the voice that cried, ' For the pomp of pride,
    We haste to an early tomb!

" ' For the pomp and pleasure of pride,
    We toil like Afric slaves,
And only to earn a home at last
    Where yonder cypress waves; '
And then they pointed — I never saw
    A ground so full of graves!

' And still the coffins came,
    With their sorrowful trains and slow;
Coffin after coffin still,
    A sad and sickening show;
From grief exempt, I never had dreamt
    Of such a world of woe!

" Of the hearts that daily break,
    Of the tears that hourly fall,
Of the many, many troubles of life,
    That grieve this earthly ball —
Disease, and Hunger, and Pain, and Want —
    But now I dreamt of them all!

" For the blind and the cripple were there,
    And the babe that pined for bread,
And the houseless man, and the widow poor
    Who begged — to bury the dead;
The naked, alas! that I might have clad,
    The famished I might have fed!

" The sorrow I might have soothed,
    And the unregarded tears;
For many a thronging shape was there,
    From long-forgotten years —
Ay, even the poor rejected Moor,
    Who raised my childish fears!

" Each pleading look, that long ago,
    I scanned with a heedless eye,
Each face was gazing as plainly there
    As when I passed it by;
Woe, woe for me, if the past should be
    Thus present when I die!

" No need of sulphureous lake,
    No need of fiery coal,
But only that crowd of human kind
    Who wanted pity and dole —
In everlasting retrospect —
    Will wring my sinful soul!

" Alas! I have walked through life
　　Too heedless where I trod;
Nay, helping to trample my fellow-worm,
　　And fill the burial sod —
Forgetting that even the sparrow falls
　　Not unmarked of God!

" I drank the richest draughts,
　　And ate whatever is good —
Fish, and flesh, and fowl, and fruit,
　　Supplied my hungry mood;
But I never remembered the wretched ones
　　That starve for want of food!

" I dressed as the noble dress,
　　In cloth of silver and gold,
With silk, and satin, and costly furs,
　　In many an ample fold;
But I never remembered the naked limbs
　　That froze with winter's cold.

" The wounds I might have healed!
　　The human sorrow and smart!
And yet it was never in my soul
　　To play so ill a part;
But evil is wrought by want of thought,
　　As well as want of heart! "

She clasped her fervent hands,
　　And the tears began to stream;
Large, and bitter, and fast they fell,
　　Remorse was so extreme;
And yet, O yet, that many a dame
　　Would dream the Lady's Dream!

Thomas Hood.

AULD ROBIN GRAY.

[This touching little ballad has received many tributes of commendation from eminent bards and critics. Sir Walter Scott wrote: " Auld Robin Gray is the real pastoral which is worth all the dialogues which Coridon and Phillis have had together, from the days of Theocritus downwards;" and Leigh Hunt said of it, " It has suffused more eyes with tears of the first water than any other ballad that ever was written." For a long time the poem was of unknown authorship, and so general was the interest exhibited regarding it that its author was advertised for in the public press, a reward being offered for the discovery.

The first part of the ballad has appeared in several works on elocution, but it is believed that the piece is now printed entire for the first time in this country.]

I.

WHEN the sheep are in the fauld, and the kye's
    come hame,
And a' the warld to rest are gane,
The waes o' my heart fa' in showers frae my e'e,
Unkent by my gudeman, who sleeps sound by me.

Young Jamie lo'ed me weel, and he sought me for his
    bride,
But saving a crown-piece, he had naething beside;
To make the crown a pound, my Jamie gaed to sea,
And the crown and the pound they were baith for me.

He hadna been gane a twelvemonth and a day,
When my father broke his arm, and the cow was stown
    away;
My mither she fell sick — my Jamie at the sea;
And auld Robin Gray came a-courting me.

My father couldna work, and my mither couldna spin;
I toiled day and night, but their bread I couldna win; —
Auld Rob maintained them baith, and, wi' tears in his
    e'e,
Said, " Jeanie, oh, for their sakes, will ye no marry me? "

My heart it said na, and I looked for Jamie back;
But hard blew the winds, and his ship was a wrack;
The ship was a wrack—why didna Jamie dee?
Or why am I spared to cry, Wae is me?

My father urged me sair — my mither didna speak;
But she looked in my face till my heart was like to break;
They gied him my hand — my heart was in the sea —
And so Robin Gray he was gudeman to me.

I hadna been his wife a week but only four,
When, mournfo' as I sat on the stane at my door,
I saw my Jamie's ghaist, for I couldna think it he,
Till he said, " I'm came hame, love, to marry thee."

Oh, sair, sair did we greet, and mickle say of a';
I gied him a kiss, and bade him gang awa';—
I wish that I were dead, but I'm wae like to dee;
For though my heart is broken, I'm but young, **wae is me**.

I gang like a ghaist, and carena much to spin;
I darena think o' Jamie, for that wad be a sin;
But I'll do my best a gude wife to be,
For oh, Robin Gray, he is kind to me.

II.

The spring had passed over, 'twas summer nae **mair**,
And, trembling, were scattered the leaves in the air.
" Oh, winter," cried Jeanie, " we kindly agree,
For wae looks the sun when he shines upon me."

Nae longer she wept, her tears were a' spent;
Despair it was come, and she thought it content;
She thought it content, but her cheek was grown pale,
And she drooped like a snow-drop broke down by the hail.

Her father was sad, and her mother was wae,
But silent and thoughtfu' was auld Robin Gray;
He wandered his lane, and his face was as lean
As the side of a brae where the torrents have been.

He gaed to his bed, but nae physic would take,
And often he said, " It is best, for her sake !"
While Jeanie supported his head as he lay,
The tears trickled down upon auld Robin Gray.

" Oh, greet nae mair, Jeanie !" said he, wi' a groan;
" I'm nae worth your sorrow — the truth maun be known;
Send round fur your neebors — my hour it draws near,
And I've that to tell that it's fit a' should hear:

" I've wranged her," he said, " but I kent it o'er late;
I've wranged her, and sorrow is speeding my date;
But a's for the best, since my death will soon free
A faithfu' young heart, that was ill-matched wi' me.

" I lo'ed and I courted her mony a day,
The auld folks were for me, but still she said nay;
I kentna o' Jeanie, nor yet o' her vow ; —
In mercy forgi'e me, 'twas I stole the cow!

" I cared not for crummie, I thought but o' thee;
I thought it was crummie stood 'twixt you and me;
While she fed your parents, oh! did you not say,
You never would marry wi' auld Robin Gray?

" But sickness at hame, and want at the door —
You gi'ed me your hand, while your heart it was sore;
I saw it was sore, why took I her hand?
Oh, that was a deed to my shame o'er the land!

" Now truth, soon or late, comes to open daylight!
For Jamie cam' back, and your cheek it grew white;
White, white grew your cheek, but aye true unto me—
Oh, Jeanie, I'm thankfu'— I'm thankfu' to dee!

" Is Jamie came here yet?" and Jamie he saw;
" I've injured you sair, lad, so I leave you my a';
Be kind to my Jeanie, and soon may it be !
Waste no time, my dauties, in mournin' for me."

They kissed his cauld hands, and a smile o'er his face
Seemed hopefu' of being accepted by grace ;
" Oh, doubtna," said Jamie, " forgi'en he will be,
Wha wauldna be tempted, by love, to win thee ?"

*   *   *   *   *

The first days were dowie, while time slipt awa';
But saddest and sairiest to Jeanie of a'
Was thinking she couldna be honest and right,
Wi' tears in her e'e, while her heart was sae light.

But nae guile had she, and her sorrow away,
The wife of her Jamie, the tear couldna stay;
A bonnie wee bairn — the auld folks by the fire —
Oh, now she has a' that her heart can desire!

Lady Anne (Lindsay) Barnard.

Scotland, 1750–1825.

A SONG OF PRAISES.

SPIRIT haunted me long years ago,
  And played his fairy pranks with thought and
      feeling;
  Through the rosy light's bewitching glow,
  I saw all things were beautiful, and kneeling
At the shrine of Beauty, I adored
  The world so full of loveliness and gladness.
A few short years of youth sometimes afford
  Sad change! I had my change of sadness.
Then all things took the same sad hue,
  While yet the spirit haunted me a season,
Still discoloring the Beautiful and True,
  Till I awoke from poetry to reason.

Then years went by in prose, so true, so real,
  That the spirit moved my song no more,
And I had wandered from the false Ideal;
  And my dreamy days of life were o'er,
When yet once more my spirit claimed my measure,
  Waking me to other songs than those
I sung in early years of youth and pleasure;
  Unto God my new-waked song arose!
      Praise to the God of Beauty!

For the lily, and the race of flowers,
  For the forest and its monarch trees,
For the tangled brake and shady bowers,
  For all their warbling birds and humming bees,
For the dew-drop and the radiant cloud,
  For the rainbow and the gentle rain,
For summer's mantle and for winter's shroud —

For all that's beautiful on hill or plain,
    We praise thee, God of Beauty.

For the surges of the rolling ocean,
    For the rivers and their tumbling tide,
For the thunder's roar and lightning's motion;
    For the mountain's and the glacier's slide.
For the boreal and the austral ices,
    For the lava from the crater's fire,
For Day, when all his gorgeousness entices,
    For starry Night, with all her bright attire,
        We praise thee, God of Grandeur.

For all the joys of Home's endearing altar,
    For parents, children, brothers, sisters, all!
For the tried and true fast friends who never falter,
    For all who minister at mourning's call,
For succor, and for sympathizing sorrow,
    For love, hope, memory, hours of joy and gladness,
        We praise thee, God of Love.
Thou who didst make earth, air, and everything that is,
Sun, moon and stars — the universe is His,
    Praise to the God, Jehovah.
Thou who didst limit the illimitable void,
    And plant the boundaries of time and space,
Thou who didst make all things to be enjoyed,
    O may we feel the glory of thy grace.

        O God of light and love,
    For the earth, the air, the ocean,
    We offer thee devotion,
        Thou God above.

For our bodies, for our spirit,
For the life that we inherit,
For existence and salvation,
We offer adoration,
Now and forever,
To the glorious giver,
      GOD.   *Edward R. Roe.*

AIRY VISIONS.

I WATCHED a summer cloud dissolve —
  It brought no rain;
But like my simple heart's resolve,
  'Twas formed in vain.

Floating in its azure sea
  With gold it gleamed,
And rather than a cloud to me
  A boat it seemed —

A far off phantom fairy sail,
  But growing near —
Oh, in that azure calm how frail!
  To disappear.

Across my soul's calm sea there floats
  A golden dream,
All bright and fair as cloudlet boats
  In azure gleam.

'Tis far away and hard to solve —
  But why my fear?
Do all things bright and fair dissolve
  In growing near?
              E. T. R

CLEOPATRA.

HERE, Charmion, take my bracelets –
    They bar with a purple stain
My arms; turn over my pillows—
    They are hot where I have lain;
Open the lattice wider,
    A gauze on my bosom throw,
And let me inhale the odors
    That over the garden blow.
I dreamed I was with my Antony,
    And in his arms I lay;
Ah, me! the vision has vanished —
    Its music has died away;
The flame and the perfume have perished,
    As this spiced aromatic pastille,
That wound the blue smoke of its odor,
    Is now but an ashy hill.
Scatter upon me rose leaves,
    They cool me after my sleep,
And with sandal odors fan me
    Till into my veins they creep;
Reach down the lute, and play me
    A melancholy tune,
To rhyme with the dream that has vanish'd,
    And the slumbering afternoon.
There, drowsing in golden sunlight,
    Loiters the slow, smooth Nile,
Through slender papyri, that cover
    The sleeping crocodile.
The lotus rolls on the water,
    And opens its heart of gold,

And over its broad leaf pavement
  Never a ripple is rolled.
The twilight breeze is too lazy
  Those feathery palms to wave,
And yon little cloud is as motionless
  As stone above a grave.
Ah me! this lifeless nature
  Oppresses my heart and brain!
Oh! for a storm and thunder —
  For lightning and wild, fierce rain!
Fling down that lute — I hate it!
  Take rather this buckler and sword,
And crash and clash them together
  Till this sleeping world is stirred!
Hark! to my Indian beauty —
  My cockatoo, creamy white,
With roses under his feathers,
  That flash across the light.
Look! listen! as backward and forward
  To his hoop of gold he clings,
How he climbs with crest uplifted,
  And shrieks as he madly swings!
O cockatoo, shriek for Antony!
  Cry, " Come, my love, come home!"
Shriek, " Antony! Antony! Antony!"
  Till he hears you even in Rome.
There — leave me, and take from my chamber
  That wretched little gazelle,
With its bright black eyes so meaningless,
  And its silly tinkling bell!
Take him — my nerves he vexes —
  The thing without blood or brain —

Or, by the body of Isis,
   I'll snap his thin neck in twain!
Leave me to gaze at the landscape
   Mistily stretching away,
When the afternoon's opaline tremors
   O'er the mountains quivering play,
Till the fiercer splendor of sunset
   Pours from the West its fire
And melted, as in a crucible,
   Their earthly forms expire;
And the bald, blear skull of the desert
   With glowing mountains is crowned,
That, turning like molten jewels,
   Circle its temples round.

I will lie and dream of the past time,
   Æons of thought away,
And through the jungle of memory
   Loosen my fancy to play;
When, a smooth and velvety tiger,
   Ribbed with yellow and black,
Supple and cushioned-footed,
   I wandered, where never the track
Of a human creature had rustled
   The silence of mighty woods,
And fierce in a tyrannous freedom,
   I knew but the law of my moods;
The elephant, trumpeting, started
   When he heard my footsteps near,
And the spotted giraffe fled wildly
   In a yellow cloud of fear.

I sucked in the noontide splendor,
   Quivering along the glade,

Or yawning, panting, and dreaming,
  Basked in the tamarisk shade,
Till I heard my wild mate roaring,
  As the shadows of night came on,
To brood in the trees' thick branches,
  And the shadow of sleep was gone;
Then I roused and roared in answer,
  And unsheathed from my cushioned feet
My curving claws, and stretched me,
  And wandered my mate to greet.
We toyed in the amber moonlight,
  Upon the warm, flat sand,
And struck at each other our massive arms —
  How powerful he was and grand!
His yellow eyes flashed fiercely
  As he crouched and gazed at me,
And his quivering tail, like a serpent,
  Twitched, curving nervously;
Then like a storm he seized me,
  With a wild, triumphant cry,
And we met, as two clouds in heaven
  When the thunders before them fly.
We grappled and struggled together,
  For his love, like his rage, was rude;
And his teeth in the swelling folds of my neck
  At times, in our play, drew blood.
Often another suitor —
  For I was flexile and fair —
Fought for me in the moonlight,
  While I lay crouching there,
Till his blood was drain'd by the desert;
  And, ruffled with triumph and power,

He licked me, and lay beside me
  To breathe him a vast half-hour.
Then down to the fountain we loitered,
  Where the antelopes came to drink ;
Like a bolt we sprang upon them,
  Ere they had time to shrink.
We drank their blood and crushed them,
  And tore them limb from limb,
And the hungriest lion doubted
  Ere he disputed with him.
That was a life to live for!
  Not this weak human life,
With its frivolous, bloodless passions,
  Its poor and petty strife!
Come to my arms, my hero;
  The shadows of twilight grow,
And the tiger's ancient fierceness
  In my veins begins to flow.
Come not cringing to sue me!
  Take me with triumph and power,
As a warrior that storms a fortress!
  I will not shrink nor cower.
Come as you came in the desert,
  Ere we were women and men,
When the tiger passions were in us,
  And love as you loved me then!

                By W. W. Story.

KATYDID.

SULTRY was the summer evening,
  And the weather hot and dry;
Here and there a small cloud lingered
  In the crimson western sky.

But when night had spread her mantle
  Over woodland, vale, and hill,
Not a zephyr was then wafting,
  E'en the aspen leaf was still.

Languidly I sat reposing,
  Half asleep, within the glade,
When methought I heard a murmuring
  Voice amidst the maple shade.

Silently I sat and listened,
  Wondering if there could be
Dryad, sylvan elf, or fairy,
  Hiding in the maple tree;

Not a leaf to me seemed moving,
  But amidst the branches hid,
Something in a voice mysterious,
  Softly whispered " Katydid."

What? But not another sentence
  Fell upon my anxious ear;
Could some disembodied spirit
  From another world be near?

Half ashamed, I asked the question,
  Is it friend or foe that's hid?
Or is there a spirit present?
  Still the answer " Katydid."

Who was Kate? and where her dwelling?
    Was there any one could tell?
Was she some lone Indian maiden,
    And the fairest of the dell?

Seriously I put the query,
    To what seemed so strangely hid,
" *Can a woman keep a secret?* "
    Still the answer " Katydid."

What could be the solemn mystery,
    So religiously concealed?
Katydid, but what? who knew it?
    Would it ever be revealed?

Stranger still, a woman's secret,
    From the babbling world is hid;
For the wisest village gossip
    Cannot tell what " Katydid."

Peter Peppercorn.

THE NAKED TRUTH.

I DO not fear to follow out the truth,
Albeit along the precipice's edge;
Let us speak plain: there is more force in names
Than most men dream of; and a lie may keep
Its throne a whole age longer, if it skulk
Behind the shield of some fair seeming name.
Let us call tyrants *tyrants*, and maintain
That only freedom comes by grace of God,
And all that comes not by his grace must fall;
For men in earnest have no time to waste
In patching fig leaves for the naked truth.

James Russell Lowell.

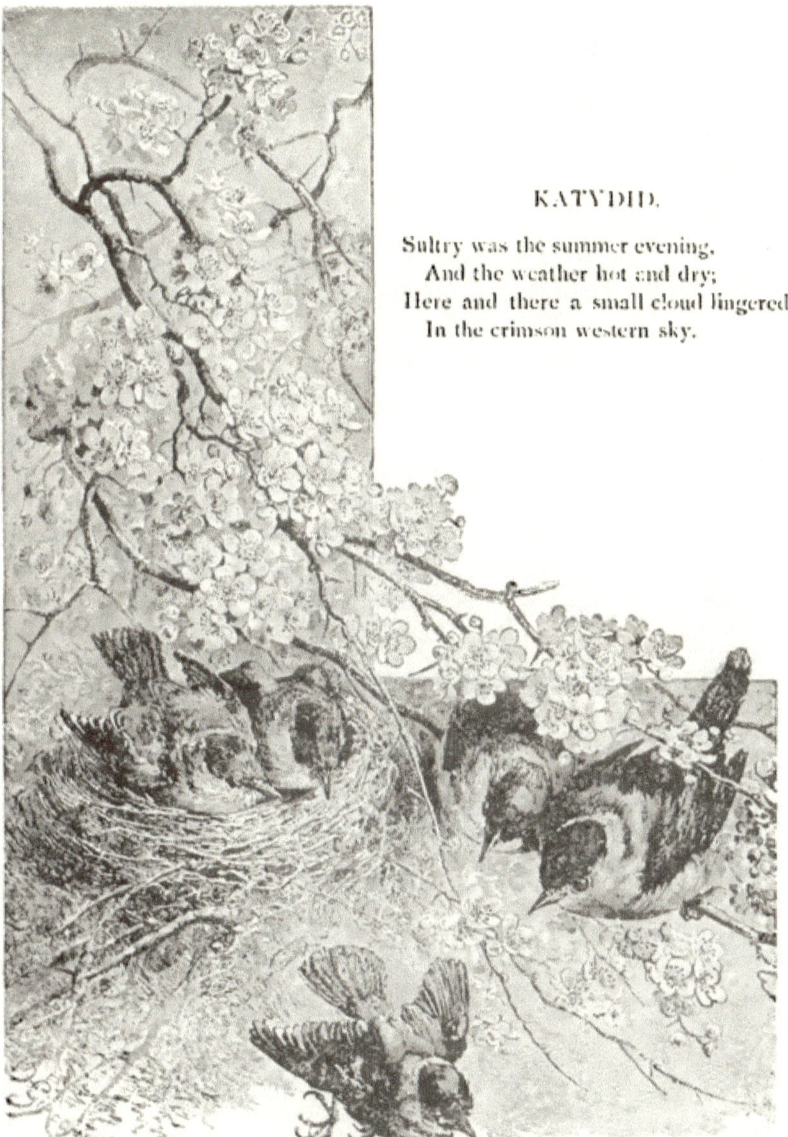

KATYDID.

Sultry was the summer evening,
 And the weather hot and dry;
Here and there a small cloud lingered
 In the crimson western sky.

WILLIAM AND HELEN.

[In the preface to the edition published anonymously in 1796, Sir Walter Scott says: "The first two lines of the forty-seventh stanza, descriptive of the speed of the lovers, may perhaps bring to the recollection of many a passage extremely similar in a translation of 'Leonora,' which first appeared in the *Monthly Magazine.* In justice to himself, the translator thinks it his duty to acknowledge that his curiosity was first attracted to this truly romantic story by a gentleman, who, having heard 'Leonora' once read in manuscript, could only recollect the general outlines, and part of a couplet, which, from the singularity of its structure and frequent recurrence, had remained impressed upon his memory. For the information of those to whom such obsolete expressions may be less familiar, it may be noticed that the word *serf* means a vassal; and that to *busk* and *boune* is to dress and prepare one's self for a journey."]

FROM heavy dreams fair Helen rose
   And eyed the dawning red:
"Alas, my love, thou tarriest long!
   Oh, art thou false, or dead?"

With gallant Frederick's princely power
   He sought the bold crusade;
But not a word from Judah's wars
   Told Helen how he sped.

With Paynim and with Saracen,
   At length a truce was made,
And every knight returned to dry
   The tears his love had shed.

Our gallant host was homeward bound,
   With many a song of joy:
Green waved the laurel in each plume,
   The badge of victory.

And old and young, and sire and son,
   To meet them crowd the way,
With shouts, and mirth, and melody,
   The debt of love to pay.

Full many a maid her true love met,
  And sobbed in his embrace,
And fluttering joy in tears and smiles
  Arrayed full many a face.

Nor joy nor smile for Helen sad:
  She sought the host in vain;
For none could tell her William's fate,
  If faithless, or if slain.

The martial band is passed and gone:
  She rends her raven hair,
And in distraction's bitter mood
  She weeps with wild despair.

" Oh, rise, my child," her mother said,
  " Nor sorrow thus in vain;
A perjured lover's fleeting heart
  No tears recall again."

" O mother, what is gone, is gone,
  What's lost, forever lorn:
Death, death alone can comfort me;
  Oh had I ne'er been born!

" Oh, break, my heart, oh, break at once!
  Drink my life-blood, Despair!
No joy remains on earth for me,
  For me in Heaven no share."

" Oh, enter not in judgment, Lord!"
  The pious mother prays;
" Impute not guilt to thy frail child!
  She knows not what she says.

" Oh, say thy Pater Noster, child!
    Oh, turn to God and grace!
His will that turned thy bliss to bale,
    Can change thy bale to bliss."

" O mother, mother! what is bliss?
    O mother, what is bale?
My William's love was heaven on earth,
    Without it, earth is hell.

" Why should I pray to ruthless Heaven,
    Since my loved William's slain?
I only prayed for William's sake,
    And all my prayers were vain."

" Oh, take the sacrament, my child,
    And check these tears that flow;
By resignation's humble prayer,
    Oh, hallowed be thy woe!"

" No sacrament can quench this fire,
    Or slake this scorching pain:
No sacrament can bid the dead
    Arise and live again.

" Oh, break, my heart, oh, break at once!
    Be thou my god, Despair!
Heaven's heaviest blow has fallen on me,
    And vain each fruitless prayer."

" Oh, enter not in judgment, Lord,
    With thy frail child of clay!
She knows not what her tongue has spoke;
    Impute it not, I pray!

" Forbear, my child, this desperate woe,
    And turn to God and grace;
Well can devotion's heavenly glow
    Convert thy bale to bliss."

" O mother, mother, what is bliss?
    O mother, what is bale?
Without my William, what were heaven,
    Or, with him, what were hell? "

Wild she arraigns the eternal doom,
    Upbraids each sacred power,
Till, spent, she sought her silent room
    All in the lonely tower.

She beat her breast, she wrung her hands,
    Till sun and day were o'er,
And through the glimmering lattice shone
    The twinkling of the star.

Then, crash! the heavy drawbridge fell,
    That o'er the moat was hung;
And clatter! clatter! on its boards
    The hoof of courser rung.

The clank of echoing steel was heard
    As off the rider bounded;
And slowly on the winding stair
    A heavy footstep sounded.

And hark! and hark! a knock—Tap! tap!
    A rustling, stifled noise:
Door-latch and tinkling staples ring; —
    At length a whispering voice.

" Awake, awake, arise, my love!
   How, Helen, dost thou fare?
Wakest thou, or sleep'st? laugh'st thou, or weep'st?
   Hast thought on me, my fair? "

" My love! my love! — so late by night! —
   I waked, I wept for thee:
Much have I borne since dawn of morn;
   Where, William, couldst thou be?"

" We saddle late — from Hungary
   I rode since darkness fell;
And to its bourne we both return
   Before the matin-bell."

" Oh, rest this night within my arms,
   And warm thee in their fold!
Chill howls through hawthorn-bush the wind: —
   My love is deadly cold."

" Let the wind howl! through hawthorn-bush!
   This night we must away ;
The steed is wight, the spur is bright;
   I cannot stay till day.

" Busk, busk, and boune ! Thou mount'st behind
   Upon my black Barb steed :
O'er stocks and stiles, a hundred miles,
   We haste to bridal bed."

" To-night — to-night a hundred miles!
   O dearest William, stay!
The bell strikes twelve — dark, dismal hour !
   Oh, wait, my love, till day!"

" Look here, look here — the moon shines clear —
   Full fast I ween we ride;
Mount and away ! for ere the day
   We reach our bridal bed.

" The black Barb snorts, the bridle rings;
   Haste, busk, and boune, and seat thee!
The feast is made, the chamber spread,
   The bridal guests await thee."

Strong love prevailed : she busks, she bounes,
   She mounts the Barb behind,
And round her darling William's waist
   Her lily arms she twined.

And, hurry! hurry! off they rode,
   As fast as fast might be;
Spurned from the courser's thundering heels
   The flashing pebbles flee.

And on the right, and on the left,
   Ere they could snatch a view,
Fast, fast each mountain, mead, and plain,
   And cot, and castle flew.

" Sit fast — dost fear? — The moon shines clear —
   Fleet rides my Barb — keep hold!
Fear'st thou?" — " Oh no!" she faintly said;
   " But why so stern and cold?

" What yonder rings? what yonder sings?
   Why shrieks the owlet gray? "—
" 'Tis death-bells' clang, 'tis funeral song,
   The body to the clay.

" With song and clang, at morrow's dawn,
 Ye may inter the dead:
To-night I ride, with my young bride,
 To deck our bridal bed.

" Come with thy choir, thou coffined guest,
 To swell our nuptial song!
Come, priest, to bless our marriage feast!
 Come all, come all along! "

Ceased clang and song; down sunk the bier;
 The shrouded corpse arose:
And, hurry, hurry! all the train
 The thundering steed pursues.

And, forward! forward! on they go;
 High snorts the straining steed;
Thick pants the rider's laboring breath,
 As headlong on they speed.

" O William, why this savage haste?
 And where thy bridal bed? " —
" 'Tis distant far." — " Still short and stern?"
 " 'Tis narrow, trustless maid."

" No room for me? " — " Enough for both; —
 Speed, speed, my Barb, thy course!"
O'er thundering bridge, through boiling surge,
 He drove the furious horse.

Tramp! tramp! along the land they rode
 Splash! splash! along the sea;
The steed is wight, the spur is bright,
 The flashing pebbles flee.

Fled past on right, and left how fast,
    Each forest, grove, and bower;
On right and left fled past how fast
    Each city, town, and tower.

" Dost fear? dost fear? — The moon shines clear; —
    Dost fear to ride with me? —
Hurrah! hurrah! the dead can ride! "
    " O William, let them be!

" See there, see there!   What yonder swings
    And creaks 'mid whistling rain? " —
" Gibbet and steel, the accursed wheel;
    A murderer in his chain.

" Hollo! thou felon, follow here:
    To bridal bed we ride;
And thou shalt prance a fetter dance
    Before me and my bride. "

And hurry, hurry! clash, clash, clash!
    The wasted form descends;
And fleet as wind through hazel-bush
    The wild career attends.

Tramp! tramp! along the land they rode,
    Splash! splash! along the sea;
The scourge is red, the spur drops blood,
    The flashing pebbles flee.

How fled what moonshine faintly showed!
    How fled what darkness hid!
How fled the earth beneath their feet,
    The heaven above their head!

" Dost fear? dost fear? — the moon shines clear,
    And well the dead can ride;
Does faithful Helen fear for them?"
    " Oh, leave in peace the dead!"

" Barb! Barb! methinks I hear the cock;
    The sand will soon be run:
Barb! Barb! I smell the morning air;
    The race is well nigh done."

Tramp! tramp! along the land they rode,
    Splash! splash! along the sea;
The scourge is red, the spur drops blood,
    The flashing pebbles flee.

" Hurrah! hurrah! well ride the dead,
    The bride, the bride is come!
And soon we reach the bridal bed,
    For, Helen, here's my home."

Reluctant on its rusty hinge
    Revolved an iron door,
And by the pale moon's setting beam
    Were seen a church and tower.

With many a shriek and cry whiz round
    The birds of midnight, scared;
And, rustling like autumnal leaves,
    Unhallowed ghosts were heard.

O'er many a tomb and tombstone pale
    He spurred the fiery horse,
Till sudden at an open grave
    He checked the wondrous course.

The falling gauntlet quits the rein,
  Down drops the casque of steel,
The cuirass leaves his shrinking side,
  The spur his gory heel.

The eyes desert the naked skull,
  The moldering flesh the bone,
Till Helen's lily arms entwine
  A ghastly skeleton.

The furious Barb snorts fire and foam,
  And, with a fearful bound,
Dissolves at once in empty air,
  And leaves her on the ground.

Half seen by fits, by fits half heard,
  Pale specters fleet along;
Wheel round the maid in dismal dance,
  And howl the funeral song.

" E'en when the heart's with anguish cleft,
  Revere the doom of Heaven.
Her soul is from her body reft;
  Her spirit be forgiven!"

Walter Scott.

THE PRINCIPAL RULES OF ORATORY.

(IN A NUTSHELL.)

BE brief, be pointed; let your matter stand
Lucid in order, solid, and at hand;
Spend not your words on trifles, but condense;
Strike with the mass of thought, not drops of sense;
Press to the close with vigor once begun,
And leave (how hard the task!) leave off when done;
Who draws a labor'd length of reasoning out,
Puts straws in lines for winds to whirl about;
Who draws a tedious tale of learning o'er,
Counts but the sands on ocean's boundless shore;
Victory in law is gained as battles fought,
Not by the numbers, but the forces bro't.
What boots success in skirmishes or in fray,
If rout and ruin following close the day?
What worth a hundred posts maintained with skill,
If, these all held, the foe is victor still?
He who would win his cause, with power must frame
Points of support, and look with steady aim;
Attack the weak, defend the strong with art,
Strike but few blows, but strike them to the heart;
All scattered fires but end in smoke and noise,
The scorn of men, the idle play of boys.
Keep, then, this first great precept ever near,
Short be your speech, your matter strong and clear;
Earnest your manner, warm and rich your style,
Severe in taste, yet full of grace the while;
So may you reach the loftiest heights of fame,
And leave, when life is past, a deathless name.

Anonymous.

EROS ATHANATOS.

[A GARDEN, THE NUPTIAL NIGHT OF HYACINTHUS AND IRENE.]

Two shapes that walk together, and caress,
Amid a garden sweet with silentness,
And, watching every flower and pulsing star,
Share their souls' rapture with all things that are.
Through the wide casement, open to the sky,
White-footed gleams the bed where they shall lie;
And from the chamber, luminously dim,
Red marble steps slope downward to the brim
Of a white-fountain in the garden, where
A marble Dryad glimmers through the air.
Scented the garden lies and blossom-strewn,
And still as sleep beneath the rising Moon,
Save from a blooming rose-grove, warm and still,
Soft steals the nightingale's thick, amorous trill.

HYACINTHUS.

SEEST thou two waifs of cloud in the dim blue
     Meandering moonward in the vap'rous light?
     Methinks they are two spirits bright and true,
     Blending their silvern breaths, and born anew,
In the still rapture of this heavenly night!
See! how like flowers the stars their paths bestrew,
Till the moon turns, and smiles, and looks them through,
     Breathing upon them, when with bosoms white
     They melt on one another, and unite.
Now they are gone! they vanish from our view,
     Lost in that rapture exquisitely bright!
O love! my love! methinks that thou and I
Resemble those thin waifs in heaven astray;
     We meet, we blend, grow bright!

IRENE.

                And we must die!

HYACINTHUS.

Nay, sweet, for love can never pass away!

IRENE.

Are *they* not gone? and, dear, shall we not go?
  Oh, love is life, but after life comes death!

HYACINTHUS.

No flower, no drop of rain, no flake of snow,
No beauteous thing that blossometh below,
  May perish, though it vanish, ev'n as breath!
The bright Moon drinks those wanderers of the west,
They melt in her warm beauty, and are blest;
We see them not, yet, in that light divine
Upgathered, they are happy, and they shine;
Not lost, but vanished, grown ev'n unawares,
A part of a diviner life than theirs!

NIGHTINGALES SING.

Through our throats the raptures rise,
    In the scented air they swim;
From the skies,
    With their own love-luster dim,
Gaze innumerable eyes! —
    Sweet, oh, sweet,
Grows the music from each throat,
    Thick and fleet,
Note on note,
Till in ecstasy we float!

IRENE.

How vast looks Heaven! how solitary and deep!
  Dost thou believe that Spirits walk the air,

Treading those azure fields, and downward peep
With sad, great eyes when Earth is fast asleep?

HYACINTHUS.

One spirit, at least, immortal LOVE, walks there!

A SHOOTING STAR.

Swift from my bliss, in the silence above,
I slip to thy kiss, O my star! O my love!

SPIRITS IN THE LEAVES.

Who are these twain in the garden bowers?
They glide with rapture rich as ours.
Touch them, feel them, and drink their sighs,
Brush their lips and their cheeks and eyes!

How their hearts beat! how they glow!
Brightly, lightly, they come and go;
Upward gazing they look in bliss,
Save when softly they pause, to kiss.

Kiss them also and share the light
That fills their breathing this golden night.
Touch them! clasp them! round them twine,
Their lips are burning with dews divine.

HYACINTHUS.

Love, tread this way with rosy feet,
And, resting on the shadowy seat,
'Neath the laburnum's golden rain,
Watch how with murmurous refrain
The fountain leaps, its basin dark
Flashing in many a starry spark.

With such a bliss, with such a light,
With such an iteration bright,
Our souls, upbubbling from the clay,
Leap, sparkle, blend in silvern spray,
Gleam in the Moon, and falling still,
Sink duskily with a thick thrill,
Together blent with kiss and press,
In the dark silence of caress,
Yet there they pause not, but cast free
After surcease of ecstacy,
Heavenward they leap together clinging,
And like the fountain flash, upspringing!

THE FOUNTAIN LEAPING.

Higher, still higher!
  With a trembling and gleaming
  Still upward streaming,
In the silvern fire
Of a dim desire;
Still higher, higher!
  With a bright pulsation
  Of aspiration—
Higher!
Higher, still higher!
  To the lights above me;
  They gleam, they love me;
They beckon me nigher,
And my waves aspire,
Still higher, higher; —
  But I fall down failing,
  Still wildly wailing —
Higher!

NIGHTINGALES SING.

Deeper let the glory glow;
  Sweeter let our voices croon!
Yet more slow,
Let our happy music flow,
Sweet and slow, hushed and low.
  Now the gray cloud veils the Moon.
Sweet, oh, sweet!
Watch her as our wild hearts beat.
  See! she quits the clasping cloud,
Forth she moves on silvern feet,
  Smiling with her bright head bowed?
Pour the living rapture loud!
Thick and fleet,
Sweet, oh, sweet,
  Let the notes of rapture crowd!

IRENE (*to herself*).

And *this* is love! — Until this hour
I never lived; but, like a flower
Close prest i' the bud, with sleeping senses,
I drank the dark, dim influences
Of sunlight, moonlight, shade, and dew.
At last I open thrilling through
With Love's strange sense, which seemeth part
Of the warm life within my heart,

Part of the air around.   Oh bliss!
Was ever night so sweet as this?
It is enough to breathe, to be,
As if one were a flower, a tree,
A leaf o' the bough, just stirring light
With the warm breathing of the night!

SPIRITS IN THE LEAVES.

Whisper, what are they doing now?
He is kissing his lady's brow,
Holding her face up to the light
Like a beautiful tablet, marble-white.

The Moon is smiling upon it — lo!
Whiter it is than driven snow.
He kisses again and speaketh gay;
Whisper, whisper, what doth he say?

HYACINTHUS.

Forever and ever! forever and ever!
  As the fount that upleaps, as the breezes that blow,
      Love thou me!
Forever and ever, forever and ever,
  While the nightingales sing and the rose garlands glow,
      Love I thee!
Forever and ever, with all things to prove us,
In this world, in that world that bendeth above us,
Asleeping, awaking, in earth, as in Heaven,
By this kiss, this other, by thousands ungiven,
By the hands which now touch thee, the arms that enfold
      thee,
By the soul in my eyes that now swoons to behold thee,
By starlight, by moonlight, by scented rose-blossoms,
By all things partaking the joy in our bosoms,
By the rapture within us, the rapture around us,
By God who hath made us, and Love who hath crowned us,
By one sense and one soul we are blent, ne'er to sever —
Forever and ever! forever and ever!
More kisses to seal it.   Forever and ever.

THE WOOD ECHOES.

Forever and ever.

THE WIND SINGS.

Hush, no more — for they have fled;
Foot by foot and tread by tread
I pursue them; all is said,
Till Apollo rises red.

Here they sat, and there, and there!
Here stood clinging thou may'st swear,
For the spirit of the air
Still their scented breath doth bear.

All is done, and all grows chill.
Here upon the window-sill
I will lean and feel a thrill
From the sleeping chamber still.

Blow the curtain back and peep:
Silvern bright the moonbeams creep.
Hush! Still pale with passion deep,
See them lying fast asleep.

Robert Buchanan.

NOW THE OLD WIFE'S GONE.

LONE, ay, masters, I live alone in this old small
    room that you see,
    For, now my old woman is laid to rest, I have no
    one to think of me;
We were wedded a long, long while ago, full fifty years and
    more,
And folks find changes hard to bear when nigh upon
    fourscore.

Ah, she was a handsome and winsome lass in the days of
    the far-back past,
And a beauty lingered on her old face for me to the very
    last;
True, she sometimes had a bit of tongue, but maybe I had
    one too,
And I find out, now she is dead and gone, what worries
    a wife goes through.

Ay, the petty troubles of a woman's life a man can only
    learn
When he has to light his fire himself, and finds green
    wood won't burn;
When he has to wash out his bits of things, and cook his
    food himself,
And keep his crockware free from dust, and ranged on a
    nice clean shelf.

And then the needle that seemed to fly with magic speed
    through her work,
Sticks tightly in mine, as if rusted in, and I pull it out
    with a jerk;

And my cotton ties in a thousand knots, and as for
    worsted yarn,
I know I could dig up an acre of ground while I'm doing
    a little darn.

The old gray cat that my dead wife loved, comes rubbing
    against my hand,
And I often find myself talking to her as if she could
    understand;
But 'tis comfort to speak when my heart is full, for it
    softens my grief away;
And I don't want to hear other people preach, for there's
    nothing new they can say.

Of course I know she's better off, but a man at the close
    of life
Seems beginning his working days over again when he
    loses his long-time wife;
I shall go to her, ay, I'm thinking of that, and I'll
    patiently here abide
Till under the shade of the church we both loved, I am
    laid by my old wife's side.

Mary Frances Adams.

" Ay, the petty troubles of a woman's life."

75

DEAD.

"My son Absalom! My son, my son!"

EAD : turned at once into clay;
  Dead he that drew life from my breast ;
Whom I clasp'd to my heart yesterday,
  And close to its pulses had press'd !
Dead : and his face ashen gray !
  Dead : the wild spirit at rest !
    My son, my son !

Dead : but not shot through the heart
  In battle 'gainst wrong for the right —
'Twere noble from life thus to part,
  And fall slain in a chivalrous fight;
But to think *how* he died is the smart,
  A darkness unbroken by light!
    My son, my son!

Hadst thou died in a cause that was good,
  Standing up for the right and the true,
Thy mother had said — ay, she *would* —
  Let death make a gap 'twixt us two:
I swear, by the cross and the rood,
  Without tears I had bade thee adieu!
    My son, my son!

Dead : stricken down by a blow
  Dealt out by a passionate hand;
In the wink of an eyelid laid low,
  His blood welling out on the sand,
And crawling all red in its flow,
  Till it crept to my feet where I stand!
    My son, my son!

Dead: killed in a wild drunken brawl—
  Ah, *here* is the sting and the shame;
Ah, here is the wormwood and gall;
  This burns in my bosom like flame!
Would that tears had dropped on my pall
  Ere this blot had blackened his name.
        My son, my son!

Thus to die with a wine-maddened brain,
  Besotted, befooled, and beguiled!
I curse, from the heart of my pain,
  In words that sound frantic and wild;
I curse—but my curses are vain;
  They cannot restore me my child.
        My son, my son!

Yet my grief is but common, they say,
  Others feel the same anguish and woe;
Sad mothers and wives face the day,
  And their eyes with hot tears overflow,
As weeping, they pass on their way,
  And cursing the wine as they go,
        My son, my son!

I tell you, in God's holy name,
  That *this* is the scourge of the land,
Its burden, its sorrow, its shame,
  Burnt deep on its brow like a brand;
Striking hard at its honor and fame,
  And crumbling its strength into sand.
        My son, my son!

We mothers and wives lift the cry,
  And pray ye, O men, for your grace;

Come, help from your stations on high.
  As ye hope to look God in the face,
Who sees us, as weeping we lie,
  And ask you for ruth from your place!
    My son, my son!

O poets, *your* aid we implore:
  Chant no longer the praises of wine;
Dash the wine-cup down on the floor,
  You dishonor a craft so divine!
Ah, indeed, you would praise it no more,
  If your son lay dead there like mine!
    My son, my son!

O singers, well skilled in the song,
  Who stir the sweet air with your breath
As your voices move thrilling along,
  Dare you laud the cup that is death?
Dare ye lend your great gifts to such wrong:
  If so, from your brows tear the wreath!
    My son, my son!

Hear the cry from the mad-house and jail,
  Hear the moan of the starving and poor,
Hear the widows' and orphans' sharp wail,
  Who, like martyrs that groan and endure,
Lift to God their white faces so pale,
  And, though speechless, His pity adjure.
    My son, my son!

Help all! Free the slaves from their bands;
  Help, and take part in this fight;
Strike the fetters from paralyzed hands!
  Like Samson, rise up in your might,

Break the chains like green willow-wands:
Do this in God's name, and the right!
My son, my son!

Oh, scorn not, I pray you the cry
Of a mother, a widow undone;
But even though *you* pass it by,
It will move the great God on His throne:
He hears from the dust where I lie,
Where in ashes I weep for my son.
My son, my son!

Rev. Canon Bell.

―――――

STEEPLE FOLK.

THE wonderful people
That live in the steeple,
There chanting and singing
With the great bells swinging,
Swaying with a pond'rous motion to and fro,
With a mighty cling! clang!
A sullen clash and bang!
A booming of noises,
Myriads of voices,
Smitten out from dull metal with a blow.

And then the wild, wild glee
Of elf folk frolic free!
As they skip on the rope,
It will verily smoke,
And they hang head down in a spider's web,

Or gambol on the beams
Like weird pigmies in dreams,
These goblin rope-dancers
And marvelous prancers
That leap to and fro on a shining thread.

Oh, the sound of far bells,
Borne in on windy swells,
The faint, silver chiming,
The sweet broken rhyming,
Like some poet's lines that run in the head;
We walk in grassy fields,
And the brain almost reels
With the mem'ry of bliss:
A fond word or a kiss,
And the rose she wore — the rose was ripe red.

And now there comes a hum
When all the air is dumb,
Like innumerable bees
In freshly blossomed trees;
What is it those elves are whisp'ring to each other
In a secret low sound,
That seems to heave the ground,
A soft buzz and tingle —
No jangle or jingle —
Like a baby crooned to sleep by its mother?

Weird music not of earth,
Thin and fine as elf mirth,
Comes winding round and round,
In a spiral of sound,
And moves us to tears with its haunting strain,

By its intimations,
And faint reverberations,
Of tenderest heart thrills,
That the grave alone stills —
That quicken the cells of the coldest brain.

Strange wailings and sighings,
Loud sobbings and cryings,
And then a plaintive knell
From the great tolling bell,
Heard over the green, daisy-sprinkled mead;
Yes, there is some one dead
And she was newly wed;
A fortnight but just gone,
Bells rang clearly ding! dong!
To this woful day did the elves give heed!

They knew it was coming,
And woke a strange humming,
That prophesies of ill
When the wind blasts are still;
And, if hearts do break, what is it to them?
It is, I ween, the same,
For their loss or their gain,
Whether bells merry go,
Or bells toll sad and slow;
They care not what happens to ants of men.

Fantasies of motion,
High in that great ocean
Of blue, pellucid air
With a calm everywhere;
Above this earth is the vast serenity,

Above the want and woe,
And running to and fro,
Above the pain and loss,
And dragging heavy cross,
Above the dull cares of poor humanity.

Good, church-going people
Gaze up at yon steeple,
As it seems to reel and rock
They hear voices that mock;
And " hush! was that a whisper in the breast?
Or was it wicked fays
That heed not prayer or praise
That never bow the knee,
But live Godless and free,
In the holy house of worship and rest? "

The ills we cannot know,
Like the gathering of snow,
These elves see advancing,
When sunbeams are dancing,
A wisp of vapor, a wreath of smoke;
And they laugh to see us play
And sport the time away
Till thunder gusts and showers
Have spoiled our pretty bowers,
Or out of a clear heaven falls the stroke.

But from the over-soul,
The great enduring whole,
There falls a sweeter chime,
A more entrancing rhyme,
Far, far above the clanging of the bell,

Above the blended strain
Of human joy and pain,
From that eternal calm
The universal psalm,
Sounds, all is well! all is well! all is well!

      Augusta Larned.

ONLY A WOMAN.

"She loves with love that cannot tire ;
 And if, ah, woe! she loves alone
Through passionate duty love flames higher,
 As grass grows taller around a stone."

      Coventry Patmore.

O, the truth's out. I'll grasp it like a snake —
It will not slay me. My heart shall not break
Awhile, if only for the children's sake.

For his, too, somewhat. Let him stand unblamed;
None say, he gave me less than honor claimed,
Except — one trifle scarcely worth being named —

The *heart*. That's gone. The corrupt dead might be
As easily raised up, breathing — fair to see,
As he could bring his whole heart back to me.

I never sought him in coquettish sport,
Or courted him as silly maidens court,
And wonder when the longed-for prize falls short.

I only loved him — any woman would;
But shut my love up till he came and sued,
Then poured it o'er his dry life like a flood.

I was so happy I could make him blest!
So happy that I was his first and best,
As he mine—when he took me to his breast.

Ah me! if only then he had been true!
If for one little year, a month or two,
He had given me love for love, as was my due!

Or had he told me, 'ere the deed was done,
He only raised me to his heart's dear throne —
Poor substitute—because the queen was gone!

O, had he whispered, when his sweetest kiss
Was warm upon my mouth in fancied bliss,
He had kissed another woman even as this —

It were less bitter! Sometimes I could weep,
To be thus cheated, like a child asleep;
Were not my anguish far too dry and deep.

So I built my house upon another's ground;
Mocked with a heart just caught at the rebound —
A cankered thing, that looked so firm and sound.

And when that heart grew colder, colder still,
I, ignorant, tried all duties to fulfill,
Blaming my foolish, pain-exacting will.

All—anything but him. It was to be
The full draught others drink up carelessly
Was made this bitter Tantalus-cup for me.

I say again—he gives me all I claimed,
I and my children never shall be shamed;
He is a just man—he will live unblamed.

Only — O God, O God, to cry for bread,
And get a stone! Daily to lay my head
Upon a bosom where the old love's dead!

Dead? Fool! It never lived. It only stirred,
Galvanic, like an hour-cold corpse. None heard;
So let me bury it without a word.

He'll keep that other woman from my sight.
I know not if her face be foul or bright;
I only know that it was his delight —

As his was mine; I only know he stands
Pale, at the touch of their long-severed hands,
Then to a flickering smile his lip commands,

Lest I should grieve, or jealous anger show.
He need not. When the ship's gone down, I trow,
We little reck whatever wind may blow.

And so my silent moan begins and ends,
No world's laugh or world's taunt, no pity of friends,
Or sneer of foes, with this my torment blends.

None knows — none heeds. I have a little pride;
Enough to stand up, wifelike, by his side,
With the same smile as when I was his bride.

And I shall take his children to my arms;
They will not miss these fading, worthless charms;
Their kiss — ah! unlike his — all pain disarms.

And haply as the solemn years go by,
He will think sometimes, with regretful sigh,
The other woman was less true than I.

Dinah Mariah Mulock.

CASTLES IN SPAIN.

OW much of my young heart, O Spain,
  Went out to thee in days of yore!
What dreams romantic filled my brain,
  And summoned back to life again
The Paladins of Charlemagne,
  The Cid Campeador!

And shapes more shadowy than these,
  In the dim twilight half revealed ;
Phœnician galleys on the seas,
The Roman camps like hives of bees,
The Goth uplifting from his knees
  Pelayo on his shield.

It was these memories, perchance,
  From annals of remotest eld,
That lent the colors of romance
To every trivial circumstance,
And changed the form and countenance
  Of all that I beheld.

Old towns, whose history lies hid
  In monkish chronicle or rhyme —
Burgos, the birthplace of the Cid,
Zamora and Valladolid,
Toledo, built and walled amid
  The wars of Wamba's time;

The long, straight line of the highway,
  The distant town that seems so near,
The peasants in the fields, that stay
Their toil to cross themselves and pray,
When from the belfry at midday
  The Angelus they hear;

White crosses in the mountain pass,
  Mules gay with tassels, the loud din
Of muleteers, the tethered ass
That crops the dusky wayside grass,
And cavaliers with spurs of brass
  Alighting at the inn;

White hamlets hidden in fields of wheat,
  White cities slumbering by the sea,
White sunshine flooding square and street,
Dark mountain-ranges, at whose feet
The river-beds are dry with heat —
  All was a dream to me.

Yet something somber and severe
  O'er the enchanted landscape reigned;
A terror in the atmosphere,
As if King Philip listened near,
Or Torquemada, the austere,
  His ghostly sway maintained.

The softer Andalusian skies
  Dispelled the sadness and the gloom;
There Cadiz by the seaside lies,
And Seville's orange-orchards rise,
  Making the land a paradise
    Of beauty and of bloom.

There Cordova is hidden among
  The palm, the olive, and the vine;
Gem of the South, by poets sung,
And in whose Mosque Almanzor hung,
As lamps, the bells that once had rung
  At Compostella's shrine.

CASTLES IN SPAIN.

But over all the rest supreme,
  The star of stars, the cynosure,
The artist's and the poet's theme,
The young man's vision, the old man's dream —
Granada by its winding stream,
  The city of the Moor!

And there the Alhambra still recalls
  Aladdin's palace of delight:
Allah il Allah! through its halls
Whispers the fountain as it falls,
The Darro darts beneath its walls,
  The hills with snow are white.

Ah yes, the hills are white with snow,
  And cold with blasts that bite and freeze;
But in the happy vale below
The orange and pomegranate grow,
And wafts of air toss to and fro
  The blossoming almond-trees.

The Vega cleft by the Xenil,
  The fascination and allure
Of the sweet landscape chains the will;
The traveler lingers on the hill,
His parted lips are breathing still
  The last sigh of the Moor.

How like a ruin overgrown
  With flowers that hide the rents of time,
Stands now the Past that I have known;
Castles in Spain, not built of stone,
But of white summer cloud, and blown
  Into this little mist of rhyme!

Henry Wadsworth Longfellow.

THE LAST BANQUET.

1793.

[The incident narrated in the poem is based on fact, a tragedy of the kind being reported to have occurred, during the French Revolution, in the north of France.]

ITAUT, the Norman marquis,
 Sat in his banquet-hall,
When the shafts of the autumn sunshine
 Gilded the castle-wall;
While in through the open windows
 Floated the sweet perfume,
Borne in from the stately garden
 And filling the lofty room;

And still, like a strain of music
 Breathed in an undertone,
The ripple of running water
 Rose, with its sob and moan,
From the river, swift and narrow,
 Far down in the vale below,
That shone like a silver arrow
 Shot from a bended bow.

Yonder, over the poplars,
 Lapped in the mellow haze,
Lay the roofs of the teeming city,
 Red in the noonday blaze ;
While ever, in muffled music,
 The tall cathedral-towers
Told to the panting people
 The story of the hours.

His was a cruel temper:
  Under his baneful sway
Peasant and maid and matron
  Fled from his headlong way,
When down from his rocky eyric,
  Spurring his foaming steed,
Galloped the haughty noble,
  Ripe for some evil deed.

But when the surging thousands,
  Bleeding at every pore,
Roused by the wrongs of ages,
  Rose with a mighty roar —
Ever the streets of cities
  Rang with a voice long mute;
Gibbet and tree and *lanterne*
  Bearing their bleeding fruit.

Only one touch of feeling —
  Hid from the world apart,
Locked with the key of silence —
  Lived in that cruel heart;
For one he had loved and worshiped,
  Dead in the days of yore,
Who slept in the lonely chapel,
  Hard by the river-shore.

High on a painted panel,
  Set in a gilded shrine,
Shone her benignant features
  Lit with a smile divine;

Under the high, straight forehead,
  Eyes of the brightest blue,
Framed in her hair's bright masses,
  Rivaled the sapphire's hue.

" Why do you come, Breconi? "
  " Marquis, you did not call;
But Mignonne is waiting yonder,
  Down by the castle-wall."
" Bid her begone! " — " But, master —
  Poor child! *she loves you so!*
And broken with bitter weeping,
  She told me a tale of woe.

" She says there is wild work yonder,
  There in the hated town,
Where the crowds of frenzied people
  Are shooting the nobles down.
And to-night, ere the moon has risen,
  They come with burning brand,
With the flame of the blazing castle
  To light the lurid land.

" But first you must spread the banquet —
  Host for the crew abhorred —
Ere out from the topmost turret
  They fling my murdered lord.
Flee for thy life, Lord Marquis,
  Flee from a frightful doom,
When the night has hid the postern
  Safe in its friendly gloom! "

" Tush! are you mad, Breconi?
    Spread them the banquet here,
With flowers and fruit and viands,
    Silver and crystal clear;
Let not a touch be wanting —
    Hasten those hands of thine!
Haste to the task, Breconi;
    And I will draw the wine!"

S.owly the sun went westward,
    Till all the city's spires
Flamed in the flood of splendor —
    A hundred flickering fires.
Over the peaceful landscape,
    Clasped by the girdling stream,
Quivered, in mournful glory
    The last expiring beam.

Then up from the rippling river
    Sounded the tramp of feet
That rose o'er the solemn stillness
    Laden with perfume sweet;
While high o'er the sleeping city,
    And over the garden gloom,
Towered the grim, black castle,
    Still as the silent tomb.

Leaning over the casement,
    Heark'ning the busy hum,
Smiling, the haughty marquis
    Knew that his time was come:

And he turned to the paneled picture —
  That answered his look again,
And beamed with a smile of welcome —
  Humming a low refrain.

Under the echoing archway,
  And up o'er the stairs of stone,
Ever the human torrent
  Shouted, in strident tone —
Curses and gibes and threat'nings,
  With snatches of ribald jest,
Stirring the blood to fury
  In many a brutal breast.

There, under the lighted tapers
  Set in the banquet-hall,
Smiling and calm and steadfast,
  Towered the marquis tall.
Dressed in his richest costume,
  Facing the gibing host,
He wore on its broad blue ribbon
  The star of " The Holy Ghost."

" Welcome, fair guests — be seated! "
  He cried to the motley crowd
That drew to the loaded table
  With curses long and loud;
Waving a graceful welcome,
  The gleaming lights reveal
The rings on his soft, white fingers,
  Strung with their nerves of steel.

Turned to the paneled picture,
    Calm in his icy hate,
He stood, in his pride of lineage,
    Cold as a marble Fate;
Smiling in hidden meaning —
    In his rich garments dressed —
As cold and hard and polished
    As the brilliants on his breast.

Pouring a brimming beaker,
    He cried: " Drink, friends, I pray!
Drink to the toast I give you!
    Pledge me my proudest day!
Here, under the hall of banquet —
    Drink, drink to the festal news! —
Stand twenty casks of powder
    Set with a lighted fuse!"

Frozen with sudden horror,
    They saw, like a fleecy mist,
As he quaffed the purple vintage,
    The ruffles at his wrist.
Turned to the smiling picture,
    Clear as a silver bell
Echoed his last fond greeting —
    " I drink to thee, *ma belle!*"

Down crashed the crystal goblet,
    Flung on the marble floor;
Back rushed the stricken revelers,
    Back to the close-barred door!

Up through its yawning crater
  The mighty earthquake broke,
Dashing its spume of fire
  Up through its waves of smoke!

Out through the deep'ning darkness,
  A wild, despairing cry
Rang as the riven castle
  Lighted the midnight sky;
Then down o'er the lurid landscape,
  Lit by those fires of hell —
Buttress and roof and rafter —
  The smoking ruin fell!

*   *   *   *   *   *   *

Over the Norman landscape
  The summer sun looks down,
Gilding the gray cathedral,
  Gilding the teeming town.
Still shines the rippling river
  Lapped in its bands of green;
Still hangs the scent of roses
  Over the peaceful scene:

But high o'er the trembling poplars,
  Blackened and burned and riven,
Those blasted battlements and towers
  Frown in the face of heaven;
And still in the sultry August
  I seem at times to feel
The smile of that cruel marquis,
  Keen as his rapier's steel!

Edward Renaud.

BABY'S SHOES.

THOSE little, those little, blue shoes!
Those shoes that no little feet use,
    O, the price were high
    That those shoes would buy,
Those little blue unused shoes!

For they hold the small shape of feet
That no more their mother's eyes meet,
    That, by God's good will,
    Years since, grew still,
And ceased from their totter so sweet.

And O, since that baby slept,
So hushed, how the mother has kept,
    With a tearful pleasure
    That little dear treasure,
And o'er them thought and wept!

For they mind her forevermore
Of a patter along the floor;
    And blue eyes she sees
    Look up from her knees
With a look that in life they wore.

As they lie before her there,
There babbles from chair to chair
    A little sweet face
    That's a gleam in the place,
With its little gold curls of hair.

Then O wonder not that her heart
From all else would rather part
   Than those tiny blue shoes
   That no little feet use,
And whose sight makes such fond tears start.

William C. Bennett.

DOLORES.

HER old boat loaded with oranges,
   Her baby tied on her breast,
   Minorcan Dolores bends to her oars,
   Noting each reed on the slow-moving shores ;
But the way is long, and the inlet wide —
Can two small hands overcome the tide
   Sweeping up into the west?

  Four little walls of coquina-stone,
   Rude thatch of palmetto-leaves;
There have they nestled, like birds in a tree,
From winter, and labor, and hunger free;
Taking from earth their small need, but no more,
No thought of the morrow, no laying in store,
   No gathering patient sheaves.

  Alone in their southern island-home,
   Through the year of summer days,
The two love on; and the bountiful beach
Clusters its sea-food within his reach;
The two love on, and the tropical land
Drops its wild fruit in her indolent hand,
   And life is a sunshiny haze:

101   DOLORES.

Luiz, Dolores, and baby brown,
    With dreamy, passionate eyes—
Far in the past, lured by Saxon wiles,
A simple folk came from the Spanish sea-isles,
Now, tinged with the blood of the creole quadroon,
Their children live idly along the lagoon,
    Under the Florida skies.

Luiz, Dolores, and baby brown,
    Ah, their blossoming life of love!—
But fever falls with its withering blight;
Dolores keeps watch through the sultry night,
In vain her poor herbs, in vain her poor prayers —
Her Luiz is mounting the spirit-winged stairs
    That lead to her heaven above.

So, her old boat loaded with oranges,
    Her baby tied on her breast,
Dolores rows off to the ancient town,
Where the blue-eyed soldiers come marching down
From the far cold north; they are men who know —
Thus Dolores thinks — how to cure all woe;
    Nay, their very touch is blest.

" Oranges! oranges! " hear her cry,
    Through the shaded plaza path;
But the northern soldiers come marching in
Through the old Spanish city with stir and din;
And the silent people stand sullen by,
To see the old flag mount again to the sky —
    The flag they had trampled in wrath.

Ah, brown Dolores! will no one hear,
    And buy thy poor little store?
Now north, now south, on the old sea wall —
But her pitiful tones unheeded fall;
Now east, now west, through the angry town,
Patient she journeys up and down,
    Nor misses one surly door.

Then desperate, up to the dreaded ranks
    She carries her passionate suit;
" I have no money, for none would buy;
But come, for God's sake, or he will die!
Save him, my Luiz, he is so young! "
She pleads in her liquid Minorcan tongue,
    And proffers her store of fruit.

But the northern soldiers move steadily on,
    They hear not nor understand;
The last blue rank has passed down the street,
She sees but the dust of their marching feet;
They have crossed a whole country by night and by day,
And marked, with their blood, every step of the way,
    To conquer this southern land.

They are gone — O despair! she turns to the church,
    Half-fainting, her fruit wet with tears;
" Perhaps the old saint, who is always there,
May wake up and take them to pay for a prayer;
They are very sweet, as the saint will see,
If he would but wake up, and listen to me;
    But he sleeps so, he never hears."

She enters, the church is filled with men,
    The pallid men of the north;
Each dingy old pew is a sick man's bed,
Each battered old bench holds a weary head,
The altar-candles are swept away
For vials and knives in shining array,
    And a new saint is stepping forth.

He must be a saint, for he comes from the shrine,
    A saint of a northern creed —
Clad in a uniform — army blue,
But surely the saints may wear any hue
Dolores thinks, as he takes her hands
And hears all her story, and understands
    The cry of her desperate need.

An orange he gives to each weary man,
    To freshen the fevered mouth,
Then forth they go down the old sea-wall,
And they hear in the dusk the picket's call;
The row-boat is moored on the shadowy shore,
The northern saint can manage an oar,
    And the boat glides fast to the south.

A healing touch and a holy drink,
    A bright little heavenly knife,
And this strange northern saint, who prays no prayers,
Brings back the soul from the spirit-winged stairs,
And once more Minorcan Luiz's dark eyes,
In whose depths the warmth of the tropics lies,
    Rest calm on the awe-stricken wife.

" Oh, dear northern saint! a shrine will I build,
    Wild roses I'll bring from afar,
The jessamine, orange-flower, wood-tulips bright,
And those will I worship each morning and night.
" Nay, nay, poor Dolores, I am but a man,
A surgeon, who binds up with what skill he can
    The wounds of this heart-breaking war.

" See, build me no shrines, but take this small book,
    And teach the brown baby to read."
He is gone; and Dolores is left on the shore,
She watches the boat till she sees it no more,
She hears the quick musketry all through the night,
She holds fast the book in her pine-knot's red light,
    The book of the northerner's creed.

    *   *   *   *   *   *

The sad war is over, the dear peace has come,
    The blue-coated soldiers depart;
The brown baby reads the small book, and the three
Live on in their isle in the Florida sea;
The brown baby learns many things wise and strange,
But all his new English words never can change
    The faith of Dolores' fond heart.

A boat with a load of oranges
    In a flower-decked shrine doth stand
Carved in coquina, and thither she goes,
To pray to the only real saint she knows,
The northern surgeon in army blue;
And there she was found in the morning's dew,
    Dead, with the book in her hand.

                     Constance Fenimore Woolson.

THE MAIDEN'S ARMOR.

'TIS chastity, my brother, chastity:
She that has that, is clad in complete steel;
And, like a quiver'd nymph, with arrows keen,
May trace huge forests, and unharbor'd heaths,
Infamous hills, and sandy perilous wilds,
Where, through the sacred rays of chastity,
No savage fierce, bandit, or mountaineer,
Will dare to soil her virgin purity:
Yea, there, where very desolation dwells,
By grots and caverns shagged with horrid shades,
She may pass on with unblench'd majesty,
Be it not done in pride, or in presumption.
Some say, no evil thing that walks by night
In fog or fire, by lake or moorish fen,
Blue, meager hag, or stubborn unlaid ghost
That breaks his magic chain at curfew time,
No goblin, or swart fairy of the mine,
Hath hurtful power o'er true virginity.
Do ye believe me yet, or shall I call
Antiquity from the old schools of Greece,
To testify the arms of chastity?
Hence had the huntress Dian her dread bow,
Fair silver-shafted queen, forever chaste,
Wherewith she tamed the brinded lioness
And spotted mountain-pard, but set at naught
The frivolous bolt of Cupid; gods and men
Feared her stern frown, and she was queen of the woods.
What was that snaky-headed Gorgon shield
That wise Minerva wore, unconquer'd virgin,
Wherewith she freezed her foes to congeal'd stone,
But rigid looks of chaste austerity,

And noble grace, that dash'd brute violence
With sudden adoration and blank awe?
So dear to Heaven is saintly chastity,
That, when a soul is found sincerely so,
A thousand liveried angels lackey her,
Driving far off each thing of sin and guilt;
And, in clear dream and solemn vision,
Tell her of things that no gross ear can hear,
Till apt converse with heavenly habitants
Begin to cast a beam on the outward shape,
The unpolluted temple of the mind,
And turns it, by degrees, to the soul's essence,
Till all be made immortal.   *Milton.*

IF THAT HIGH WORLD.

If that high world which lies beyond
  Our own, surviving love endears;
If there the cherished heart be fond,
  The eye the same, except in tears—
How welcome those untrodden spheres!
  How sweet this very hour to die!
To soar from earth, and find all fears
  Lost in thy light—eternity.
It must be so: 'tis not for self
  That we so tremble on the brink;
And, striving to o'erleap the gulph,
  Yet cling to Being's severing link.
Oh! in that future let us think
  To hold each heart the heart that shares,
With them the immortal waters drink,
  And soul in soul grow deathless theirs.
                                Lord Byron.

" A thousand liveried Angels lackey her,
Driving far off each thing of sin and guilt."

CUDDLE DOON.

THE bairnies cuddle doon at nicht,
   Wi' mickle faucht an' din;
" O, try and sleep, ye waukrife[1] rogues,
   Your faither's comin' in."
They never heed a word I speak;
   I try to gie a froon,
But aye I hap[2] them up, an' cry,
   " O bairnies, cuddle doon."

Wee Jamie wi' the curly head —
   He aye sleeps next the wa',
Bangs up an' cries, " I want a piece —"
   The rascal starts them a'.
I rin' an' fetch them pieces, drinks;
   They stop awee the soun',
Then draw the blankets up an' cry,
   " Noo, weanies, cuddle doon."

But ere five minutes gang, wee Rab
   Cries out frae' 'neath the claes,
" Mither, ma'k' Tam gie ower at ance,
   He's kittlin[3] wi' his taes."
The mischief's in that Tam for tricks,
   He'd bother half the toon;
But aye, I hap them up, an' cry,
   " O bairnies, cuddle doon."

---

1 Wakeful.   2 Cover.   3 Tickling.

At length they hear their father's fit,
    An' as he steeks[4] the door,
They turn their faces to the wa',
    While Tam pretends to snore.
" Hae a' the weans been gude?" he asks,
    As he pits off his shoon;
" The bairnies, John, are in their beds,
    An' lang since cuddled doon."

An' just afore we bed oursel's,
    We look at oor wee lambs;
Tam has his airm roun' wee Rab's neck,
    An' Rab, his airm roun' Tam's.
I lift wee Jamie up the bed,
    An' as I straik each croon,
I whisper, till my heart fills up,
    " O bairnies, cuddle doon."

The bairnies cuddle doon at nicht,
    Wi' mirth that's dear to me;
But sune the big warld's cark an' care,
    Will quaten[5] doon their glee.
Yet coom what will to ilka ane,
    May he who sits aboon,
Aye whisper, though their pows[6] be bauld,
    " O bairnies, cuddle doon."

Alexander Anderson.

---

4 Shuts.   5 Quiet.   6 Heads.

YE NEEDNA' BE COURTIN' AT ME.

YE needna' be courtin' at me, auld man,
  Ye needna' be courtin' at me;
Ye're threescore an' three, an' ye're blin' o' an' ee,
  Sae ye needna' be courtin' at me, auld man,
    Ye needna' be courtin' at me.

" Stan' aff, noo, an' just lat me be, auld man,
  Stan' aff, noo, an' just lat me be;
Ye're auld an' ye're cauld, an' ye're blin' an' ye're bald,
  An' ye're nae for a lassie like me, auld man,
    Ye're nae for a lassie like me."

" Ha'e patience, an' hear me a wee, sweet lass,
  Ha'e patience, an' hear me a wee;
I've gowpens o' gowd, an' an aumy weel stowed,
  An' a heart that lo'es nane but thee, sweet lass,
    A heart that lo'es nane but thee.

" I'll busk you as braw as a queen, sweet lass,
  I'll busk you as braw as a queen;
I've guineas to spare, an', hark ye, what's mair,
  I'm only two-score an' fifteen, sweet lass,
    Only two-score an' fifteen."

" Gae hame to your gowd an' your gear, auld man,
  Gae hame to your gowd an your gear;
There's a laddie I ken has a heart like mine ain,
  And to me he shall ever be dear, auld man,
    To me he shall ever be dear.

8

" Get aff, noo, an' fash me nae mair, auld man,
      Get aff, noo, an' fash me nae mair;
There's a something in love that your gowd canna
         move —
      I'll be Johnie's although I gang bare, auld man,
         I'll be Johnie's although I gang bare."

Peter Still.

<hr>

THE CITY OF THE HEART.

HE heart is a city teeming with life —
Through all its gay avenues, rife
         With gladness
         And innocent madness,
Bright beings are passing along,
Too fleeting and fair for the eye to behold,
   While something of Paradise sweetens their song,
They are gliding away with their wild gushing ditty,
         Out of the city,
      Out of the beautiful gates of gold !
         Through gates that are ringing
         While to and fro swinging,
      Swinging and ringing ceaselessly,
Like delicate hands that are clapped in glee,
      Beautiful hands of infancy !

The heart is a city — and gay are the feet
         That dance along
         To the joyous beat
Of the timbrel that giveth a pulse to song.

Bright creatures enwreathed
    With flowers and mirth,
Fair maidens bequeathed
    With the glory of earth,
Sweep through the long street, and singing await,
A moment await at the wondering gate;
Every second of time there comes to depart
Some form that no more shall revisit the heart!
They are gliding away and breathing farewell —
    How swiftly they pass
    Through the gates of brass,
    Through gates that are ringing
    While to and fro swinging,
And making deep sounds, like that half-stifled swell
Of the far-away ring of a gay marriage bell!

The heart is a city with splendor bedight,
Where tread martial armies arrayed for the fight,
    Under banner-hung arches,
    To war-kindling marches,
    To the fife and the rattle
    Of drums, with gay colors unfurled,
    On, eager for battle,
To smite their bright spears on the spears of the world!
Through noontime, through midnight, list and thou'lt hear
The gates swing in front, then clang in the rear.
    Like a bright river flowing,
    The war host is going,
    And like to that river,
    Returning, ah, never!
Through daylight and darkness low thunder is heard
    From the city that flings
    Her iron-wrought wings,

Flapping the air like the wings of a bird!
　　The heart is a city — how sadly and slow,
　　　　To and fro,
　　Covered with rust, the solemn gates go!
　　　　　With meek folded arms,
　　　　　With heads bending lowly,
　　　　　Strange beings pass slowly
Through the dull avenues, chanting their psalms;
Sighing and mourning, they follow the dead
Out of the gates that fall heavy as lead—
Passing, how sadly, with echoless tread,
　　　　The last one is fled!
No more to be opened, the gates softly close,
And shut in a stranger who loves the repose;
With no sigh for the past, with no countenance of pity,
He spreads his black flag o'er the desolate city!

T. Buchanan Read.

THE PROBLEM OF ETERNITY.

ANOTHER annual circle is complete!
   Another year is added to the past!
   The unit of all time has reached its mete,
      And we may measure all years by the last.
   And I have questioned it: " Canst thou not cast
The ratio of eternity for me?
   'Tis infinitely long; but thou art vast,
And *time* reveals its mysteries to thee:
O Year! what is thy ratio to eternity? "

The Old Year fell into the tomb of Time
   Without reply — it would not answer me.
And then I sought, in fair and sunny clime,
   Where shores are washed by broad Pacific's sea,
   And giant forests grow, and found a tree —
A brave old pine — which soared into the blue
   An hundred fathoms high; for I would see
If that old giant could not give the clue
By which the finite might the infinite pursue.

The giant waved his hoary head on high,
   But answered not from all his life, so long!
And then I sought the sea, that murmured by
   And seemed to struggle in its muttering song
   To utter things unutterable, along
The hoary rocks upon the echoing coast —
   And questioned that: " O deep, and strong,
And boundless Ocean! surely thou art, most
Of all things known and finite, in the infinite lost!

Thou didst behold the natal day of Earth,
    And hear the annual chimes of time strike One.—
Thou didst behold the primal man go forth,
    The first to look upon the kindling sun;
    And when the seas were gathered into one,
And mountains rose, and infant rivers ran,
    Ere nature's countless ages had begun—
Thy life was running through its lengthy span!
O Ocean, tell the wondrous mystery to man! "

But still the rolling ocean answered naught;
    Its life was all too short, and finite still—
It could not solve the infinite, nor aught
    Unravel of the All-Eternal will.
    O vast Eternity! with what a thrill
The longing mind conceives the infinite,
    And faints, and fails, while yet it strives to fill
Eternity in all its depth and height—
Smitten to blindness by its own alluring light.

Thou deathless Mind! wilt thou not answer me?
    Undying as thou art, and measuring all—
What is thy ratio to Eternity?
    Thou dost compute the ages as they fall;
    Earth yields her hidden mysteries to thy call,
And suns, and stars, and systems, have been weighed
    In thy far-reaching balance, and the pall
Which lies upon the age, long decayed,
Has vanished, even at the light thyself hast made.

But still the eternal problem is unsolved!
    Back o'er departed years, the longing thought
Retraces ages ere the earth revolved;
    Beholds the infant world before it caught

The earliest blush of primal day, or aught
Of life had moved upon the rolling sphere—
    Beholds the long succeeding ages, fraught
With myriad changes, as they each appear;
Yet finds no clue to make the eternal problem clear.

Eternity! submissive let me bow
    Before the awful problem of thy round.
O vast Eternity—eternal now!—
    No ratio in the universe is found
    To estimate the infinite profound.
The finite cannot solve the infinite;
    And One alone, who knows nor mete nor bound
To wisdom, love, or majesty, or might,
Can solve the problem of Eternity aright.

Edward R. Roe.

MY HEART LEAPS UP.

My heart leaps up when I behold
    A rainbow in the sky:
    So was it when my life began;
    So is it now I am a man;
So be it when I shall be old,
        Or let me die!
    The child is father of the man;
And I could wish my days to be
Bound each to each by natural piety.

William Wordsworth.

CLEOPATRA'S SOLILOQUY.

WHAT care I for the tempest?   What care I for
the rain?
If it beat upon my bosom, would it cool its burning
pain—
This pain that ne'er has left me since on his heart I lay,
And sobbed my grief at parting as I'd sob my soul away?
O Antony! Antony! Antony! when in thy circling arms
Shall I sacrifice to Eros my glorious woman's charms,
And burn life's sweetest incense before his sacred shrine
With the living fire that flashes from thine eyes into mine?
O when shall I feel thy kisses rain down upon my face,
As, a queen of love and beauty, I lie in thy embrace,
Melting - - melting — melting, as a woman only can
When she's a willing captive in the conquering arms of man,
As he towers a god above her, and to yield is not defeat,
For love can own no victor, if love with love shall meet?
I still have regal splendor, I still have queenly power,
And more than all — unfaded is woman's glorious dower;
But what care I for pleasure? what's beauty to me now,
Since Love no longer places his crown upon my brow?
I have tasted its elixir, its fire has through me flashed,
But when the wine glowed brightest from my eager lip
'twas dashed,
And I would give all Egypt but once to feel the bliss
Which thrills through all my being whene'er I meet his
kiss;
The tempest wildly rages, my hair is wet with rain,
But it does not still my longing, nor cool my burning pain,
For Nature's storms are nothing to the raging of my soul
When it burns with jealous frenzy beyond a queen's control.

I fear not pale Octavia — that haughty Roman dame —
My lion of the desert — my Antony can tame.
I fear no Persian beauty, I fear no Grecian maid:
The world holds not the woman of whom I am afraid.
But I'm jealous of the rapture I tasted in his kiss,
And I would not that another should share with me that
    bliss;
No joy would I deny him, let him cull it where he will,
So, mistress of his bosom is Cleopatra still;
So that he feels forever, when he Love's nectar sips,
'Twas sweeter — sweeter — sweeter when tasted on my
    lips;
So that all other kisses, since he has drawn in mine,
Shall be unto my loved as " water after wine."
Awhile let Cæsar fancy Octavia's pallid charms
Can hold Rome's proudest consul a captive in her arms,
Her cold embrace but brightens the memory of mine,
And for my warm caresses he in her arms shall pine.
'Twas not for love he sought her, but for her princely
    dower;
She brought him Cæsar's friendship, she brought him
    kingly power,
I should have bid him take her had he my counsel sought.
I've but to smile upon him, and all her charms are naught;
For I would scorn to hold him by but a single hair,
Save his own longing for me when I'm no longer there;
And I will show you, Roman, that for one kiss from me,
Wife — fame — and even honor to him shall nothing be!

Throw wide the window, Eros — fling perfumes o'er me now,
And bind the lotus blossoms again upon my brow,
The rain has ceased its weeping, the driving storm is past,
And calm are Nature's pulses, that lately beat so fast.

Gone is my jealous frenzy, and Eros reigns serene,
The only god e'er worshiped by Egypt's haughty Queen.
With Antony — my loved — I'll kneel before his shrine
'Till the loves of Mars and Venus are naught to his and
    mine;
And down through coming ages, in every land and tongue,
With them shall Cleopatra and Antony be sung.
Burn sandal-wood and cassia, let the vapor round me
    wreathe
And mingle with the incense the lotus blossoms breathe.
Let India's spicy odors, and Persia's perfumes rare,
Be wafted on the pinions of Egypt's fragrant air.
With the sighing of the night breeze, the river's rippling
    flow,
Let me hear the notes of music in cadence soft and low,
Draw round my couch its curtains; I'd bathe my soul in
    sleep:
I feel its gentle languor upon me slowly creep.
O let me cheat my senses with dreams of future bliss,
In fancy feel his presence, in fancy taste his kiss,
In fancy nestle closely against his throbbing heart,
And throw my arms around him, no more — no more to
    part.
Hush ! hush ! his spirit's pinions are rustling in my ears;
He comes upon the tempest to calm my jealous fears;
He comes upon the tempest in answer to my call.
Wife — fame — and even honor — for me he leaves them
    all;
And royally I'll welcome my lover to my side.
I have won him — I have won him from Cæsar and his
    bride.

Mary Bayard Clarke.

REUBEN AND ROSE — "Two days she wandered."

REUBEN AND ROSE.

A TALE OF ROMANCE.

HE darkness which hung upon Willumberg's walls
   Had long been remember'd with awe and dismay!
For years not a sunbeam had play'd in its halls,
   And it seem'd as shut out from the regions of day!

Though the valleys were brighten'd by many a beam,
   Yet none could the woods of the castle illume;
And the lightning which flash'd on the neighboring stream
   Flew back, as if fearing to enter the gloom!

" Oh! when shall this horrible darkness disperse?"
   Said Willumberg's lord to the seer of the cave; —
" It ne'er can dispel," said the wizard of verse,
   " Till the bright star of chivalry's sunk in the wave! "

And who was the bright star of chivalry then?
   Who could be but Reuben, the flower of the age?
For Reuben was first in the combat of men,
   Though Youth had scarce written his name on her page.

For Willumberg's daughter his bosom had beat;
   For Rose who was bright as the spirit of dawn,
When with wand dropping diamonds, and silvery feet,
   It walks o'er the flowers of the mountain and lawn!

Must Rose, then, from Reuben so fatally sever?
   Sad, sad were the words of the man in the cave,
That darkness should cover the castle forever,
   Or Reuben be sunk in the merciless wave!

She flew to the wizard —" And tell me, oh tell !
 Shall my Reuben no more be restored to my eyes?" —
" Yes, yes — when a spirit shall toll the great bell
 Of the moldering abbey, your Reuben shall rise! "

Twice, thrice he repeated, " Your Reuben shall rise! "
 And Rose felt a moment's release from her pain;
She wiped, while she listen'd, the tears from her eyes,
 And she hoped she might yet see her hero again!

Her hero could smile at the terrors of death,
 When he felt that he died for the sire of his Rose;
To the Oder he flew, and there plunging beneath,
 In the lapse of the billows soon found his repose.

How strangely the order of destiny falls! —
 Not long in the waters the warrior lay,
When a sunbeam was seen to glance over the walls!
 And the castle of Willumberg bask'd in the ray!

All, all but the soul of the maid was in light —
 There sorrow and terror lay gloomy and blank;
Two days did she wander, and all the long night,
 In quest of her love, on the wide river's bank.

Oft, oft did she pause for the toll of the bell,
 And she heard but the breathings of night in the air;
Long, long did she gaze on the watery swell,
 And she saw but the foam of the white billow there.

And often as midnight its veil would undraw,
 As she look'd at the light of the moon in the stream,
She thought 'twas his helmet of silver she saw,
 As the curl of the surge glitter'd high in the beam.

And now the third night was begemming the sky,
  Poor Rose on the cold, dewy margent reclined,
There wept till the tear almost froze in her eye,
  When—hark!—'twas the bell that came deep in the
    wind.

She startled, she saw, through the glimmering shade,
  A form o'er the waters in majesty glide;
She knew 'twas her love, though his cheek was decay'd,
  And his helmet of silver was wash'd by the tide.

Was this what the seer of the cave had foretold!—
  Dim, dim through the phantom the moon shot a gleam;
'Twas Reuben, but ah! he was deathly and cold,
  And fleeted away like the spell of a dream!

Twice, thrice did he rise, and as often she thought
  From the bank to embrace him, but never, ah! never;
Then springing beneath, at a billow she caught,
  And sunk to repose on its bosom forever!

Tom Moore.

MEASURING THE BABY.

WE measured the riotous baby
　　Against the cottage wall—
A lily grew at the threshold,
　　And the boy was just as tall.
A royal tiger lily,
　　With spots of purple and gold,
And a heart like a jeweled chalice,
　　The fragrant dew to hold.

Without the bluebirds whistled
　　High up in the old roof-trees,
And to and fro at the window
　　The red rose rocked her bees;
And the wee pink fists of the baby
　　Were never a moment still,
Snatching at shine and shadow
　　That danced on the lattice sill.

His eyes were wide as bluebells—
　　His mouth like a flower unblown—
Two little bare feet, like funny white mice
　　Peeped out from his snowy gown;
And we thought, with a thrill of rapture,
　　That yet had a touch of pain,
When June rolls around with her roses,
　　We'll measure the boy again.

Ah me!　In a darkened chamber,
　　With the sunshine shut away,
Through tears that fell like a bitter rain
　　We measured the boy to-day;

And the little bare feet that were dimpled
　And sweet as a budding rose,
Lay side by side together,
　In the hush of a long repose.

Up from the dainty pillow,
　White as the risen dawn,
The fair little face lay smiling,
　With the light of Heaven thereon —
And the dear little hands, like rose leaves
　Dropped from a rose, lay still,
Never to snatch at the sunshine
　That crept to the shrouded sill.

We measured the sleeping baby
　With ribbons white as snow,
For the shining rosewood casket
　That waited him below;
And out of the darkened chamber
　We went with a childless moan —
To the height of the sinless angels
　Our little one had grown.

Emma Alice Browne.

A LONDON IDYL.

HEY, rain, rain, rain!
  It patters down the glass and on the sill,
    And splashes underneath, along the lane —
      Then gives a kind of scream, and lies quite still;
  One likes to hear it, tho', when one is ill;
Rain, rain, rain, rain!
  Hey, how it pours and pours!
Rain, rain, rain, rain!
  A weary day for poor girls out-o' doors.

Ah, don't! that kind of comfort makes me cry,
And, Parson, since I'm bad, I want to die.
    The roaring of the street,
    The tramp, tramp, tramp of feet,
The sobbing, sobbing of the weary Rain,
Have gone into the aching of my brain.
I'm lost and weak, and can no longer bear
To wander like a shadow here and there —
  As useless as a stone — tired out - - and sick!
  So that they put me down to slumber quick,
It does not matter where.
No one will miss me; all will hurry by,
  And never cast a thought on one so low;
  Fine gentles miss fine ladies when they go,
But folk care nought for such a thing as I.

'Tis bad, I know, to talk like that —too bad!
  Joe, tho' he's often hard, is strong and true —
  (Ah, Joe meant well!) and there's the baby too!
But I'm so tired and sad.

I'm glad it was a boy, sir, very glad.
A man can fight along, can say his say,
  Is not looked down upon, holds up his head,
  And at a push can always earn his bread;
Men have the best of it, in many a way.

But ah! 'tis hard indeed for girls to keep
  Decent and honest, tramping in a town,
  Their best but bad — made light of — beaten down,
Forever wearying, wearying for sleep.
If they grow hard, go wrong, from bad to badder,
  Why, Parson dear, they're happier being blind:
  They get no thanks for being good and kind —
The better that they are, they feel the sadder!

Nineteen! Nineteen!
  Only nineteen, and yet so old, so old; —
I feel like fifty, Parson — I have been
  So wicked, I suppose, and life's so cold!
Ah, cruel are the wind and rain and snow,
  And I've been out for years among them all:
  I scarce remember being weak and small
Like Baby there — it was so long ago.
It does not seem that I was born, but woke
        One day in a dark room
        High up among the smoke,
And trembling at the roaring of the gloom
That hung around me (for you could not see
  The people from our window — only stone —
Deep walls, black pits, and lanes — tho' drearily
  You heard the deep streets groan);
And I was all alone, and looking out,
  And listening in a dream;

And far between the housetops was a gleam
Of water winding silver-like about.
That was the River.   It look'd cool and deep,
    And as I watch'd, I felt it slipping past,
As if it smoothly swept along in sleep,
    Gleaming and gliding fast;
And so I lean'd upon the sill and hearken'd
    To the strange hum, while all the roofs became
    Cover'd with thin, sick flame,

And with a dusky thrill the River darken'd;
Till coldly, coldly, on the roofs there lighten'd
    A pale, sad silver light from heaven shed,
And with a sweep that made me sick and frighten'd
    The Yellow Moon roll'd up above my head;
And down below me groan'd the noise and trade
And O! I felt alive, and was afraid,
    And cold, and hungry, shrieking out for bread.
All that is like a dream!   It don't seem *true!* —
    Father was dead and mother left, you see,
    To work for little brother Ned and me,
And up among the roofs we grew and grew;
Lock'd in whole days high up, while mother char'd
    In people's houses; only now and then
We slipt away into the streets, and stared
    At the big crowds of women and of men.
And I was six, but Ned was only three,
    And thin and weak and weary; and one day,
    While mother was away.
        He put his little head upon my knee,
And went to sleep, and would not stir a limb,
    But look'd quite strange and old,
For when I touch'd him, shook him, spoke to him,

He smiled and grew so cold;
Then I was frighten'd and cried out, and none
   Could hear me, and I sat and nursed his head,
Watching the smoky window while the sun
   Peep'd in upon his face and made it red;
And I began to cry;—till mother came,
Knelt down and scream'd, and named the great God's
         name,
   And told me he was dead.
Well, when she put his night-gown on, and weeping
   Put him among the rags upon his bed,
I thought that brother Ned was only sleeping,
   And took his little hand and felt no fear;
   But, when the place grew gray and cold and drear,
And the round moon came creeping, creeping, creeping,
   Over the roofs and put a silver shade
   All round the cold, cold bed where he was laid,
   I sobb'd and was afraid.
Ah, yes, it's like a dream! for time pass'd by,
   And I went out into the smoky air,
Fruit-selling, Parson —trudging wet or dry--
   Winter and summer—weary, cold, and bare;
And when old mother laid her down to die,
And parish buried her, I did not cry,
   And hardly seem'd to care;
I was too hungry and too dull; beside,
   The roar o' streets had made me dry as dust;
It took me all my time, howe'er I tried,
   To keep my limbs alive and earn a crust;
I had no time for weeping,
   And when I was not out amid the roar,
   Or standing frozen at the play-house door,
Why, I was coil'd upon my straw, and sleeping.

Ah, pence were hard to gain!
Some girls were pretty, too, but I was plain!
Fine ladies never stopp'd and looked and smil'd,
    And gave me money for my face's sake;
That made me hard and angry when a child,
    But now it thrills my heart and makes it ache!
The pretty ones, poor things, what could they do,
    Fighting and starving in the wicked town,
    But go from bad to badder — down, down, down —
Being so poor and yet so pretty too?
Never could bear the like of that — ah, no!
Better have starved outright than gone so low!
For often late at night
    A face that I had known when mild and meek
    Pass'd by with fearful smile and painted cheek,
Gleam'd in the gas, and faded out of sight.

But I've no call to boast.   I might have been
    As wicked, Parson, dear, in my distress,
But for your friend — you know the one I mean?
    The tall, pale lady in the mourning dress.
Though we were cold at first, that wore away —
        She was so mild and young,
        And had so soft a tongue,
And eyes to sweeten what she loved to say,
She never seem'd to scorn one, no, not she,
And (what was best) she seem'd as sad as me!
Not one of those that make a girl feel base,
And call her names, and talk of her disgrace,
And frighten one with thoughts of flaming Hell
    And fierce LORD GOD with black and angry brow,
But soft and mild, and sensible as well,
    And O I loved her, and I love her now.

She did me good for many and many a day —
  More good than pence could ever do, I swear,
  For she was poor, with little pence to spare —
Learn'd me to read and quit low words — and pray.
And, Parson, tho' I never understood
How such a life as mine was meant for good,
    And could not understand
How one she said was wicked ever could
    Go to your better land
    Among a troop so grand,
I liked to hear her talk of such a place,
  And thought of all the angels she was best,
Because her soft voice soothed me, and her face
  Made my words gentle, put my heart at rest.

Ah! sir, 'twas very lonesome night and day,
  Save when the sweet Miss came, I was alone:
  Moved on and hunted thro' the streets of stone,
And even in dreams afraid to rest or stay.
Then the girls had lads to work and strive for,
  I envied them, and did not know 'twas wrong,
  And often, very often, used to long
For some one I could like and keep alive for.
Marry? Not they!
  They can't afford to be so good, you know;
But many of them, tho' they step astray,
  Indeed don't mean to sin so much, or go
Against what's decent. Only 'tis their way.
And many might do worse than that, may be.
  If they had ne'er a one to fill a thought —
It sounds half wicked, but poor girls like me
  Must sin a little, to be good in aught.

So I was glad when I began to see
That costermongering Joe had fancied me;
And when, one night, he took me to the play,
    Over on Surrey side, and offer'd fair,
    That we should take a little room and share
Our earnings, why, I could not answer " nay "!
And that's a year ago; and tho' I'm bad,
    I've been as true to Joe as girl could be ;
I don't complain a bit of Joe, dear lad,
    Joe never, never meant but well; and we
Have had as fresh and fair a time, I think,
    As one could hope, since we are both so low:
    Joe likes me, never gave me push or blow,
When sober — only he was wild in drink.

But then, we don't mind beating when a man
    Is angry, if he likes us and keeps straight,
Works for his bread and does the best he can;—
    'Tis being left and slighted that we hate.
And so the baby's come, and I shall die!
    And tho' 'tis hard to leave poor Baby here,
    Where folk will think him bad, and all's so drear,
The great LORD GOD knows better far than I.
    Ah, don't! — 'tis kindly, but it pains me so!
    You say I'm wicked, and I want to go!
" GOD's kingdom," Parson, dear?   Ah nay, ah nay!
    That must be like the country — which I fear;
I saw the country once, one summer day,
    And I would rather die in London here.

For I was sick of hunger, cold and strife,
    And took a sudden fancy in my head
    To try the country, and to earn my bread

Out among fields, where, I had heard, one's life
Was easier and brighter.   So, that day,
I took my basket up and stole away,
Early at morning.   As I went along,
  Trembling and loath to leave the busy place,
I felt that I was doing something wrong,
  And fear'd to look policemen in the face.
And all was dim: the streets were gray and wet
  After a rainy night: and all was still;
  I held my shawl around me with a chill,
And dropt my eyes from every face I met;
Until the streets began to fade, the road
  Grew fresh and clean and wide,
Fine houses where the gentlefolk abode,
  And gardens full of flowers, on every side:
That made me walk the quicker — on, on, on—
  As if I were asleep with half-shut eyes,
  And all at once I saw to my surprise
The houses of the gentlefolk were gone,
And I was standing still,
Shading my face upon a high green hill.
  And the bright sun was blazing,
And all the blue above me seem'd to melt
  To burning, flashing gold, while I was gazing
On the great smoky cloud where I had dwelt.

I'll ne'er forget that day.   All was so bright
  And strange.   Upon the grass around my feet
The rain had hung a million drops of light ;
  The air, too, was so clear and warm and sweet
It seem'd a sin to breathe it.   All around
  Were hills and fields, and trees that trembled thro'
  A burning, blazing fire of gold and blue;

And there was not a sound,
  Save a bird singing, singing, and a kind
Of sighing from the grass upon the ground,
  I turn'd away, like one grown deaf and blind.
Then, with my heavy hand upon my chest,
  Because the bright air pain'd me trembling, sighing,
I stole into a dewy field to rest,
  And O the green, green grass where I was lying
Was fresh and living — and the birds sang loud.
Out of a golden cloud —
  And I was looking up at him and crying !

The hours they slipt away; and by and by
The sun grew red, big shadows fill'd the sky,
  The air grew damp with dew,
And the dark night was coming down, I knew.
Well, I was more afraid than ever then,
  And I felt that I should die in such a place; —
  So back to London town I turned my face,
And crept into the great, black streets again;
And when I breathed the smoke and heard the roar,
  Why, I was better, for in London here
  My heart was busy, and I felt no fear.
I never saw the country any more.
And I have staid in London well or ill,
  I dared not stay out yonder if I could,
  For one feels dead, and all looks pure and good —
I could not bear a life so bright and still.
All that I want is sleep,
Under the flags and stones, so deep, so deep!
GOD won't be hard on one so mean, but He
  Perhaps will let a tired girl slumber sound
  There in the deep, cool darkness underground;

And I shall waken up in time, may be,
Better and stronger, not afraid to see
  The great Still Light that folds Him round and round.

See! there's a bit of sunshine thro' the pane —
How cool and moist it looks amid the rain!
I like to hear the splashing of the drops
On the house tops,
And the loud humming of the folks that go
Along the streets below!
I like the smoke and roar — I am so bad —
  They make a low one hard and still her cares —
  There's Joe!   I hear his foot upon the stairs!
He must be wet, poor lad!
He will be angry, like enough, to find
  Another little life to clothe and keep,
But show him baby, Parson — speak him kind —
  And tell him Doctor thinks I'm going to sleep.
A hard, hard life is his — he need be strong
And rough, to earn his bread and get along; —
I think he will be sorry when I go,
  And leave the little one and him behind.
  I hope he'll see another to his mind
To keep him straight and tidy.   Poor old Joe!

Robert Buchanan.

THE FROGS.

For Recitation — with Imitations.

WHY should the birds have all the words
　　Of song and praise in poets' lays,
While all unstrung the lyre has hung,
And all incog, the tuneful frog
　　Is croaking all his days? —
　　Croaking with a *croak, cro-ack, croak* —
　　　Trilling with a *trill, ter-ril, trill* —
　　Joking with a *joke, jo-ack, joke* —
Waking every echoing hill
With his merry music still!

Chirping in the tree-tops all the night
　　Chirping, chirruping, chirping!
Never in the sunshine's gairish light
　　Chirping.
Hiding from each curious eye,
Dappled green and gray they lie,
Seeming, as we pass them by,
Only moss-tufts gray and dry.
Still, when night-fall's shades appear,
Wakes the tree-frog's piping clear —
　　Chirp — chirp — chirruping.

When the spring rains fill the pond;
When the wild ducks vagabond,
Fly to regions far beyond —
　　Hear the merry serenaders!
Nestling groups along the shore,
Forth their trilling concert pour —
Trilling, trilling, trilling more —
　　Spring-time's evening merry-makers.

Then, when summer on the bog
Decks with verdure every log,
See the sunshine-loving frog,
   Sitting — sitting, like a ghoul!
'Till some stealthy step comes nigh;
Then, with single gurgling cry,
Leaping with a quick good-bye,
   Chug! he sinks into the pool.

Sitting in the green lagoon
Musing on the evening moon,
Body half immersed they lie,
Glinting with each glimmering eye,
Tuning for the concert's din —
Never ready to begin!
   Each one anxious to prepare;
      Twanging never two together!
   Twanging here, and *twanging* there,
      Like wet strings in rainy weather.

All of those are known and heard,
Common as a household word.
Others rarely trill or mutter,
Sounds no other throat can utter —
Soldiers camped by Bayou Pierre,*
Listening for the foeman there,
Heard discordant cow-bells near —
Heard them tinkling sharp and clear
Forth, at risk of death or wounding,
Crept they where the bells were sounding —
Searched they all the brake surrounding;
Listening still, and still confounding

* On White River, Arkansas.

Every *tingle* in the bog;
   Tinkled by the " cow-bell frog "!
Tingling, tingling in the bog —
   Only by the cow-bell frog.

Giant of the Rana race,
   Lo, the bull-frog, grave and grim!
See his wonted lurking place
   By the pool's o'er-shaded rim —
By the stagnant bayou bank —
   By the river or lagoon —
By the margins, drear and dank,
   Where he nightly bays the moon.
Eyes like diamonds set in gold;
Neckless head on body cold;
Throat like pouch of pelican;
Arms and legs which mimic man;
Dappled skin, black, gray, and green —
Uglier elf was never seen!
Yet, when evening shades appear,
How he startles every ear!
How he times the loud response —
Thrills a hundred throats at once —
Echoing deep in concert true —
Bool-yer-o-boo! bool-yer-o-boo! bool-yer-o-boo!

               Edward R. Roe.

THE COTTER'S SATURDAY NIGHT.

INSCRIBED TO R. AIKEN, ESQ.

" Let not ambition mock their useful toil,
  Their homely joys and destiny obscure;
Nor grandeur hear, with a disdainful smile,
  The short but simple annals of the poor."

Gray.

I.

MY loved, my honor'd, much respected friend,
  No mercenary bard his homage pays:
With honest pride I scorn each selfish end ;
  My dearest meed, a friend's esteem and praise.
To you I sing, in simple Scottish lays,
  The lowly train in life's sequester'd scene;
The native feelings strong, the guileless ways;
  What Aiken in a cottage would have been ;
Ah! tho' his worth unknown, far happier there, I ween.

II.

November chill blaws loud wi' angry sugh ;
  The short'ning winter-day is near a close;
The miry beasts retreating frae the pleugh;
  The black'ning trains o' craws to their repose;
The toil-worn Cotter frae his labor goes,
  This night his weekly moil is at an end —
Collects his spades, his mattocks, and his hoes —
Hoping the morn in ease and rest to spend,
And weary, o'er the moor, his course does homeward
    bend.

III.

At length his lonely cot appears in view,
　Beneath the shelter of an aged tree;
Th' expectant wee things, toddlin', stacher through
　To meet their dad, wi' flichterin' noise and glee.
His wee bit ingle, blinkin' bonnily,
　His clean hearth-stane, his thriftie wifie's smile,
The lisping infant prattling on his knee,
　Does a' his weary carking cares beguile,
And makes him quite forget his labor and his toil.

IV.

Belyve the elder bairns come drapping in,
　At service out amang the farmers roun';
Some ca' the pleugh, some herd, some tentie rin
　A cannie errand to a neibor town;
Their eldest hope, their Jenny, woman grown,
　In youthfu' bloom, love sparklin' in her e'e,
Comes hame, perhaps, to show a bra' new gown,
　Or deposit her sair-won penny fee,
To help her parents dear, if they in hardship be.

V.

Wi' joy unfeigned, brothers and sisters meet,
　An' each for other's weelfare kindly spiers:
The social hours, swift wing'd, unnotic'd fleet;
　Each tells the uncos that he sees or hears;
The parents, partial, eye their hopeful years;
　Anticipation forward points the view.
The mother, wi' her needle an' her shears,
　Gars auld claes look amaist as weel's the new;
The father mixes a' wi' admonition due.

"Th' expectant wee things, toddlin', stacher through
To meet their dad, wi' flichterin' noise and glee."

VI.

Their masters' an' their mistress' command,
    The younkers a' are warned to obey;
And mind their labors wi' an eydent hand,
    An' ne'er, tho' out o' sight, to jauk or play;
" An' oh, be sure to fear the Lord alway!
    An' mind your duty, duly, morn an' night!
Lest in temptation's path ye gang astray,
    Implore His counsel and assisting might:
They never sought in vain that sought the Lord aright!"

VII.

But, hark! a rap comes gently to the door.
    Jenny, wha kens the meanin' o' the same,
Tells how a neibor lad cam o'er the moor,
    To do some errands and convoy her hame.
The wily mother sees the conscious flame
    Sparkle in Jenny's e'e, and flush her cheek;
Wi' heart-struck anxious care inquires his name,
    While Jenny hafflins is afraid to speak;
Weel pleas'd the mother hears it's nae wild, worthless rake.

VIII.

Wi' kindly welcome, Jenny brings him ben;
    A strappin' youth; he taks the mother's e'e;
Blithe Jenny sees the visit's no ill ta'en;
    The father cracks of horses, pleughs, and kye.
The youngster's artless heart o'erflows wi' joy,
    But blate and laithfu', scarce can weel behave;
The mother, wi' a woman's wiles, can spy
    What makes the youth sae bashfu' an sae grave;
Weel pleas'd to think her bairn's respected like the lave.

IX.

Oh happy love! where love like this is found!
    Oh heartfelt raptures! bliss beyond compare!
I've paced this weary mortal round,
    And sage experience bids me this declare: —
If Heav'n a draught of heavenly pleasure spare,
    One cordial in this melancholy vale,
'Tis when a youthful, loving, modest pair
    In other's arms breathe out the tender tale,
Beneath the milk-white thorn that scents the ev'ning gale.

X.

Is there, in human form, that bears a heart,
    A wretch, a villain, lost to love and truth,
That can, with studied, sly, ensnaring art,
    Betray sweet Jenny's unsuspecting youth?
Curse on his perjured arts! dissembling smooth!
    Are honor, virtue, conscience, all exil'd?
Is there no pity, no relenting ruth,
    Points to the parents fondling o'er their child,
Then paints the ruin'd maid, and their distraction wild?

XI.

But now the supper crowns their simple board,
    The halesome parritch, chief o' Scotia's food;
The soupe their only hawkie does afford,
    That 'yont the hallan snugly chows her cood;
The dame brings forth, in complimental mood,
    To grace the lad, her weel-hain'd kebbuck fell,
An' aft he's prest, an' aft he ca's it guid;
    The frugal wifie, garrulous, will tell,
How 'twas a towmond auld, sin' lint was i' the bell.

XII.

The cheerfu' supper done, wi' serious face,
   They round the ingle, form a circle wide;
The sire turns o'er, wi' patriarchal grace,
   The big ha'-Bible, ance his father's pride;
His bonnet rev'rently is laid aside,
   His lyart haffets wearing thin an' bare:
Those strains that once did sweet in Zion glide,
   He wales a portion with judicious care;
And "Let us worship GOD!" he says, with solemn air.

XIII.

They chant their artless notes in simple guise:
   They tune their hearts, by far the noblest aim;
Perhaps "Dundee's" wild-warbling measures rise,
   Or plaintive "Martyrs," worthy of the name:
Or noble "Elgin" beats the heav'n ward flame,
   The sweetest far of Scotia's holy lays:
Compared with these, Italian trills are tame;
   The tickl'd ears no heart-felt raptures raise;
Nae unison hae they with our Creator's praise.

XIV.

The priest-like father reads the sacred page —
   How Abram was the friend of GOD on high;
Or Moses bade eternal warfare wage
   With Amalek's ungracious progeny,
Or how the royal bard did groaning lie
   Beneath the stroke of Heav'ns avenging ire;
Or Job's pathetic plaint, and wailing cry;
   Or rapt Isaiah's wild, seraphic fire;
Or other holy seers that tune the sacred lyre.

XV.

Perhaps the Christian volume is the theme —
   How guiltless blood for guilty men was shed ;
How He who bore in Heaven the second name,
   Had not on earth whereon to lay his head :
How his first followers and servants sped ;
   The precepts sage they wrote to many a land ;
How he, who lone in Patmos banished,
   Saw in the sun a mighty angel stand,
And heard great Bab'lon's doom pronounced by Heaven's
     command.

XVI.

Then, kneeling down, to HEAVEN'S ETERNAL KING,
   The saint, the father, and the husband prays:
Hope " springs exulting on triumphant wing,"
   That thus they all shall meet in future days;
There ever bask in uncreated rays,
   No more to sigh, or shed the bitter tear,
Together hymning their Creator's praise,
   In such society, yet still more dear;
While circling Time moves round in an eternal sphere.

XVII.

Compar'd with this, how poor Religion's pride,
   In all the pomp of method and of art,
When men display to congregations wide
   Devotion's ev'ry grace, except the heart!
The Power, incensed, the pageant will desert,
   The pompous strain, the sacerdotal stole;
But haply, in some cottage far apart,
   May hear, well pleas'd, the language of the soul;
And in his Book of Life the inmates poor enroll.

XVIII.

Then homeward all take off their sev'ral way;
　The youngling cottagers retire to rest;
The parent-pair their secret homage pay,
　And proffer up to Heaven the warm request,
That HE who stills the raven's clam'rous nest,
　And decks the lily fair in flow'ry pride,
Would, in the way his wisdom sees the best,
　For them and for their little ones provide;
But, chiefly, in their hearts with grace divine preside.

XIX.

From scenes like these old Scotia's grandeur springs,
　That makes her loved at home, revered abroad:
Princes and lords are but the breath of kings,
　" An honest man's the noblest work of GOD! "
And certes, in fair Virtue's heav'nly road,
　The cottage leaves the palace far behind:
What is a lordling's pomp? — a cumbrous load,
　Disguising oft the wretch of human kind,
Studied in arts of hell, in wickedness refined!

XX.

Oh, Scotia! my dear, my native soil!
　For whom my warmest wish to Heaven is sent,
Long may thy hardy sons of rustic toil
　Be blest with health, and peace, and sweet content!
And, oh, may Heav'n their simple lives prevent
　From luxury's contagion, weak and vile!
Then, howe'er crowns and coronets be rent,
　A virtuous populace may rise the while,
And stand a wall of fire around their much-lov'd Isle.

XXI.

Oh, Thou! who pour'd the patriotic tide,
  That stream'd thro' Wallace's undaunted heart:
Who dared to nobly stem tyrannic pride,
  Or nobly die, the second glorious part,
(The patriot's God peculiarly thou art,
  His friend, inspirer, guardian and reward!)
Oh, never, never Scotia's realm desert;
  But still the patriot and the patriot bard
In bright succession raise, her ornament and guard!

Robert Burns.

CIVIL WAR.

" RIFLEMAN, shoot me a fancy shot
      Straight at the heart of yon prowling vidette;
    Ring me a ball in the glittering spot
      That shines on his breast like an amulet!"

" Ah, captain! here goes for a fine drawn bead,
    There's music around when my barrel's in tune!"
Crack! went the rifle, the messenger sped,
    And dead from his horse fell the ringing dragoon.

" Now, rifleman, steal through the bushes, and snatch
    From your victim some trinket to handsel first blood;
A button, a loop, or that luminous patch
    That gleams in the moon like a diamond stud."

" Oh captain! I staggered, and sunk on my track,
    When I gazed on the face of that fallen vidette,
For he looked so like you, as he lay on his back,
    That my heart rose upon me, and masters me yet.

" But I snatched off the trinket — this locket of gold;
   An inch from the center my lead broke its way,
Scarce grazing the picture, so fair to behold,
   Of a beautiful lady in bridal array."

" Ha! rifleman, fling me the locket! — 'tis she,
   My brother's young bride — and the fallen dragoon
Was her husband — Hush! soldier, 'twas Heaven's decree,
   We must bury him there, by the light of the moon!

" But, hark! the far bugles their warnings unite;
   War is a virtue — weakness a sin;
There's a lurking and loping around us to-night;
   Load again, rifleman, keep your hand in!"

Anonymous.

HOW TO BECOME CONSEQUENTIAL

A BROW austere, a circumspective eye,
A frequent shrug of the *os humeri*,
A nod significant, a stately gait,
A blust'ring manner, and a tone of weight,
A smile sarcastic, an expressive stare;
Adapt all these as time and place will bear.
Then rest assur'd that those of little sense
Will set you down — a man of consequence.

Anonymous.

AN ODE TO THE RAIN.

[Composed before daylight, on the morning appointed for the departure of a very worthy, but not very pleasant, visitor; whom it was feared the rain might detain.]

I.

KNOW it is dark; and though I have lain
Awake, as I guess, an hour or twain,
I have not once opened the lids of my eyes,
But I lie in the dark, as a blind man lies.
O Rain! that I lie listening to,
    You've but a doleful sound at best;
I owe you little thanks, 'tis true,
    For breaking thus my needful rest!
Yet if, as soon as it is light,
O Rain, you will but take your flight,
I'll neither rail, nor malice keep,
Though sick and sore for want of sleep;
But only now, for this one day,
Do go, dear Rain! do go away!

II.

O Rain! with your dull two-fold sound,
The clash hard by, and the murmur all round!
You know, if you know aught, that we,
Both night and day, but ill agree:
For days, and months, and almost years,
Have limped on through this vale of tears,
Since body of mine, and rainy weather,
Have lived on easy terms together.
Yet if, as soon as it is light,
O Rain! you will but take your flight.

Though you should come again to-morrow,
And bring with you both pain and sorrow;
Though stomach should sicken and knees should
    swell —
I'll nothing speak of you but well.
But only now for this one day,
Do go, dear Rain! do go away.

III.

Dear Rain! I ne'er refused to say
You're a good creature in your way,
Nay, I could write a book myself
Would fit a parson's lower shelf,
Showing, how very good you are —
What then?   Sometimes it must be fair!
And if sometimes, why not to-day?
Do go, dear Rain! do go away!

IV.

Dear Rain! if I've been cold and shy,
Take no offense! I'll tell you why.—
A dear old Friend e'en now is here,
And with him came my sister dear;
After long absence now first met,
Long months by pain and grief beset —
We three dear friends! in truth, we groan
Impatiently to be alone.
We three, you mark! and not one more!
The strong wish makes my spirit sore.
We have so much to talk about,
So many sad things to let out;

So many tears in our eye-corners,
Sitting like little Jacky Horners —
In short, as soon as it is day,
Do go, dear Rain! do go away!

V.

And this I'll swear to you, dear Rain!
Whenever you shall come again,
Be you as dull as e'er you could
(And by the by 'tis understood,
You're not so pleasant as you're good),
Yet knowing well your worth and place,
I'll welcome you with cheerful face;
And though you staid a week or more,
We're ten times duller than before,
Yet with kind heart, and right good will,
I'll sit and listen to you still;
Nor should you go away, dear Rain,
Uninvited to remain,
But only now, for this one day,
Do go, dear Rain! do go away!

Samuel Taylor Coleridge.

THE OLD STAGER'S STORY.

AH, good evening to you again! So you've brought the proof then, eh?
   "MACBETH, MR. HUBERT VILLERS." Yes, that's better, I must say.
Now, what'll you take! Hot whisky? Right! What, ho there, Polly, my dear!
Two fours of Irish warm for me and this other gentleman here.

Not half bad tipple, is it, my boy? 'Tain't often I drink from choice,
But I fancy a drop of Irish warm softens and mellers the voice:
So you liked my Claud last night, you say? Well, 'tis fairish they all allow;
But I'm getting a bit too old and fat for the lover business now.

Ah, well, I mustn't complain, I suppose! I can stick to the heavy line,
And I've got a few browns put by, you know, in that old stocking o' mine;
Though, mind you, with a company near a dozen strong, or quite,
If business is slack, 'tis a tightish fit when it comes to Saturday night.

See some queer things, we traveling folks? Well, yes, that's perfectly true:
Why, 'twas only now while sitting here, smoking and waiting for you,

I was thinking over a curious scene you may have heard
      about,
That shows how the real thing after all beats acting out-
      and-out!

I know it's true, for it all took place under my eyes, you
      know:
Let's see, 'twas at — yes, at Doncaster — about two years
      ago,
Me and the missus was sitting down at our lodgin's one
      day at tea,
When the slavey told me a lady had called, and wanted to
      speak to me,

" Show her up here," I says, for I thought, 'tis one of our
      folks look'd round
To ask me something about to-night but I was wrong, I .
      found;
For there entered, blushing up to her eyes, shrinking,
      tremulous, coy,
A lady I'd never seen before, with a charming little boy.

A beautiful blonde she was, not more than two and twenty
      or so.
With 'witching eyes of a lustrous brown, but ah, how full
      of woe!
And she and her boy were dressed in black, and she wore
      in mournful mood
On her flaxen hair, that was tinged with gold, the weeds
      of widowhood.

She took the chair I gave her, and spoke in a low, sweet
    voice —
I could see that she was a lady born, she seemed so gentle
    and nice;
She'd had some knowledge of the stage as an amateur, she
    said,
And could I give her something to do to find her boy in
    bread ?

" O that's how the wind lays, is it? " I thought.   " Well,
    p'r'aps I might do worse:
If she only acts as well as she looks, she'd nicely line my
    purse;"
And I took good stock of her as she sat with her boy
    beside her chair,
And stroked with dainty, tremulous hand his bonny golden
    hair.

Bit by bit her story came out.   Long back her mother had
    died,
And left her, an only child, to be her father's darling and
    pride;
He was in the law, and thought to be rich, and was held
    in high repute;
But, ah! he died a ruined man, and left her destitute.

Then the only relative she had — an aunt, who was well-
    to-do —
Had taken her in, and had found for her a wealthly suitor,
    too.

But she loved another — a sailor lad — who, like herself,
    was poor;
And when they married, her haughty aunt had spurned
    her from her door

They were very happy at first, she said, and her voice was
    tearful and low,
But, O, she had lost her husband too — he was drown'd
    four months ago;
His ship was wrecked, and all were lost; and now, in her
    need and care,
She'd no one left in all the world, but her little Charlie
    there!

And here she drooped her head, poor girl, and her voice
    was choked with sighs—
Hem, hem! confound the smoke; how it gets in a fellow's
    throat and eyes!
Then she finished her tale: She felt at first all stunned
    and dazed, she said;
And even to think aught but of him seemed treachery to
    the dead.

But by-and-by, for the sake of her boy, now doubly pre-
    cious and dear,
She nerved herself to look beyond to the future that seemed
    so drear:
She thought of a governess' place at last, but then they
    would have to part,
And to give up her only darling now would almost break
    her heart!

Little by little her things had gone to meet their daily need,
Till her home too had to be given up, and all seemed lost
    indeed;
Then she thought of how she loved the stage in the
    happy Long Ago,
And how well she played as an amateur — at least they
    told her so.

She'd called at all the theaters she knew, but 'twas still the
    same old tale —
A novice had no chance at all where even vet'rans fail;
Then some one had told her to come to me, and she'd
    traveled here to-day
To see if I could take her on, in however humble a way.

I should find her quick and willing, she said, in all I wanted
    done;
And all she wanted was lodging and food for her and her
    little one:
She'd nothing left but her wedding-ring and one poor
    half-a-crown,
And, O, there was only the work-house, if — and here she
    quite broke down.

Well, there, the parsons give it sometimes to we " poor
    players " hot,
But whatever our faults may be, my boy, we ain't a hard-
    hearted lot!
There was the missis a-crying too, with the little kid on
    her knee,
And I — well this weeping business, somehow, always gits
    over me!

11

And the end of it was that I took her on, as a super, so to
    speak,
And found her board and lodging with us, and a shilling
    or two a week.
She helped the missis in different ways, and did it capi-
    tally, too.
And we sent her on in little parts where she hadn't much
    to do.

But a quicker " study " I never knew, and she'd something
    better and higher —
I could see that she was an actress born — the woman had
    passion, fire!
She took with the public from the first, and with her sweet
    young face,
And passion, and power, and we gave her soon the leading
    lady's place.

Some of our ladies was jealous-like when they see her
    taking the lead,
And used to sneer at her ring and weeds, and mutter,
    " Mrs. indeed!"
But she was so gentle, obliging, meek, this soon wore off,
    it did,
And they all of 'em got to love her at last, and to almost
    worship the kid.

She seemed transformed with passion and power when
    once she got on the stage,
And Mrs. Mowbray, as she was called, came to be quite
    the rage;

She'd only to show herself for the cheers to thunder out,
    and lor'!
She always was good for three recalls of a night, and often
    more!

'Twas the best day's work I ever did when I lent her a help-
    ing hand:
By Jove, sir, as Constance in *King John* that woman was
    something grand!
And as for Ophelia, where she sings that song before she
    dies,
Hardened old stager as I am, it brought the tears to my
    eyes.

One night I happened to be in the front when she was
    extra fine;
'Twas in *East Lynne*, and she'd just come on, with her boy,
    as Madame Vine:
She's supposed, as the Lady Isabel, to have wronged her
    husband and fled,
But takes the governess' place disguised, after he thinks
    she's dead.

She'd got to the crowning scene of all, where the mother
    longs to stretch
Her arms to her boy, but has to check and school herself,
    poor wretch!
And the house was hushed in pity and awe, when I saw
    her stare and start,
Then stagger, and turn as white as death, and put her
    hand to her heart.

I followed her eyes, and there close by in the pit, looking
    pale and thin,
Was a tall young fellow in naval dress, who had only just
    come in:
He sprang to the stage, and bounded on, and you can
    guess the rest.—
" O Alice, Alice!"   " O Harry, dear!"—and she swooned
    away on his breast!

I think for the moment the people thought 'twas part of
    the play, forsooth,
But her story, you see, had been whispered about, and
    they easily guessed the truth,
And then — ah! talk of a scene, my boy! such cheers you
    never heard —
I thought the roof would have fallen in — I did, upon my
    word*!*

Of course the curtain had to be dropped, and I whispered
    to the band
To strike up something, and hurried behind at once, you
    understand,
To find her just " coming-to," dear heart, with the women
    all weeping there,
And her husband, with her hand in his, kneeling beside
    her chair.

And her little one clinging to her —ah! what a tarblow
    that would have been!
'Twould have made the fortune of a piece to have brought
    in such a scene!

I've come to look at it now, you see, in a sort of profes-
    sional light;
But then I was very nearly as weak as the women were, or
    quite.

His story was short: his ship was wrecked, and 'twas
    thought that all were drown'd,
But he and another clung to a spar, and were picked up
    safe and sound;
'Twas more like the Tichborne story again than anything
    else I know:
Do I believe in the Claimant? Yes — I believe he's
    Arthur O!

They landed him close to the Diamond Fields, and he
    wrote to his wife, but she
Believed he was dead, and had changed her name, and
    taken service with me;
Then he took a turn at the diggin's, and there good luck
    came thick and fast,
And he'd come back rich to find her gone, but they'd met
    at last — at last!

Then her story was told, and how good I'd been, and all
    the rest, dear heart,
And she would insist on going on again to finish her
    part:
So I went to the front myself, you know, and told the
    people all,
And, upon my soul, I thought this time the roof must
    surely fall.

And when she came on again at last, what deafening thun-
    der o' cheers!
Men a-waving their hats like mad — women and kids in
    tears!
I thought of the night when Kean first set all England's
    heart astir:
" Sir, the pit ROSE AT ME! " he said; and so it did at her!

And she seemed inspired, so grand she was, so passionate,
    true and warm;
From the time she opened her mouth again, she took the
    house by storm;
Three times they had her back at the end, and I shall never
    forget
How he had to lead her on at the last — I can see and hear
    'em yet.

A bonnie couple they were, my boy, and to see 'em to-
    gether then —
Hem! bother the smoke; it's been and got into my eyes
    again!
He dropped me a " fiver " for a feed for the company next
    day,
And she brought me this here diamond ring — up to the
    knocker, eh?

He took a nice little place in Kent, where thy're living in
    style, you know;
And there's always a knife and fork for me, whenever I
    like to go.

It ain't so very long ago — perhaps two or three months,
    or more —
Since me and the missus was there for a week, and was
    treated " up to the door."

I had their story put in a play, and it answered pretty
    well,
But, bless your heart, it wasn t a patch on the genuine
    article!
Well, good-bye for the present, old friend, if you won't
    have any more:
You won't forget about the bills? Good on yer! *Orevwar!*
                        Edwin Coller.

THE BALLAD OF THE SHAMROCK.

MY BOY left me just twelve years ago,
'Twas the black year of famine, of sickness and woe,
When the crops died out, and the people died too,
    And the land into one great graveyard grew;
And our neighbors' faces were as white and thin,
As the face of the moon, when she first comes in;
And honest men's hearts were rotten with blight,
And they thieved, and prowled, like wolves at night;
When the whole land was as dark as dark could be,
'Twas then that Donald my boy left me.
We were turned from the farm, where we'd lived so long,
For we couldn't pay the rent, and the law was strong;
From the low meadow land, and flax fields blue,
And the handsome green hill, where the yellow furze
    grew;

And the honest old cow, that each evening would stand
At the little gate, lowing, to be milked by my hand;
And the small patch of garden at the end of the lawn,
Where Donald grew sweet flowers for his Colleen Bawn.
But Donald and I had to leave all these,
I to live with father, and he to cross the seas,
For Donald was as proud as any king's son,
And swore he'd not stand by, and see such wrongs done,
But would seek a fortune out in the wide west,
Where the honest can find labor and the weary rest;
And as soon as he was able, why then he'd send for me,
To come and rest my poor old head in his home across the
    sea;
And then his young face flushed like a June sky at dawn,
As he said, he was thinking how his Colleen Bawn
Could come along to help him to keep the house straight,
For he knew how much she loved him, and she'd promised
    him to wait.
I think I see him now, as he stood one blessed day,
With his pale, smiling face upon the Limerick quay,
And I lying on his breast, with his long curly hair
Blowing all about my shoulders, as if to keep me there,
And the quivering of his lips that he tried to keep so proud,
Not because of his old mother, but the idle, curious crowd.
Then the hoisting of the anchor, and the flapping of the sail,
And the stopping of my heart, when the wild Irish wail
From the mothers and the kinsfolk on the quay,
Told me plainer than all words, that my darling was away.
Ten years went dragging by, and I heard but now and
    then,
For my Donald, though a brave boy, was no scholar with
    the pen;
But he sent me kindly words, and bade me not despair,

And sometimes sent me money, perhaps more than he
    could spare.
So I waited and I prayed, until it came to pass
That Father Pat he wanted me one Sunday after mass;
When I went a little fearsome, to the back vestry room,
Where his reverence sat a smiling, like a sun-flower in the
    gloom;
And then he up and told me, God bless him, that my boy
Had sent to bring me over, and I nearly died for joy.
All day I was half crazed, as I wandered through the house,
The dropping of the sycamore seeds, or the scrambling of
    a mouse,
Thrilled through me like a gun shot, and I durst not look
    behind,
For the pale face of my darling was always in my mind;
The pale face so sorrowful, the eyes so large and dark,
And softly shining as the deers' are, in young Lord Marsy's
    park,
And the long chestnut hair blowing loosely by the wind,
All this seemed at my shoulder, and I did not look behind;
But I said in my own heart, it is but the second-sight,
Of the day when I shall see him, all beautiful and bright.
Then I made my box ready to go across the sea;
My boy had sent a ticket, so my passage it was free.
But all the time I longed that some little gift I had,
To take across the ocean to my own dear lad;
A pin, or a chain, or something of the kind,
Just to mind the poor boy of the home he'd left behind.
But I was too poor to buy them, so I'd nothing left to
    do,
But to go to the old farm, the homestead that he knew,
To the handsome green hill where my Donald used to
    play,

And cut a sod of shamrock for the exile far away.
All through the voyage I nursed it, and watered it each
    day,
And kept its green leaves sheltered from the salt sea
    spray,
And I'd bring it up on deck, when the sun was shining
    fair,
And watch its triple leaflets open slowly in the air.
At first the sailors laughed at my little sod of grass,
But when they knew my object, they gently let me pass;
And the ladies in the cabin were very kind to me,
And made me tell my story of my boy across the sea;
So I told them of my Donald and his fair manly face,
Till bare speaking of my darling made a sunshine in the
    place.
We landed at the Battery, in New York's big bay,
The sun was shining grandly, and the wharves looked
    gay,
But I could see no sunshine nor beauty in the place,
What I only cared to look on, was Donald's sweet face.
And in all that great crowd, and I turned everywhere,
I could not see a sign of him, my darling was not there
I asked the men around me to go and find my son,
But they only stared and laughed, and left me one by
    one,
Till at last an old-country man came to me and said,
(How could I live to hear it?) that Donald was dead.
The shamrock sod is growing on Greenwood's hillside,
It grows upon the heart of my darling and my pride,
And on summer days I sit by the headstone all day,
With my heart growing old and my head growing gray,
And I watch the dead leaves whirl from the sycamore
    trees,

And wonder why it is that I can't die like these.
But I think that this same winter, and in my heart I
   hope,
I'll be lying nice and quiet upon Greenwood's slope,
With my darling close beside me, underneath the trick-
   ling dew,
And the shamrock creeping pleasantly above us two.

Fitz James O'Brien.

COME REST IN THIS BOSOM.

COME rest in this bosom, my own stricken deer,
Though the herd have fled from thee, thy home is still
   here. —
Here still is the smile that no cloud can o'ercast,
And a heart and a hand all thy own to the last

Oh! what was love made for, if 'tis not the same
Through joy and through torment, through glory and
   shame?
I know not, I ask not, if guilt's in that heart,
I but know that I love thee, whatever thou art.

Thou hast called me thy angel in moments of bliss,
And thy angel I'll be 'mid the horrors of this—
Through the furnace, unshrinking, thy steps to pursue,
And shield thee, and save thee, or perish there too.

Thomas Moore.

THE HOLLOW OAK.

HOLLOW is the oak beside the sunny waters
      drooping;
  Thither came, when I was young, happy children
      trooping;
Dream I now, or hear I now—far, their mellow whoop-
  ing?

Gay below the cowslip bank, see, the billow dances,
There I lay beguiling time—when I lived romances—
Dropping pebbles in the wave, fancies into fancies;—

Farther, where the river glides by the wooded cover,
Where the merlin singeth love, with the hawk above her,
Came a foot and shone a smile—woe is me, the Lover!

Leaflets on the hollow oak still as greenly quiver,
Musical amid the reeds murmurs on the river;
But the footsteps and the smile?—woe is me forever!

               E. Bulwer Lytton.

MAUNA LOA.

OVER the girdling sea
  We sail for MAUNA LOA;
To windward lies Maui,
  To leeward Mauna Loa;
And swift we glide with wind and tide,
  Pilgrims to Mauna Loa;
We watch no moon or star for guide,
  But only Mauna Loa.

The mountain fumes five watery leagues away,
Around his head the hovering halos play:

"Thither came, when I was young, happy children trooping."

Our island boatmen court the fitful breeze,
And trim our buoyant bark to skim the seas.
League after league we speed our wondering way;
We leave the night behind; before us play
The lurid sparkles tipped with mountain light,
Reflected o'er the sea from Loa's height.
'Tis morning on the sea: Hawaii
Looms up from out the waters and the sky,
And Mauna Loa lifts his head on high,
  Mauna Loa wakens from his sleep —
    Mauna Loa clothes his head with cloud —
  Mauna Loa lightens o'er the deep —
    Mauna Loa's crater thunders loud !
The clouds about his head are clouds of smoke:
  They came not from the ocean's summer mist ;
The thunders which his lofty dome awoke
    Are Vulcan's peals, not Jupiter's; —
    The glowing beams are Lucifer's;
And not the rays of Sol illume the lurid smoke.

So swift we sail till morning struggles nigh,
Contending with the fire-illumed sky;
And so, while showers of ashy cinders pour,
We moor our vessel near the island shore.

For days we trod the isle of Hawaii ;
For days we climbed the wondrous mountain high;
And night and day we felt, and saw, and heard,
Beyond all speech or utterable word !

Passing the snowy girdle of the mount,
We stood to windward of the fiery fount —
The vast, abysmal crater, deep and broad —
Which uttered thunders like the voice of God.

The outer elements beneath our feet
Were storming in the clouds of summer heat ;
But in the deaf'ning, deep volcano's roar,
The atmospheric thunders seemed no more
Than mimic storms upon th' illusive stage
Where mimic elements in strife engage.
Over the burning pit for miles abroad,
A canopy above the fiery god
In smoky curtains hung, or rolled away
To Mauna Kea in their fitful play,
Disclosing changeful hues of fiery blue,
Scarlet and purple in commingling hue;
And in their scenic counterfeit displayed
Inverted image, in the heavens portrayed,
Of burning mountains, rent and all aglow
With bright volcanic fire like that below.

Anon, the glowing pillar of fire and cloud,
With lightnings vivid and with thunders loud,
Shot upward straight an hundred fathoms high,
And outward curved like comets in the sky.
Over the ocean smoky clouds were blown,
Bearing volcanic ashes, raining down
Dust and blown cinders on the darkened sea
And o'er the decks of distant ships a-lee;
Within the crater's vast and fiery verge,
The white-hot molten lava, surge on surge,
Heaved, raged, and dashed with thundering roar,
Like surging ocean on a rock-bound shore.

Then suddenly a calm came on; and all
The lava waves were still; the lurid pall
In mid-air hovered o'er the dread abyss;
The thunders ceased; the roar, the howl, the hiss,

And all the sounds of simulated dole
Fell down into a smothered rumbling roll.
Illusive calm!   An earthquake broke the spell.
A new-formed crater in the mountain hell
Burst forth, and midway down the mountain side
Poured out a molten river, deep and wide,
Of white-hot lava, struggling to be free,
And rolling downward to the distant sea.
Around its fiery rim the crater built
A cone of scoria, ashes, pumice, silt,
Cinders, slag, and lava cooled; and out
Of this dread throat threw fitfully about,
Or shot sheer upward tow'rd th' astonished sky
Its fiery columns thundering on high,
A deep, infernal subterranean sound —
A smothered rumbling, awful and profound,
Alternate with explosion's mingled roar,
Convulsed th' abysmal fire from shore to shore,
Filling the air with lava spouting high,
Like fiery surf into a fiery sky.
Again the gleaming lava rose in towers,
Cones, columns, spires, or minarets and showers
Of glowing slag and cooling ashes fell
Back in the mouth of that volcanic hell.
Up with the molten columns as they rose,
Myriads of shining fragments interpose,
And back, down-falling in fantastic lines —
Recurving — shooting intersecting sines,
And streaking all the hot, volcanic air —
Make gleaming phantasms in th' infernal glare.

With senses surfeited with wonder there,
We turned our 'wildered wanderings to where

12

The stream of molten lava, rolling free,
Poured through the distant forest to the sea.
And what a flood was there! A lava flood,
Slow-rolling, like a stream of smoking blood,
Clotted, and sluggish as the surface cooled,
Bursting in crimson spouts where pooled
In deep depressions, broke the thickening crust,
Or rushing madly down where'er it must,
A river of fire, quick-moving, broad and deep,
In thundering cascade down the mountain steep.
Into the forest plunged th' impetuous stream,
Upheaving rocks, and burning trees which gleam,
And scintillate, and light the murky air
With showery stars out-bursting through the glare.
Vast trees enveloped in the burning flood,
Surrounded at the base, brief moment stood,
Then bursting with a cannon's sudden roar,
O'er-toppled in the flood they fell before.
And so the lava river, surging free,
Plunged through the blazing forest to the sea.
Reluctant sea! unwonted to receive
The fiery flood, its wildered waters heave
In waves tumultuous, shivering like glass
White-hot in water, all the molten mass;
Throwing a vitreous hailstorm upon high,
With thunders echoing from sea to sky.
From all the fiery firmament night fled away
From gory light reflected from the spray.
And glowing clouds of steam and sulphury smoke
Careered before the wind, and red waves broke
In deaf'ning thunders on the shining shore,
While sky, and earth, and ocean, mingled in the roar.
Was 't not enough! No — while th' volcano raged

Contending men in direful war engaged;
And Mauna Loa's slope saw deeds of death
Within the shadow of his sulphury breath.
Ka-meha-meha, king of Hawaii,
Compelled a bold, rebellious chief to fly
With all his followers up the mountain slope —
Too few and feeble with his king to cope.
Keoua divided up his band
Of flying braves — one company to stand
In feint of battle with the irate king;
Another in advance to fly, and bring
Their wives and children to a safe retreat.
And now the ground beneath their hurrying feet
Rocked wildly with a sudden earthquake's throes.
The thundering crater joined their human foes;
Belched forth black clouds of blinding smoke, which rose
Before the treacherous winds, which blew their breath
Of deadly sulphur, dooming all to death.
And so they perished!   And around them all
The rolling blackness spread its inky pall
And banished day; while through the deadly gloom
Fierce lightnings played around their stifling tomb.

Anon, the comrades of the stricken band —
The deadly sulphur clouds blown over,—stand
Appalled in presence of their kindred dead!
At first so life-like looked the scene of dread,
They seemed but resting from the hasty flight.
Some lay in silent groups; some sat upright,
But stiff in death; some held their harmless spears
Gripped tightly, resting on their rocky biers.
Dead mothers clasped dead children in their grasp,
And not a soul survived that sulphury gasp!

While over all the faces of the dead,
The mingled ashes, dust, and sulphur spread
Appalling pallor death could never show!
So perished there Ka-meha-meha's foe.

Over the girdling sea
We sail from Mauna Loa;
To windward lies Maui,
To leeward Mauna Loa;
And slow we glide 'gainst wind and tide,
Pilgrims from Mauna Loa;
Watching, as over the waves we ride,
Receding Mauna Loa.

Edward R. Roe.

THE DEATH OF THE OWD SQUIRE.

'TWAS a wild, mad kind of night, as black as the
bottomless pit,
The wind was howling away like a Bedlamite in a
fit,
Tearing the ash boughs off, and mowing the poplars down
In the meadows beyond the old flour-mill, where you turn
off to the town.

And the rain (well it *did* rain) dashing against the window
glass,
And the deluging on the roof, as the Devil were come to
pass;
The gutters were running in floods outside the stable-door,
And the spouts splashed from the tiles, as they would
never give o'er.

Lor' how the winders rattled! you'd almost ha' thought
    that thieves
Were wrenching at the shutters; while a ceaseless pelt of
    leaves
Flew to the doors in gusts; and I could hear the beck
Falling so loud I knew at once it was up to a tall man's
    neck.

We was huddling in the harness-room, by a little scrap of
    fire,
And Tom, the coachman, he was there, a practicing for the
    choir;
But it sounded dismal, anthem did, for Squire was dying
    fast,
And the Doctor said, " Do what he would, Squire's break-
    ing up at last. "

The death watch, sure enough, ticked loud just over th'
    owd mare's head,
Though he had never once been heard up there since
    master's boy lay dead;
And the only sound, beside Tom's toon, was the stirring in
    the stalls,
And the gnawing and the scratching of the rats in the old
    walls.

We couldn't hear Death's foot pass by, but we knew that
    he was near;
And the chill rain, and the wind and cold made us all
    shake with fear;
We listened to the clock up-stairs, 'twas breathing soft
    and low,
For the nurse said " At the turn of night the old Squire's
    soul would go."

Master had been a wildish man, and led a roughish life;
Didn't he shoot the Bowton Squire, who dared write to
      his wife?
He beat the Rads at Hindon town, I heard in twenty-nine,
When every pail in market-place was brimmed with red
      port wine.

And as for hunting, bless your soul, why for forty years or
      more
He'd kept the Marley hounds, man, as his fayther did
      afore;
And now to die, and in his bed — the season just begun —·
" It made him fret," the doctor said, " as it might do any
      one."

And when the young sharp lawyer came to see him sign
      his will,
Squire made me blow my horn outside as we were going
      to kill;
And we turned the hounds out in the court — that seemed
      to do him good;
For he swore, and sent us off to seek a fox in Thornhill
      wood.

But then the fever it rose high, and he would go see the
      room
Where mistress died ten years ago when Lammastide
      shall come;
I mind the year, because our mare at Saulsbury broke
      down;
Moreover the town hall was burnt at Steeple Dinton town.

It might be two, or half-past two, the wind seemed quite
    asleep;
Tom, he was off, but I awake, sat watch and ward to keep;
The moon was up, quite glorious like, the rain no longer fell,
When, all at once, out clashed and clanged the rusty
    turret bell.

That hadn't been heard for twenty years, not since the
    Luddite days;
Tom he leaped up, and I leaped up, for all the house ablaze
Had sure not scared us half so much, and out we ran like
    mad,
I, Tom, and Joe the whipper in, and t' little stable lad.

" He's killed himself," that's the idea that came into my
    head;
I felt as sure as though I saw Squire Barrowly was dead;
When all at once a door flew back, and he met us face to
    face;
His scarlet coat was on his back, and he looked like the
    old race.

The nurse was clinging to his knees, and crying like a
    child;
The maids were sobbing on the stairs, for he looked fierce
    and wild;
" Saddle me Lightning Bess, my men," that's what he
    said to me:
" The moon is up, we're sure to find at Stop or Etterly.

" Get out the dogs; I'm well to-night, and young again
    and sound,
I'll have a run once more before they put me under
    ground;
They brought my father home feet first, and it never shall
    be said
That his son Joe, who rode so straight, died quietly in
    his bed.

" Brandy ! " he cried; " a tumbler full, you women howling
    there; "
Then clapped the old black velvet cap upon his long gray
    hair,
Thrust on his boots, snatched down his whip, though he
    was old and weak,
There was a devil in his eye, that would not let me speak.

We loosed the dogs to humor him, and sounded on the
    horn:
The moon was up above the woods, just east of Haggard
    Bourne;
I buckled Lightning's throat-lash fast; the Squire was
    watching me;
He let the stirrups down himself so quick, yet carefully.

Then up he got and spurred the mare, and, ere I well
    could mount,
He drove the yard gate open, man; and called to old
    Dick Blount,
Our huntsman, dead five years ago — for the fever rose
    again,
And was spreading like a flood of flame, fast up into his
    brain.

Then off he flew before, the dogs yelling to call us on,
While we stood there, all pale and dumb, scarce knowing
    he was gone;
We mounted, and below the hill we saw the fox break out,
And down the covert ride we heard the old Squire's part-
    ing shout.

And in the moon-lit meadow mist we saw him fly the rail
Beyond the hurdles by the beck, just half-way down the
    vale;
I saw him breast fence after fence — nothing could turn
    him back;
And in the moonlight after him streamed out the brave
    old pack.

'Twas like a dream, Tom cried to me, as we rode free and
    fast,
Hoping to turn him at the brook, that could not well be
    past,
For it was swollen with the rain; but ah, 'twas not to be;
Nothing could stop old Lightning Bess but the broad breast
    of the sea.

The hounds swept on, and well in front the mare had got
    her stride;
She broke across the fallow land that runs by the down
    side;
We pulled up on Chalk Linton Hill, and as we stood us
    there,
Two fields beyond we saw the Squire fall stone dead from
    the mare.

Then she swept on, and in full cry, the hounds went out
    of sight;
A cloud came over the broad moon, and something dimmed
    our sight,
As Tom and I bore master home, both speaking under
    breath;
And that's the way I saw th' owd Squire ride boldly to his
    death.

Anonymous.

COMMODITY.

From Shelley's " Queen Mab."

COMMERCE has set the mark of selfishness,
  The signet of its all-enslaving power,
  Upon a shining ore, and called it gold;
  Before whose image bow the vulgar great,
The vainly rich, the miserable proud,
The mob of peasants, nobles, priests and kings,
And with blind feelings reverence the power
That grinds them to the dust of misery.
But in the temple of their hireling hearts
Gold is a living god, and rules in scorn
    All earthly things but virtue

Since tyrants, by the sale of human life,
Heap luxuries to their sensualism, and fame
To their wide-wasting and insatiate pride,
Success has sanctioned to a credulous world
The ruin, the disgrace, the woe, of war.
His hosts of blind and unresisting dupes
The despot numbers; from his cabinet
These puppets of his schemes he moves at will
(Even as the slaves by force of famine driven

Beneath a vulgar master) to perform
A task of cold and brutal drudgery; —
Hardened to hope, insensible to fear,
Scarce living pulleys of a dead machine,
Mere wheels of work, and articles of trade,
That grace the proud and noisy pomp of wealth!

The harmony and happiness of man
Yield to the wealth of nations; that which lifts
His nature to the heaven of its pride
Is bartered for the poison of his soul,
The weight that drags to earth his towering hopes;
Blighting all prospect but of selfish gain,
Withering all passion but of slavish fear,
Extinguishing all free and generous love
Of enterprise and daring.   Even the pulse
That fancy kindles in the beating heart
To mingle with sensation, it destroys; —
Leaves nothing but the sordid lust of self,
The groveling hope of interest and gold,
Unqualified, unmingled, unredeemed
Even by hypocrisy.

        And statesmen boast
Of wealth!   The wordy eloquence that lives
After the ruin of their hearts, can gild
The bitter poison of a nation's woe;
Can turn the worship of the servile mob
To their corrupt and glaring idol, Fame,
From Virtue, trampled by its iron tread —
Although its dazzling pedestal be raised
Amid the horrors of a limb-strewn field,
With desolated dwellings smoking round.

The man of ease, who, by his warm fireside,
To deeds of charitable intercourse,
And bare fulfillment of the common laws
Of decency and prejudice, confines
The struggling nature of his human heart,
Is duped by their cold sophistry; he sheds
A passing tear perchance upon the wreck
Of earthly peace, when near his dwelling's door
The frightful waves are driven — when his son
Is murdered by the tyrant, or religion
Drives his wife raving mad. But the poor man
Whose life is misery and fear and care;
Whom the morn wakens but to fruitless toil;
Who ever hears his famished offspring's scream ;
Whom their pale mother's uncomplaining gaze
Forever meets, and the proud rich man's eye
Flashing command, and the heart-breaking scene
Of thousands like himself; — he little heeds
The rhetoric of tyranny.   His hate
Is quenchless as his wrongs; he laughs to scorn
The vain and bitter mockery of words;
Feeling the horror of the tyrant's deeds,
And unrestrained but by the arm of power,
    That knows and dreads his enmity.

The iron rod of Penury still compels
Her wretched slave to bow the knee to wealth,
And poison with unprofitable toil
A life too void of solace, to confirm
The very chains that bind him to his doom.
Nature, impartial in munificence,
Has gifted man with all-subduing will;
Matter, with all its transitory shapes,

Lies subjected and plastic at his feet,
That, weak from bondage, trembled as they tread —
How many a rustic Milton has passed by,
Stifling the speechless longings of his heart
In unremitting drudgery and care!
How many a vulgar Cato has compelled
His energies, no longer tameless then,
To mold a pin, or fabricate a nail!
How many a Newton to whose passive ken
Those mighty spheres that gem infinity
Were only specks of tinsel fixed in heaven
To light the midnights of his native town!

Yet every heart contains perfection's germ:
The wisest of the sages of the earth
That ever from the stores of reason drew
Science, and truth, and virtue's deadliest tone
Were but a weak and inexperienced boy —
Proud, sensual, unimpassioned, unimbued
With pure desire and universal love —
Compared to that high being, of cloudless brain,
Untainted passion, elevated will,
Which death (who even would linger long in awe
Within his noble presence, and beneath
His changeless eye-beam) might alone subdue.
Him every slave now dragging through the filth
Of some corrupted city his sad life,
Pining with famine, swoln with luxury,
Blunting the keenness of his spiritual sense
With narrow schemings and unworthy cares,
Or madly rushing through all violent crime
To move the deep stagnation of his soul,
Might imitate and equal.

> But mean lust
> Has bound its chains so tight about the earth
> That all within it but the virtuous man
> Is venal.   Gold or fame will surely reach
> The price prefixed by selfishness, to all
> But him of resolute and unchanging will;
> Whom nor the plaudits of a servile crowd,
> Nor the vile joys of tainting luxury,
> Can bribe to yield his elevated soul
> To Tyranny or Falsehood, though they wield
> With blood-red hand the scepter of the world.
> All things are sold.   The very light of heaven
> Is venal: earth's unsparing gifts of love,
> The smallest and most despicable things
> That lurk in the abysses of the deep,
> All objects of our life, even life itself,
> And the poor pittance which the laws allow
> Of liberty — the fellowship of man,
> Those duties which his heart of human love
> Should urge him to perform instinctively—
> Are bought and sold as in a public mart
> Of undisguising Selfishness, that sets
> On each its price, the stamp-mark of her reign.
> Even love is sold.   The solace of all woe
> Is turned to deadliest agony: old age
> Shivers in selfish beauty's loathing arms,
> And youth's corrupted impulses prepare
> A life of horror, from the blighting bane
> Of commerce; whilst the pestilence that springs
> From unenjoying sensualism has filled
> All human life with hydra-headed woes.

Falsehood demands but gold to pay the pangs
Of outraged conscience; for the slavish priest
Sets no great value on his hireling faith;
A little passing pomp, some servile souls
Whom cowardice itself might safely chain,
Or the spare mite of avarice could bribe,
To deck the triumph of their languid zeal,
Can make *him* minister to tyranny.
More daring crime requires a loftier meed;
Without a shudder the slave-soldier lends
His arm to murderous deeds, and steels his heart
When the dread eloquence of dying men,
Low mingling on the lonely field of fame,
Assails that nature whose applause he sells
For the gross blessings of the patriot mob,
For the vile gratitude of heartless kings,
And for a cold world's good word—viler still!

There is a nobler glory which survives
Until our being fades, and, solacing
All human care, accompanies its change;
Deserts not virtue in the dungeon's gloom,
And, in the precincts of the palace, guides
His footsteps through that labyrinth of crime;
Imbues his lineaments with dauntlessness,
Even when from power's avenging hand he takes
Its sweetest, last, and noblest title—death;—
The consciousness of good, which neither gold,
Nor sordid fame, nor hope of heavenly bliss,
Can purchase; but a life of resolute good,
Unalterable will, quenchless desire
Of universal happiness, the heart
That beats with it in unison, the brain

Whose ever-wakeful wisdom toils to change
Reason's rich stores for its eternal weal.

This " commerce " of sincerest virtue needs
No mediative signs of selfishness,
No jealous intercourse of wretched gain,
No balancings of prudence, cold and long: —
In just an equal measure all is weighed;
One scale contains the sum of human weal,
And one, the good man's heart.

                        How vainly seek
The selfish for that happiness denied
To aught but virtue!   Blind and hardened they
Who hope for peace amid the storms of care,
Who covet power they know not how to use,
And sigh for pleasure they refuse to give!
Madly they frustrate still their own designs;
And, where they hope that quiet to enjoy
Which virtue pictures, bitterness of soul,
Pining regrets, and vain repentances,
Disease, disgust, and lassitude pervade
Their valueless and miserable lives.

But hoary-headed Selfishness has felt
Its death-blow, and is tottering to the grave.
A brighter morn awaits the human day;
When every transfer of earth's natural gifts
Shall be a commerce of good words and works;
When poverty and wealth, the thirst of fame,
The fear of infamy, disease, and woe,
War with its million horrors, and fierce hell,
Shall live but in the memory of Time,
Who, like a penitent libertine, shall start,
Look back, and shudder at his younger years.

THE COLISEUM.

From Byron's " Childe Harold's Pilgrimage."

RCHES on arches! as it were that Rome,
Collecting the chief trophies of her line,
Would build up all her triumphs in one dome,
Her Coliseum stands; the moonbeams shine
As 'twere its natural torches, for divine
Should be the light which streams here, to illume
This long-explored but still exhaustless mine
Of contemplation: and the azure gloom
Of an Italian night, where the deep skies assume

Hues which have words, and to speak ye of Heaven,
Floats o'er the vast and wondrous monument,
And shadows forth its glory.   There is given
Unto the things of earth, which Time hath bent,
A spirit's feeling, and where he hath leant
His hand, but broke his scythe, there is a power
And magic in the ruin'd battlement,
For which the palace of the present hour
Must yield its pomp, and wait till ages are its dower.

And here the buzz of eager nations ran,
In murmur'd pity, or loud-roar'd applause,
As man was slaughter'd by his fellow-man.
And wherefore slaughter'd? wherefore but because
Such were the bloody Circus' genial laws,
And the imperial pleasure—Wherefore not?
What matters where we fall to fill the maws
Of worms — on battle-plains or listed spot?
Both are but theaters where the chief actors rot.

13

I see before me the Gladiator lie;
He leans upon his hand — his manly brow
Consents to death, but conquers agony,
And his droop'd head sinks gradually low —
And through his side the last drops, ebbing slow
From the red gash, fall heavy, one by one,
Like the first of the thunder-shower; and now
The arena swims around him — he is gone,
Ere ceased the inhuman shout which hail'd the wretch
     who won.

He heard it, but he heeded not — his eyes
Were with his heart, and that was far away;
He reck'd not of the life he lost nor prize,
But where his rude hut by the Danube lay,
There were his young barbarians all at play,
There was their Dacian mother — he, their sire,
Butcher'd to make a Roman holiday! —
All this rush'd with his blood — Shall he expire
And unavenged? — Arise, ye Goths, and glut your ire!

But here, where murder breathed her bloody stream;
And here, where buzzing nations choked the ways,
And roar'd or murmur'd like a mountain stream
Dashing or wandering as the torrent strays;
Here, where the Roman million's blame or praise
Was death or life, the playthings of a crowd,
My voice sounds much — and fall the stars' faint rays
On the arena void — seats crush'd — walls bow'd —
And galleries, where my steps seem echoes strangely loud.

A ruin — yet what ruin! from its mass
Walls, palaces, half-cities, have been rear'd ;
Yet oft the enormous skeleton ye pass,

And marvel where the spoil could have appear'd.
Hath it indeed been plunder'd, or but clear'd?
Alas! developed, opens the decay,
When the colossal fabric's form is near'd,
It will not bear the brightness of the day,
Which streams too much on all years, man, have reft away.

But when the rising moon begins to climb
Its topmost arch, and gently pauses there;
When the stars twinkle through the loops of time,
And the low night-breeze waves along the air
The garland-forest, which the gray walls wear,
Like laurels on the bald first Cæsar's head;
When the light shines serene but doth not glare,
Then in this magic circle raise the dead;
Heroes have trod this spot —'tis on their dust ye tread.

" While stands the Coliseum, Rome shall stand;
" When falls the Coliseum, Rome shall fall;
" And when Rome falls — the World."   From our own
    land
Thus spake the pilgrims o'er this mighty wall
In Saxon times, which we are wont to call
Ancient; and these three mortal things are still
On their foundations, and unalter'd all;
Rome and her Ruin past Redemption's skill,
The World, the same wide den — of thieves, or what ye
    will.

Simple, erect, severe, austere, sublime —
Shrine of all saints and temple of all gods,
From Jove to Jesus — spared and blest by time;
Looking tranquillity, while falls or nods
Arch, empire, each thing round thee, and man plods

His way through thorns to ashes — glorious dome!
Shalt thou not last? Time's scythe and tyrant's rods
Shiver upon thee — sanctuary and home
Of art and piety — Pantheon! — pride of Rome!

Relic of nobler days, and noblest arts!
Despoiled, yet perfect, with thy circle spreads
A holiness appealing to all hearts —
To art a model, and to him who treads
Rome for the sake of ages, Glory sheds
Her light through thy sole aperture; to those
Who worship, here are altars for their beads;
And they who feel for genius may repose
Their eyes on honor'd forms, whose busts around them
    close.

THE VICTIM.

PLAGUE upon the people fell,
    A famine after laid them low,
Then thorpe and byre arose in fire,
    For on them brake the sudden foe;
So thick they died the people cried
    " The gods are moved against the land."
The Priest in horror about his altar
    To Thor and Odin lifted a hand:
            " Help us from famine
            And plague and strife!
            What would you have of us?
            Human life?
            Were it our nearest,
            Were it our dearest
            (Answer, O answer),
            We give you his life."

But still the foeman spoil'd and burn'd,
  And cattle died, and deer in wood,
And bird in air, and fishes turn'd
  And whiten'd all the rolling flood;
And dead men lay all over the way,
  Or down in a furrow scathed with flame:
And ever and aye the Priesthood moan'd
  Till at last it seemed that an answer came:
      " The King is happy
        In child and wife;
        Take you his dearest,
        Give us a life."

The Priest went out by heath and hill;
  The king was hunting in the wild;
They found the mother sitting still;
  She cast her arms about the child.
The child was only eight summers old,
  His beauty still with his years increased
His face was ruddy, his hair was gold,
  He seemed a victim due to the priest.
        The priest beheld him,
        And cried with joy,
        " The Gods have answer'd:
        We give them the boy."

The King return'd from out the wild,
  He bore but little game in hand;
The mother said: " They have taken the child
  To spill his blood and heal the land:
The land is sick, the people diseased,
  And blight and famine on all the lea:
The holy Gods, they must be appeased,
  So I pray you tell the truth to me.

They have taken our son,
They will have his life.
Is *he* your dearest?
Or I, the wife?"

The King bent low, with hand and brow,
  He stay'd his arms upon his knee:
    "O wife, what use to answer now?
  For now the Priest has judged for me."
The King was shaken with holy fear;
  "The Gods," he said, "would have chosen well;
Yet both are near, and both are dear,
  And which the dearest I cannot tell!"
        But the Priest was happy,
        His victim won:
      "We have his dearest,
        His only son!"

The rites prepared, the victim bared,
  The knife uprising toward the blow,
To the altar-stone she sprang alone.
  "Me, not my darling, no!"
He caught her away with a sudden cry;
  Suddenly from him brake his wife,
And shrieking, "*I* am his dearest, I—
  I am his dearest!" rush'd on the knife.
        And the Priest was happy,
        "O, Father Odin,
        We give you a life.
        Which was his nearest?
        Who was his dearest?
        The Gods have answer'd;
        We give them the wife!"

Tennyson.

THE TWO ARMIES.

S Life's unending column pours,
    Two marshal'd hosts are seen —
Two armies on the trampled shores
    That Death flows black between.

One marches to the drum-beat roll,
    The wide-mouthed clarion's bray,
And bear upon a crimson scroll,
    " Our glory is to slay."

One moves in silence by the stream,
    With sad yet watchful eyes,
Calm as the patient planet's gleam
    That walks the clouded skies.

Along its front no sabers shine,
    No blood-red pennons wave;
Its banner bears the single line,
    " Our duty is to save."

For those no death-bed's lingering shade;
    At honor's trumpet-call,
With knitted brow and lifted blade
    In glory's arms they fall.

For these no clashing falchions bright,
    No stirring battle-cry;
The bloodless stabber calls by night —
    Each answers, " Here am I!"

For those the sculptor's laurel'd bust,
    The builder's marble piles,
The anthems pealing o'er their dust
    Through long cathedral aisles.

For these the blossom-sprinkled turf,
  That floods the lonely graves,
When Spring rolls in her sea-green surf
  In flowery-foaming waves.

Two paths lead upward from below,
  And angels wait above,
Who count each burning life-drop's flow,
  Each falling tear of Love.

Though from the Hero's bleeding breast
  Her pulses Freedom drew,
Though the white lilies in her crest
  Sprung from that scarlet dew —

While Valor's haughty champions wait
  Till all their scars are shown,
Love walks unchallenged through the gate,
  To sit beside the Throne!

Oliver Wendell Holmes.

" On a little straw lies their grandmother
Stretched, speechless, cold, whom the winter had
Made already cold — cold enough for a grave."

HELP THE POOR.

Translated from the French by Prof. John Bach.

YE whom Fortune blessed, do you think some-
    times
  At your winter feasts, when the whirring ball
  Fills you with its fires, and on ev'ry step
You see dazzling lights, crystals, balusters,
Sparkling chandeliers, fulgent mirrors — and
Brightness and joy dance on the foreheads of
All the happy guests in the starry hall.

Ye whom Fortune blessed, do you think sometimes,
While a golden bell, ringing in your rooms,
Into joyous songs turns Time's mighty voice;
Do you think sometimes that a hungry wretch
On the gloomy square stops, perhaps, and sees
How your luminous shadows dancing pass
At the windows of the gilded hall?

Do you think that there, in the snow and river,
Stands that father whom, as he has no work,
Famine has besieged, and that he complains —
" Oh, so much for one!   And so many friends
Frolic at his feast!   Oh, how happy must
Be that man as his children smile on him?
There is everything — all, but bread for mine!"

He compares your feast in his suff'ring mind
With his hearth; no flame shines and sparkles there;
There his children are hungry, trembling, starved,
And their mother is clad in shreds and rags;
On a little straw lies their grandmother
Stretched, speechless, cold, whom the winter had
Made already cold — cold enough for a grave.

God has parceled out different human lots:
Some walk weighed down with a heavy load:
Very few are called to Fortune's feast;
Even these not all are alike at ease;
For a law there is, bad, unjust, perhaps,
Viewed from below, and which thus decrees
To a few, " Enjoy! "—" Envy! " to the crowd.

Gloomy, bitter, stern is indeed such thought;
It ferments the heart of the suff'ring poor.
Ye whom Fortune blessed, let your revels sleep,
That no violence shall one day pluck out
Of your hands those goods which you do not need.
And to which their eyes cleave tenaciously!
No, no violence; be it Charity!

Heavenly Charity, whom the poor adore!
Loving parent of Fortune's step-children,
That supports, relieves those the passers-by
Rudely push aside, and, if need should be,
Immolates herself, and, like Jesus Christ,
Whom she follows close, she would even say:
" Eat and drink ye all! 'Tis my flesh, my blood! "

Ye rich, let it be her, yes, her alone,
That with ample hands from your children's arms,
From your ladies' necks, pulls the diamonds,
Sapphires, necklaces, pearls and corals and
Cherished jewelry, always vain and false,
That you may relieve human misery,
And that you may save your immortal souls!

Ye rich, help the poor!   Understand that alms
Prayer's sisters are! — When a gray-haired man,
Stiff with cold, at your stony door-step falls
On his knees, in vain — when a little child,
With her red, cold hands at your feet the crumbs
Of your revels picks; then, remember well
That our Saviour's face turns away from you!

Help the poor, ye rich, that Almighty God,
Who endows you all, to your sons gives strength,
To your daughters grace, that your vines produce
Always luscious fruit, and that riper wheat
Make your gran'ries bend, that you every day
Better, holier be, and that you may see
How the angels pass through your dreams at night.

Help the poor, ye rich!   And a day will come
When the earth leaves you, when your alms-giving
Builds a treasury there on high for you!
Help the poor, so that they at least shall say:
" He has pitied us! " that the indigent,
Shivering with frost, and the hungry poor,
Not with jealous eyes look upon your feasts.

Help the poor, so that God Incarnate shall
Be content with you; that the godless, ev'n,
Bow and speak your name; that your hearth be calm
And fraternal, and you one day shall have
All the potent help of a beggar's prayers
At the throne of God in the Heaven above.

Victor Hugo.

THE KNIGHT AND THE LADY.

A Domestic Legend of the Reign of Queen Anne.

> " Hail, wedded love! mysterious tie! "
>
> *Thompson — or somebody.*

THE Lady Jane was tall and slim,
    The Lady Jane was fair,
  And Sir Thomas, her lord, was stout of limb,
  And his cough was short, and his eyes were dim,
And he wore green " specs," with a tortoise-shell rim,
And his hat was remarkably broad in the brim,
And she was uncommonly fond of him —
    And they were a loving pair! —
    And the name and the fame
    Of the Knight and his Dame,
Were everywhere hailed with the loudest acclaim.

    Now Sir Thomas the Good,
    Be it well understood,
Was a man of very contemplative mood —
    He would pore by the hour
    O'er a weed or a flower,
Or the slugs that come crawling out after a shower;
Black-beetles and Bumble-bees, Blue-bottle flies,
And Moths, were of no small account in his eyes;
An " Industrious Flea " he'd by no means despise,
While an " Old Daddy-long-legs," whose " long legs "
    and thighs
Passed the common in shape, or in color, or size,
He was wont to consider an absolute prize.

Well, it happened one day —
I really can't say
The particular month; but I *think* 'twas in May —
'Twas, I *know*, in the Springtime — when " Nature looks
gay,"
As the Poet observes — and on tree-top and spray
The dear little dickey-birds carol away;
When the grass is so green, and the sun is so bright,
And all things are teeming with life and with light —
That the whole of the house was thrown into affright.
For no soul could conceive what was gone with the
Knight!

It seems he had taken
A light breakfast — bacon,
An egg — with a little broiled haddock — at most
A round and a half of some hot buttered toast,
With a slice of cold sirloin from yesterday's roast.
And then — let me see! —
He had two, perhaps three,
Cups (with sugar and cream) of strong gunpowder tea,
With a spoonful in each of some choice *eau de vie* —
Which with nine out of ten would perhaps disagree —
In fact, I and my son
Mix " black " with our " Hyson,"
Neither having the nerves of a bull, or a bison,
And both hating brandy like what some call " pison."

No matter for that —
He had called for his hat,
With the brim that I've said was so broad and so flat,
And his " specs " with the tortoise-shell rim, and his cane
With the crutch-handled top, which he used to sustain

His steps in his walks, and to poke in the shrubs
And the grass, when unearthing his worms and his grubs.
Thus armed, he set out on a ramble — alack!
He *set out*, poor dear soul! — but he never came back!
The morning dawned — and the next — and the next,
And all in the mansion were still perplexed;

*　　　*　　　*　　　*　　　*　　　*　　　*

Up came running a man, at a deuce of a pace,
With that very peculiar expression of face
Which always betokens dismay or disaster,
Crying out — 'twas the gardener —" O ma'am! we've found
　　　master!"
" Where? where?" screamed the lady; and Echo screamed,
　　　" where? "
　　　　　The man couldn't say " There! "
　　　　　He had no breath to spare,
But, gasping for air, he could only respond
By pointing — he pointed, alas! TO THE POND.

'Twas e'en so — poor dear Knight! — with his " specs " and
　　　his hat,
He'd gone poking his nose into this and to that,
　　　　When, close to the side
　　　　Of the bank, he espied
An " uncommon fine " tadpole, remarkably fat!
　　　　He stooped; — and he thought her
　　　　His own; he had caught her!
Got hold of her tail — and to land almost brought her,
When — he plumped head and heels into fifteen feet water!

　　　　The Lady Jane was tall and slim,
　　　　The Lady Jane was fair,

Alas, for Sir Thomas! she grieved for him,
As she saw two serving men, sturdy of limb,
    His body between them bear:
She sobbed and she sighed, she lamented and cried,
    For of sorrow brimful was her cup;
She swooned, and I think she'd have fallen down and died,
    If Captain McBride
    Had not been by her side,
With the gardener; they both their assistance supplied,
    And managed to hold her up.

    But, when she " comes to,"
    O 'tis shocking to view
The sight which the corpse reveals!   Sir Thomas' body,
    It looked so odd — he
    Was half eaten up by the eels!
His waistcoat and hose, and the rest of his clothes,
Were all gnawled through and through!
    And out of each shoe
    An eel they drew,
And from each of his pockets they pulled out two!
And the gardener himself had secreted a few,
    As well we may suppose;
For when he came running to give the alarm,
He had six in the basket that hung on his arm.

    Good Father John
    Was summoned anon;
    Holy water was sprinkled,
    And little bells tinkled,
    And tapers were lighted,
    And incense ignited,

And masses were sung, and masses were said
All day, for the quiet repose of the dead,
And all night no one thought about going to bed.

But Lady Jane was tall and slim,
And Lady Jane was fair—
And, ere morning came, that winsome dame
Had made up her mind —or what is much the same,
Had *thought about*—once more " changing her name,"—
And she said, with a pensive air,
To Thompson the valet, while taking away,
When supper was over, the cloth and the tray:—
" Eels a many
I've ate; but any
So good ne'er tasted before!—
They're a fish, too, of which I'm remarkably fond —
Go, pop Sir Thomas again in the pond;
Poor dear!—HE'LL CATCH US SOME MORE."

Richard H. Barham.

" Did he love more than I ? "

LINES

In memory of my little daughter, Nellie Glen R.

THE fairest flower that bloomed for me
  Upon life's lonely shore,
A loving angel chanced to see —
  It blooms for me no more.

The angel saw and loved my flower —
  Did *he* love more than I?
I only know that self-same hour
  It blossomed in the sky.

Too rare a bud to thrive on earth
  And yield its sweet perfume —
The atmosphere that gave it birth
  Could not perfect its bloom.

And so God let his angel come
  And pluck the flower He'd given —
Transplanted to that fairer home,
  It blooms for aye in Heaven.

E. T. R.

THE BATTLE.

Schiller, translated by Bulwer.

EAVY and solemn,
  A cloudy column,
   Thro' the great plain they marching came!
    Measureless spread, like a table dread,
For the wild grim dice of the iron game.
Looks are bent on the shaking ground,
Hearts beat loud with a knelling sound;
Swift by the breasts that must bear the brunt
Gallops the major along the front.
     " Halt! "
And fettered they stand at the stark command,
And the warriors, silent, halt!

Proud in the blush of morning glowing,
What on the hill-top shines in flowing?
" See you the foeman's banner waving? "
" We see the foeman's banner waving."
" God be with ye, children and wife! "
Hark to the music, the trump and the fife;
How they ring thro' the ranks which they rouse to the
    strife!
Thrilling they sound, with their glorious tone;
Thrilling they go thro' the marrow and bone.
Brothers, God grant, when this life is o'er,
In the life to come that we meet once more!

See the smoke how the lightning is cleaving asunder!
Hark! the guns, peal on peal, how they boom in their
    thunder!
From host to host, with kindling sound,

The shouting signal circles round;
Ay, shout it forth to life or death –
Freer already breathes the breath!
The war is waging, slaughter raging,

And heavy through the reeking pall
    The iron death-dice fall!
Nearer they close —-foes upon foes.
" Ready!" from square to square it goes.
They kneel as one man, from flank to flank,
And the fire comes sharp from the foremost rank.
Many a soldier to earth is sent,
Many a gap by the balls is rent;
O'er the corse before springs the hinder man,
That the line may not fail to the fearless van.
To the right, to the left, and around and around
Death whirls in its dance on the bloody ground.
God's sunlight is quenched in the fiery fight,
Over the host falls a brooding night!
Brothers, God grant, when this life is o'er,
In the life to come that we meet once more!

The dead men lie bathed in the weltering blood,
And the living are blent in the slippery flood,
And the feet, as they reeling and sliding go,
Stumble still on the corses that sleep below.
" What— Francis! Give Charlotte my last farewell."
As the dying man murmurs the thunders swell.
" I'll give—O God! are the guns so near?
Ho, comrades! yon volley! look sharp to the rear!
I'll give thy Charlotte thy last farewell.
Sleep soft; where death thickest descendeth in rain
The friend thou forsakest thy side may regain! "

Hitherward, thitherward reels the fight;
Dark and more darkly day glooms into night.
Brothers, God grant, when this life is o'er,
In the life to come that we meet once more!

Hark to the hoofs that galloping go!
The adjutants flying—
The horsemen press hard on the panting foe;
Their thunder booms, in dying,
Victory!
Terror has seized on the dastards all,
And their colors fall!
Victory!

Closed is the brunt of the glorious fight,
And the day, like a conqueror, bursts on the night;
Triumph and fife swelling choral along,
The trumpet already sweeps marching in song.
Farewell, fallen brothers; though this life be o'er,
There's another, in which we shall meet you once more!

LOVE AND DEATH.

[Louis de Bourbon, Count of Montpensier, died suddenly of grief whilst viewing the tomb of his father, the Duke of Bourbon, which was opened at his command, amid all the pomp of a magnificent service, and in the presence of his victorious army.]

'T was the twilight hour! Deep silence hung,
Like a lone watcher, o'er each sainted shrine,
Where pure religion burnt her lamp divine,
Mid fair Italia's temple, and there rung
No sound upon the stillness, save, perchance,
When the slight gale, stirring the citron grove,

Displayed its silver lining to the glance
Of the enamored moon, or some bird wove,
Lured by the quivering light, a broken chain
Of wild and dreamy song.   But hark! that toll
From the old minster bell; and now the whole
Of the antique and consecrated fane
Was kindled with a red and glaring light,
Stronger than midday, while its fretted height
Returned the solemn anthem as it rose
Midst clouds of incense, blent with organ clear,
While the low dirge was echoed at its close
By voices, that grew stronger on the ear
At every moment—till the sounding aisle
Rang with the heavy tread of a full train
Of mailed men, who, through the sainted pile
Moved to one distant spot; each tinted pane
Shedding a crimson glow upon their forms,
And every steel-clad armor flashing back
The torchlight, clear as lightning 'mid the storms;
On, on they pressed! What stayed them in their tracks?
A gilded coffin! all alone it lay
Mid a full flood of brightness : its closed lid
Bearing a sword and shield, yet almost hid
Beneath the floating banners, bright and gay,
That waved around, as if they heeded not
What spoil it was they covered.   From the throng
Advanced a youthful chieftain to the spot,
And low he bowed, in silence deep and strong,
Besides the stately bier, until at length
He breathed, in hollow accents, strangely clear,
" Once more I would look on him!" With quick fear
His followers raised the lid, and back recoiled,

As chilled with death's cold presence: he alone
Shrank not away, but stood like sculptured stone,
Gazing upon that image, quite bespoiled
By time's relentless grasp.   Long, long he stood
Viewing those smoldering ashes, till his breast
Heaved like an ocean-billow, and the blood
Forsook his pallid lip and brow compressed,
As to the bier he bowed his youthful cheek,
And breathed his spirit's woe in accents weak.

" Dust! dust! and is this all
    That death has left for me?
What boots it now the shroud and pall
    So closely wrapt round thee?

" I thought once more to gaze
    Upon thy blessed face,
But, father, the rude worm that plays
    Hath left of thee no trace.

" I have brought victory's crown
    To set upon thy brow;
Oh! better 'twere to see thee frown,
    Than look on thee as now.

" Yet no, my father! no!
    This anguish grows too wild;
Better to have thee even so,
    Than frowning on thy child.

" Didst thou not know how well
    I loved thee, even to death,
And how my life was but a spell
    Bound in thy living breath?

" And yet thou could'st depart
    And leave me all alone —
Oh! take me, take me to that heart,
    Since to it I have grown.

" If the sun hide its rays,
    Must not the floweret die.
And can the wind-harp wake its lays
    Unless the breeze be nigh?

" Thou wert that sun to me,
    And thou that wakening gale,
And yet no answer comes from thee
    To soothe my spirit's wail.

" Oh! by the days of yore,
    When seated by thy side,
I drank in love's most precious lore,
    And sought no thoughts to hide:

" And for that mother's sake,
    Whose earthly course is done,
My sire! let thy cold ashes wake
    And speak unto thy son.

" Hush! hark! methought a voice
    Came from his distant home:
It calls me! now my heart rejoice —
    Father! I come! I come! "

And with a wild and piercing shriek he fell
Upon that couch of death, and closely pressed
His arms, as folding something to his breast,
With a convulsive shiver, that full well

Told of the inward strife; until at last,
Crushed, like a reed beneath the tempest's blast,
His slight frame yielded to the awe-struck band
That crowded round him, and each trembling hand
Unloosed his heavy breast-plate, and then took
The plume-crowned helmet from the drooping head,
That sank beneath it; but one single look
Told 'twas in vain — the youthful prince was dead!

                              Mary E. Lee.

MARY STUART AND HER MOURNER.

Mary Stuart perished at the age of forty-four years and two months. Her remains were taken from her weeping servants, and a green cloth, torn in haste from an old billiard table, was flung over her once beautiful form. Thus it remained, unwatched and unattended, except by a poor little lap-dog, which could not be induced to quit the body of its mistress. This faithful little animal was found dead two days afterward; and the circumstance made such an impression even on the hard-hearted minister of Elizabeth, that it was mentioned in the official dispatches." —*Mrs. Jamieson's Female Sovereigns — Mary Queen of Scots.*]

THE axe its bloody work had done;
    The corpse neglected lay;
This peopled world could spare not one
    To watch beside the clay.

The fairest work from Nature's hand
    That e'er on mortal shone,
A sunbeam stray'd from fairy land
    To fade upon a throne; —

The Venus of the tomb* whose form
    Was destiny and death;
The Siren's voice that stirr'd a storm
    In each melodious breath; —

Libitina, the Venus who presided over funerals.

Such *was*, what now by fate is hurl'd
    To rot, unwept, away.
A star has vanish'd from the world;
    And none to miss the ray!

Stern Knox, that loneliness forlorn
    A harsher truth might teach
To royal pomps than priestly scorn
    To royal sins can preach!

No victims now that lip can make!
    That hand how powerless now!
O God! and what's a King — but take
    A bauble from the brow?

The world is full of life and love;
    The world, methinks, might spare
From millions, one to watch above
    The dust of monarchs there.

And not one human eye — yet lo!
    What stirs the funeral pall?
What sound — it is not human woe-
    Wails moaning through the hall?

Close by the form mankind desert
    One thing a vigil keeps.
More near and near to that still heart
    It wistful, wondering, creeps.

It gazes on those glazed eyes,
    It hearkens for a breath —
It does not know that kindness dies,
    And love departs from death.

It fawns as fondly as before
　Upon that icy hand;
And hears from lips, that speak no more,
　The voice that can command.

To that poor fool, alone on earth,
　No matter what had been
The pomp, the fall, the guilt, the worth,
　The Dead was still a Queen.

With eyes that horror could not scare,
　It watched the senseless clay;
Crouch'd on the breast of Death, and there
　Moan'd its fond life away.

And when the bolts discordant clash'd,
　And human steps drew nigh,
The human pity shrunk abash'd
　Before that faithful eye.

It seemed to gaze with such rebuke
　On those who could forsake;
Then turn'd to watch once more the look
　And strive the sleep to wake.

They raised the pall — they touch'd the dead
　A cry, and *both* were still'd —
Alike the soul that Hate had sped,
　The life that Love had kill'd.

Semiramis of England, hail!
　Thy crime secures thy sway:
But when thine eyes shall scan the tale
　Those hireling scribes convey·

When thou shalt read, with late remorse,
   How one poor slave was found
Beside thy butcher'd rival's corse,
   The headless and discrown'd:

Shall not thy soul foretell thine own
   Unloved expiring hour,
When those who kneel around the throne
   Shall fly the falling tower;

When thy great heart shall silent break,
   When thy sad eyes shall strain
Through vacant space, one thing to seek,
   One thing that loved — in vain?

Though round thy parting pangs of pride
   Shall priest and noble crowd:
More worth the grief that mourn'd beside
   Thy victim's gory shroud!

E. Bulwer Lytton.

THE DECAYED FARM-HOUSE.

MID mighty ruins moldering to decay,
   The lettered traveler delights to roam;
The antique pile or column to survey,
   And trace faint legends on the crumbling dome.

They court proud cities of historic name,
   By desolation's giant arm subdued,
And meditate the spot, once dear to fame,
   Where Balbec flourished, or Palmyra stood.

The muse delights to court a lone retreat,
    And far from these illustrious scenes to stray;
Upreared by folly for ambition's seat,
    By vice and folly fall'n now tottering to decay.

She loves to meditate the humbler spot,
    Where untrick'd nature pours the rude sublime;
Where rural hands have reared the rural cot,
    Decaying now beneath the touch of time.

" Yon farm-house totters, by the tempest beat,
    The mark of age its antique chimneys bear;
Sure no sad master owns the cheerless seat.
    Say, passing shepherd, who has sojourned there?"

" Forgive the sigh," the rustic swain replied,
    " These desert scenes my happier days recall;
Forgive the tears which down my cheeks glide,
    For when I view this spot, my tears will fall.

" Stranger!" said he, " here late did Gracio dwell,
    Hast thou not heard of good old Gracio's fame?
Through all our village he was known full well,
    And even lisping infants spoke his name.

" Twice twenty years I served him as his hind,
    Twice twenty years for him I tilled the soil;
I loved my master, for I found him kind,
    My task was easy, and I blessed my toil.

" He seemed not master, but an equal friend;
    He joined our labors in the field by day,
And when the evening bade our labors end,
    He mingled freely in our rustic play.

" Ah! well I knew him from his mother's arms,
      No youth so fair, so innocent, as he;
His spring of life was deck'd with spring's best charms,
      His opening mind was like the blossom'd tree.

" His riper years with riper fruits were crown'd,
      His mellow autumn blest with genial skies;
His age, like winter's frost-ymantled ground,
      Where vigor still beneath the hoary surface lies.

" For wealth or power he breathed no prayer to
          Heaven,
      Life's every blessing industry supplied;
To him health, peace, and competence were giv'n,
      And say, can virtue form a wish beside?

" This once loved spot recalls full many a joy,
      What cheered in youth old age will ne'er forget;
But still must dote on memory's fond employ,
      And what it loved the most, the most regret.

" The spreading elm that shadows o'er the yard,
      Its parted master to my view can call;
And every object claims a soft regard,
      Since Gracio's memory sanctifies them all.

" The shady bower in yonder elmy meads,
      The vocal thicket where the throstle sung,
The little gate that through the garden leads,
      The fork now useless where the milk-pail hung.

" But Gracio's dead, and desert is the scene,
      Gracio's no more, and every charm's decayed;
Those joys are fled which gladdened once the green;
      But still fond fancy courts the fleeting shade,

15

" Still dwells tenacious on those happy hours
　　When this loved spot with social joys was crowned;
When health, content and innocence were ours,
　　And poured the song of happiness around.

" Then the glad household his return would greet,
　　And winning welcome smiled with accents bland;
The faithful house-dog gamboled round his feet,
　　To court attention from his master's hand.

To clasp his knees the prattling infants ran,
　　Proud from their sire to catch the earliest kiss;
Oh! I have seen the parent bless the man,
　　When only tears could speak his secret bliss.

" But now he's dead, the thought demands a tear,
　　I saw the good man yield his latest breath;
He fell full ripened as the autumnal ear,
　　Swept by the sickle of relentless Death.

" ' Shepherd,' said he, ' my day of life is flown; '
(Methinks ev'n now the faltering sound I hear.)
' Lay my cold corse beneath some humble stone,
　　And let no useless pomp attend my bier.'

" We tried each healing art, but could not save;
　　We bore his bier, the last sad debt to pay;
No plumy hearse bore Gracio to the grave,
　　No pompous pile was reared around his clay.

" All the sad village followed in the train,
　　We laid his bones beneath yon yew-tree's shade;
Our village curate graved the elegiac strain,
　　And lo! the stone, the spot in which he's laid."

"Twice twenty years for him I tilled the soil."

THE EPITAPH.

Here Gracio mingles with his kindred clay,
  Who lived contented, and who died resigned;
He let no slavish rule his actions sway,
  But the warm impulse of an honest mind.

Of Heaven's free blessings he bestowed a part,
  And opened wide his hospitable gate;
He fed the poor, for gen'rous was his heart;
  He soothed the sad, for pity was his mate.

To him the boon of good old age was giv'n,
  And, now, when parted from this world of woe,
He rests in holy faith of God and Heav'n,
  To meet that mercy which he gave below.

Robert Lovell.

SONG OF THE BRAVE.

From the German of Bürger.

HIGH sounds the song of valiant ones,
  As organ tones and chiming bells —
Whose lofty valor only owns —
  Not gold — but grateful song which tells.
I thank God that sing and that praise I can,
But to sing and to praise even one brave man!

The thaw-winds blow from mid-day sea,
  And drive the clouds and vapors on·
The mists before the tempests flee,
  As flocks before the gaunt wolf run;
The winds o'er the fields and the forest rush —
In sea and in river the ices crush.

On towering mountains melt the snow;
 A thousand avalanches fall;
The valley seems a sea below,
 And grows and swells the flood withal;
The waves are high-rolling away and away,
And bear the rock ice in their whirling spray.

On ponderous arch and pillars high
 Of massive free-stone resting firm,
There hangs a bridge; and midway by
 There stands a house to breast the storm,
And there live the toll-taker, children and wife
O toll-taker, toll-taker, fly for your life!

The toll-house was not tempest proof;
 Loud roared the storm which o'er it beat!
The toll-man leapt upon the roof,
 And gazed upon the tumult great:
" Merciful Heaven, have pity," he cried —
" Lost, lost! who can save! oh my children, my bride."

From either shore, on either side,
 The tempest thunders boom on boom!
On either shore the floods divide,
 Rending each pillar as they come.
The watchman, the children, the trembling wife —
They cry even louder than storm and strife.

The tempest thunders, boom on boom! –
 From either shore, on either side —
Bursting asunder doom on doom,
 The pillars and the arches wide.
And still in the midst of destruction cry
The doomed on the bridge, from earth to sky.

High on the distant shore they stand
  A host of gazers, great and small;
And each one cries and wrings the hand,
  Yet none will dare to save of all!
The watchman, the children, the trembling wife,
Still cry for deliverance thro' storm and strife.

When sounds the song of th' valiant brave,
  While organ tones and bells prolong!
Well timed! but name him —name I crave—
  When wilt'st thou name him, my fine song?
E'en in the midst of destruction's gulf
Brave one and valiant one! show thyself.

A noble count comes quickly nigh; —
  Upon a gallant steed is he.
What does the count's hand hold on high?
  A purse as full as full can be: —
" Ho! two hundred pieces of gold I give,
That watchman, and children, and wife may live!"

Was it the count? — the brave was who?
  Tell on, my noble song, tell on.
By heaven, the count was brave, 'tis true;
  But yet I knew a braver one.
O brave one — valiant one, show thyself here:
Already is terrible ruin near!

And higher yet the billows roll,
  And louder yet the whirlwinds cry,
And deeper yet will sink the soul!
  O brave deliverer, hasten nigh!
Still pillar by pillar they burst and break;
Loud crashing the tumbling arches make.

" Ho! yet I offer once again!"
    And high the count the prize upbears.
All hear — and tremble — and remain,
    And of the thousand none appears.
O, vainly the watchman, the children, the wife,
Cry frantic for aid through the storm and strife.

A plain and simple peasant, see,
    With staff in hand is hither led.
In coarse and uncouth robes is he;
    Of aspect high and bearing dread.
He heard the count's words, saw the purse in the air,
And viewed the approaching destruction there.

Then boldly, in God's name, sprung he
    Into the first small fishing boat;
Braved whirlwind, storm and raging sea;
    But leapt successfully afloat —
But alas for the watchman! — the boat was too small
To be savior at once of wife, children and all.

And thrice was he compelled to run
    Thro' whirlwind, storm and raging waves:
And thrice he drives successful on,
    Even until all his valor saves;
But scarcely to shore came they safely at last —
So rolled the rock'd boat amid billow and blast.

Who are the brave then, who the brave?
    Tell on, my noble song, tell on! —
The peasant risks his life to save —
    Yet clinking gold he looks upon.
But yet, should the count never offer reward,
The bold peasant's feat we should never have heard.

" Here!" said the count, " do not be gone!
  Here is thy prize—the purse is full!"
Say on, my noble song, say on!
  By heaven, the count's high wish is null?
But higher, in sooth, and more heavenly fair,
Is the heart that the homely-drest peasant brings there.

" My life is not on sale for gold—
  I'm poor, 'tis true, but satisfied.
Give to the saved the prize you hold—
  His was the loss; with him divide."
So gave he his heart's native goodness vent;
And rejoicingly onward he penniless went.

Edward R. Roe.

THE BACHELOR'S CANE-BOTTOMED CHAIR.

N tattered old slippers that toast at the bars,
And a ragged old jacket perfumed with cigars,
Away from the world and its toils and its cares,
I've a snug little kingdom up four pair of stairs.

To mount to this realm is a toil, to be sure,
But the fire there is bright and the air rather pure;
And the view I behold on a sunshiny day,
Is grand through the chimney-pots over the way.

This snug little chamber is crammed in all nooks,
With worthless old knickknacks and silly old books,
And foolish old odds and foolish old ends,
Cracked bargains from brokers, cheap keepsakes from
    friends.

Old armor, prints, pictures, pipes, china (all cracked),
Old rickety tables, and chairs broken-backed;
A two-penny treasure wondrous to see;
What matter? 'tis pleasant to you, friend, and me.

No better divan need the Sultan require,
Than the creaking old sofa that basks by the fire;
And 'tis wonderful, surely, what music you get
From the rickety, ramshackle, wheezy spinet.

That praying-rug came from a Turcoman's camp;
By Tiber once twinkled that brazen old lamp;
A Mameluke fierce yon dagger has drawn;
'Tis a murderous knife to toast muffins upon.

Long, long through the hours, and the night and the
    chimes,
How we talk of old books, and old friends, and old times;
As we sat in a fog made of rich Latakie
This chamber is pleasant to you, friend, and me.

But of all the cheap treasures that garnish my nest
There's one that I love and I cherish the best;
For the finest of couches that's padded with hair
I never would change thee, my cane-bottomed chair.

'Tis a bandy-legged, high-shouldered, worm-eaten seat,
With a creaking old back, and twisted old feet;
But since the fair morning when FANNY sat there,
I bless thee, and love thee, old cane-bottomed chair.

If chairs have but feeling in holding such charms,
A thrill must have passed through your withered old arms!
I looked, and I longed, and I wished, in despair,
I wished myself turned to a cane-bottomed chair.

It was but a moment she sat in this place,
She'd a scarf on her neck, and a smile on her face!
A smile on her face, and a rose in her hair,
And she sat there, and bloomed in my cane-bottomed
  chair.

And so I have valued my chair ever since,
Like the shrine of a saint, or the throne of a prince;
Saint FANNY my patroness sweet I declare,
The queen of my heart and my cane-bottomed chair.

When the candles burn low, and the company's gone,
In the silence of night as I sit here alone —
I sit here alone, but we yet are a pair —
My FANNY I see in my cane-bottomed chair.

She comes from the past and revisits my room;
She looks as she then did, all beauty and bloom;
So smiling and tender, so fresh and so fair,
And yonder she sits in my cane-bottomed chair.

W. M. Thackeray.

THE SHIPWRECK.

From Chambers' Journal.

STEADILY blows the north-east wind,
  And the harbor flag blows straight from the mast;
  And the sailors lounge and look on the pier,
  And smoke their pipes, and think it will last.

Yonder the cloud-rack lowers and glooms,
  And the sweet blue sky is hidden away;
Whilst the muttering waves grow hoarse and loud,
  And you have to shout the thing that you say.

The distant fleet of white-sailed ships
    Come hastening landward with wet, black sides,
As they lean to the push of the gusty wind,
    Now a rush, now a pause, on the weltering tides.

The spumy froth of the rock-vexed waves
    Gathers in creaming yeast on the sand;
Then away in fluttering flocks it speeds
    For edges and hillsides far inland.

The sea-birds dip and wheel in the air,
    And search the surges with greedy eyes;
They hang with tremulous wings on the brink,
    Then away on the blast with their shrill, sad cries.

Yonder the people crowd to the cliff,
    Where the long, gray grass is flattened and bent
As the stress of the hurricane passes by,
    Every eye to seaward is fixed intent.

Far down below are the cruel rocks,
    All black and slippy with black sea-weed;
And pits profound, where the whirlpools run,
    For ever revolving with hideous speed.

How the ships come! Let them come, poor barks!
    Here is the harbor quiet and still;
Once entered, the weary crew can sleep,
    And dream of their home without fear of ill.

How the ships come! What's that? A helm
    Is carried away, and she drifts to the blast;
Over her deck sweeps a roaring wave,
    And up in the rigging the crew run fast.

On she comes for the rocks! O men!
  O maids and mothers! O daughters and wives!
You are sitting at home by the hearth-fire warm,
  And the sea has a hold of your loved ones' lives!

Now she strikes on the rocks! No aid
  Can reach her there; she must tumble and roll,
Till at last a great third wave will come,
  And eat her up, and ingulf the whole

There — they are lashing themselves to the spars!
  Shrill on the wind comes their bitter cry;
They are waving their hands! Out of the main
  A billow rises, and breaks, and goes by.

All is vanished ; the ship and the men,
  Crumbled, and crushed, and hurried away!
Here are the splinters on every rock,
  All o'er the beach, and all round the bay.

There, on the sands, is a sailor's cap;
  And there, close by, a man on his face;
And there are the others! Oh, cover them quick
  And carry them off from this fatal place!

They are laid in the yard of the weather-worn church,
  And the grass will grow on their quiet grave;
But, O Lord in Heaven, hadst Thou spoke one word,
  It had stilled the wind, and curbed the wave!

But perhaps Thou *wert* speaking. Our ears are dull
  And we cannot discern in this atmosphere;
The men, as they drowned, might have clearer sense —
  Might have heard Thee well and seen Thee near.

We all must be patient, and bear our part
  In the periled toil of a wreckful world;
But some Heavenly Rest may be found at last,
  When the anchors are down, and the sails are furled.

Anonymous.

EXCELSIOR.

THE shades of night were falling fast,
  As through an Alpine village passed
A youth, who bore, 'mid snow and ice,
A banner with this strange device,
                  Excelsior!"

His brow was sad; his eye beneath,
Flashed like a falchion from its sheath,
And like a silver clarion rung
The accents of that unknown tongue,
                  " Excelsior!"

In happy homes he saw the light
Of household fires gleam warm and bright;
Above, the spectral glaciers shone,
And from his lips escaped a groan,
                  " Excelsior!"

" Try not the pass!" the old man said;
" Dark lowers the tempest overhead;
The roaring torrent is deep and wide!"
And loud that clarion voice replied,
                  " Excelsior!"

" A traveler, by the faithful hound,
Half-buried in the snow was found."

" Oh, stay," the maiden said, " and rest
Thy weary head upon this breast! "
A tear stood in his bright blue eye,
But still he answered, with a sigh,
        " Excelsior! "

" Beware the pine-tree's withered branch!
Beware the awful avalanche! "
This was the peasant's last good-night;
A voice replied, far up the height,
        " Excelsior! "

At break of day, as heavenward
The pious monks of Saint Bernard
Uttered the oft-repeated prayer,
A voice cried, through the startled air,
        " Excelsior! "

A traveler, by the faithful hound,
Half-buried in the snow was found,
Still grasping in his hand of ice
That banner with the strange device,
        " Excelsior! "

There in the twilight cold and gray,
Lifeless, but beautiful, he lay;
And from the sky, serene and far,
A voice fell, like a falling star,
        " Excelsior! "
        Henry W. Longfellow.

THE FOUNDING OF THE BELL.

HARK! how the furnace pants and roars,
  Hark! how the molten metal pours,
As, bursting from its iron doors,
    It glitters in the sun.
Now through the ready mold it flows,
Seething and hissing as it goes,
And filling every crevice up
As the red vintage fills the cup:
    Hurra! the work is done!

Unswathe him now. Take off each stay
That binds him to his couch of clay,
And let him struggle into day:
    Let chain and pulley run,
With yielding crank and steady rope,
Until he rise from rim to cope,
In rounded beauty, ribb'd in strength,
Without a flaw in all his length:
    Hurra! the work is done!

Should foemen lift their haughty hand,
And dare invade us where we stand,
Fast by the altars of our land
    We'll gather every one,
And he shall ring the loud alarm,
To call the multitudes to arm,
From distant field and forest brown,
And teeming alleys of the town:
    Hurra, the work is done!

And as the solemn boom they hear,
Old men shall grasp the idle spear,
Laid by to rust for many a year,
     And to the struggle run;
Young men shall leave their toils or books,
Or turn to sword their pruning hooks;
And maids have sweetest smiles for those
Who battle with their country's foes:
     Hurra, the work is done!

The clapper on his giant side
Shall ring no peal for blushing bride,
For birth, or death, or new-year-tide,
     Or festival begun.
A nation's joy alone shall be
The signal for his revelry;
And for a nation's woes alone
His melancholy tongue shall moan:
     Hurra! the work is done!

Borne on the gale, deep-toned and clear,
His long, loud summons shall we hear,
When statesmen to the country dear
     Their mortal race have run:
When mighty monarchs yield their breath,
And patriots sleep the sleep of death,
Then shall he raise his voice of gloom,
And peal a requiem o'er their tomb:
     Hurra! the work is done!

And when the cannon's iron throat
Shall bear the news to dells remote,
And trumpet blast resound the note,
     That victory is won;

When down the wind the banner drops,
And bonfires blaze on mountain tops,
His sides shall glow with fierce delight,
And ring glad peals from morn to night;
              Hurra! the work is done!

But of such scenes forbear to tell—
May never War awake this bell
To sound the tocsin or the knell.
              Hush'd be the alarum gun!
Sheath'd be the sword! and may his voice
But call the nations to rejoice
That War his tatter'd flag has furled,
And vanished from a wiser world:
              Hurra! the work is done!

Still may he ring when struggles cease,
Still may he ring for joy's increase,
For progress in the arts of peace,
              And friendly trophies won.
When rival nations join their hands,
When plenty crowns the happy lands,
When knowledge gives new blessings birth
And freedom reigns o'er all the earth:
              Hurra! the work is done!

                              Charles Mackay.

A LEGEND OF LAKE SUPERIOR.

MONEQUA was a chieftain's son —
  Monequa, woe-betide!
The Spirit of the Waters spun
  A charm about his bride,
And bore her off in deadly waves,
  Unknown to all beside.
And when he knew himself bereft,
He bowed him right, he bowed him left;
    He knelt toward the east;
  And thus with plea and purpose deft,
    He prayed the medicine-priest:

My bow and quiver hanging in the tent,
  My robe of skins, my all shall sure be thine;
But tell me where the water-spirit went,
  And where MEHAHA, wedded wife of mine?

Quoth thus the medicine-man: Mehaha flies
Adown the lake, among the isles that rise
    Midwater, and along each shore away,
For thirteen days of voyage, day by day!
The spirit of the waters laughs in scorn
That chief so young and bold should be forlorn,
And bids you seek in following canoe—
Where'er he lurks, still daring to pursue,
But know that not SUPERIOR's face alone
May ripple as the flying pair pass on:

But each bright lake or flowing stream may hide
Within its own o'ershaded banks your bride.
Retain your bow, your arrows, your keen knife;
Leap in the swift canoe — reck not for life —

Follow the snow-white gull where'er he flies,
And find your bride where that weird leader dies.

Monequa bears his birchen boat,
'Tis quickly in the lake afloat;
His arms, his skins, his flint and steel
Are safe within the arrowy keel;
His scanty store of pemmican,
Dried venison, corn, and earthen pan,
His sole utensil—these were all;
And swift he flew at duty's call.
A bark canoe is light and frail:
But watery wave nor stormy gale
Had power to make the boatman quail.

The waves were down, the wind was low;
  Monequa drove his light canoe
Due west, as straight as twanging bow
  Propels the arrow swift and true.
He gazed abroad upon the lake,
  And straight before his brow there stirred
A line of ripples in the wake
  Of some unwonted swimming bird.
From tail to beak 'twas snowy white;
  Its form was neither duck nor dove;
Its rounded breast threw back the light
Like shining snow-flakes in their flight;
  And wondering what the bird should prove
Which came so suddenly to sight,
He gazed and wondered as he gazed—
  The bird spread out his pinions full,
And while Monequa sat amazed,
  Up flew a snow-white gull.

What lured the snow-white gull up North,
  So far from genial wind and wave?
Had storm and tempest driven it forth
  To lands which boreal waters lave?
Or did the feathery form he bore
  But hide a spirit-bird within,
To lure Monequa from the shore,
  To waters he had never seen?
He knew not and he recked not now:
He only sought to drive his prow
Where'er the snow-white gull alluring flies,
And find his bride where that weird leader dies.

Due west the fair and treacherous pilot flew:
Due west did lorn Monequa still pursue;
Till o'er the lake Isle Royale rose to view,
And by its shore he moored his birch canoe.

Rising from out the old Silurian sea—
A rocky mount thrown up by fire's decree
Isle Royale stands amid the vasty lake,
Whose full three thousand leagues of waters break
In wintry storms, or rest in calm repose
When waves lie still and not a zephyr blows
Within the wall-rocks of a deep fiord,
Monequa gazed, but uttered ne'er a word.
Around him rose, in strange, fantastic forms,
Wrought out by time and sculptured by rude storms
Of many ages, rocks which towered on high —
Rude monuments to mark how cliffs may die.
Tall pines and hoary cedars at the base
Towered up in vain to reach the loftiest place;
While hardy shrubs adorn the craggy tops,
And boreal birds flit through the tangled copse.

Down from a cliff Monequa quick withdrew,
Shot from the shore his ready bark canoe,
And straight before him up the white gull flew!
Then over the lake in the white gull's wake
Monequa hastened to pursue.

Within a quiet harbor at Grand Isle,
Monequa moors his boat.   Around him pile
The massive rocks in rugged majesty.
But not for him the royal pageantry
Of mimic tower and monumental rock! —
Slow-swimming in the island's sheltered dock
The white gull looks into his saddened eyes
With eyes as sad as his; then flies
With gentle wing to where the Pictured Rocks
Adorn the southern shore with sculptured blocks
Of nature's architecture. — There once more
He follows, skimming eastward in his skiff
Of birchen bark, still scanning every cliff.
Skirting along the walls of sculptured rock,
Monequa sought t' avoid the breakers' shock,
And entered by an archway vast and dim
A gloomy vault, for goblins and for him.
Within he rested in his frail canoe,
And slept where none but spirits dare pursue.
The baffled light was struggling faintly in;
The throbbing waves subdued their wonted din,
And poured re-echoing murmurs through the gloom,
Marking the cavern as a cave of doom.
A white gull entered through the gaping arch;
The spirits of the place, in fitful march,

As if in answer to the bird's command —
Muttered in mystic words on every hand
Into dull ears that slept and heard them not.

Thus sang the murmuring lake Mehaha's lot:

On a cliff where spirits keep,
Fair Mehaha sank to sleep;
Started up from slumber deep,
Plunging with a deadly leap —
Sank five fathoms in the lake
In the spirit-land to wake!
O'er her gentle breezes blew,
Mourning all the night-long through;
Gently moving currents bore,
From the steep and fatal shore,
Dead Mehaha's drifting form
Deep beneath the wave and storm.
Then the buoyant body rose,
Floating where the west-wind blows.
Waters green around her—
There the breezes found her;
With the white foam crowned her,
Wafting her away!

Then came the west-wind's lay:

In the mournful moonlight—
In the glimmering starlight—
In the summer sunlight—
Eastward day by day,
Passed the gentle maiden.
Never wave was laden
With a lovelier maiden!

Never breezes blew
More for waif forbearing
With the form 'twas sparing,
  All the sad way through!
In the cavern's cover
All her ills are over;
All the rocks above her—
  All the spirits round—
Deem her body holy;
While the dead so lowly
Sinks forever slowly
  In the deep profound!

Then the cavern uttered
This sad song, and muttered:

Through my gloomy arches
  Sorrowing echoes moan;
Muffled funeral marches
  Sound from stone to stone,
Coming from the surges
  Low and woe-begone.
From the outer verges
  Where the daylight shone,
Not a beam emerges:
  But a shadowy tone,
Keeping with the dirges
  Sounding low and lone,
Funeral watch and loving guard
With apt and answering accord.
  In my deep recesses—
  In my hollow dome—

Darkness which oppresses
  Guards her silent home.
Wake, Monequa! waken!
Never sleep was taken
  In so sad a scene.
Never bird has guided
Groom from bride divided
    With so sad a mien.
    Waken — waken — waken!

Upstarting with habitual marksman's skill,
Monequa seized the bow with quickening will;
Affixed an arrow, drew it to the head —
A glance — a twang — the snow-white gull was dead!
Quick-gliding where the dead bird floating lies,
His fleet canoe shoots forward for the prize —
He finds Mehaha where the white-gull dies.

                 Edward R. Roe.

THE SWALLOWS.

From the French of Jean Pierre Claris Florian.

OW I love to see the swallows
  At my window every year,
For they bring the happy tidings,
  Smiling spring is drawing near.
" In the same nest," soft they whisper,
  " Happy love once more shall dwell;
Only lovers who are faithful
  Tidings of the spring should tell."

When beneath the icy fingers
  Of the first frosts fall the leaves,
Swallows gather on the house-tops,
  Singing as they quit the eaves,
" Haste away, the sunshine's fading,
  Cruel winds the snow will bring;
Faithful love can know no winter;
  Where it dwells is always spring."

If — unhappy! — one be taken
  By a cruel infant's hand,
Caged and parted from its lover —
  Captive in the winter land;
Soon you'll see it die of sorrow,
  While its mate, still lingering nigh,
Knows no further joy in sunshine,
  But on the same day will die.

"How I love to see the swallows
At my window every year."

TWO LOVERS.

TWO lovers by a moss-grown spring:
They leaned soft cheeks together there,
Mingled the dark and sunny hair,
And heard the wooing thrushes sing.
O budding time!
O love's blest prime!

Two wedded from the portal stept;
The bells made happy carolings,
The air was soft as fanning wings,
White petals on the pathway slept.
O pure-eyed bride!
O tender pride!

Two faces o'er a cradle bent:
Two hands above the head were locked;
These pressed each other while they rocked,
Those watched a life that love had sent.
O solemn hour!
O hidden power!

Two parents by the evening fire:
The red light fell about their knees,
On heads that rose by slow degrees,
Like buds upon the lily spire.
O patient life!
O tender strife!

The two still sat together there,
The red light shone about their knees;
But all the heads, by slow degrees,
Had gone and left that lonely pair.
O voyage fast!
O vanished past!

The red light shone upon the floor,
  And made the space between them wide;
They drew their chairs up side by side,
Their pale checks joined, and said " Once more! "
        O memories!
        O past that is!

George Eliot.

THE CHILDREN'S HOUR.

ETWEEN the dark and the daylight,
  When the night is beginning to lower,
Comes a pause in the day's occupations,
  That is known as the children's hour.

I hear in the chamber above me,
  The patter of little feet;
The sound of a door that is opened,
  And voices soft and sweet.

From my study I see in the lamplight,
  Descending the broad hall stair,
Grave Alice, and laughing Allegra,
  And Edith, with golden hair.

A whisper, and then a silence,
  Yet I know by their merry eyes
They are plotting and planning together
  To take me by surprise.

A sudden rush from the stairway;
  A sudden raid from the hall;
By three doors left unguarded,
  They enter my castle-wall.

They climb up into my turret,
    O'er the arms and back of my chair;
If I try to escape, they surround me;
    They seem to be everywhere.

They almost devour me with kisses,
    Their arms about me entwine,
Till I think of the Bishop of Bingen,
    In his Mouse-Tower on the Rhine.

Do you think, O blue-eyed banditti,
    Because you have scaled the wall,
Such an old mustache as I am
    Is not a match for you all?

I have you fast in my fortress,
    And will not let you depart,
But put you into the dungeon,
    In the Round-Tower of my heart.

And there will I keep you forever —
    Yes, forever and a day;
Till the walls shall crumble to ruin,
    And molder in dust away.

                    Henry W. Longfellow.

HAMLET AND HIS MOTHER.

From the Tragedy of Hamlet.

ACT III., SCENE IV.—The Queen's Closet.

Enter the Queen *and* Polonius.

Polo. He will come straight. Look you lay home
  to him:
Tell him his pranks have been too broad to bear with;
And that your Grace hath screened and stood between
Much heat and him. I'll sconce me even here.
Pray you, be round with him.
 Ham. [*Within.*] Mother, mother, mother!
 Queen.   I'll warrant you:
Fear me not. Withdraw; I hear him coming.
      [Polonius *hides behind the arras.*
     Enter Hamlet.
 Ham. Now, mother, what's the matter?
 Queen. Hamlet, thou hast thy father much offended.
 Ham. Mother, you have my father much offended.
 Queen. Come, come; you answer me with an idle
  tongue.
 Ham. Go, go; you question me with a wicked tongue.
 Queen. Why, how now, Hamlet? What's the matter
  now?
Have you forgot me?
 Ham.   No, by the rood, not so:
You are the Queen, your husband's brother's wife;
And — would it were not so! — you are my mother.
 Queen. Nay, then I'll set those to you that can speak.
 Ham. Come, come, and sit you down; you shall not
  budge:

You go not till I set you up a glass
Where you may see the inmost part of you.
    Queen.   What wilt thou do? thou wilt not murder me?
—Help, help, ho!
    Polo. [*Behind.*] What, ho! help, help, help!
    Ham. [*Drawing.*] How now! a rat? Dead, for a
ducat, dead!   [*Makes a pass through the arras.*
    Polo. [*Behind.*] O, I am slain!
    Queen. O me! what hast thou done?
    Ham. Nay, I know not: is it the King?
    Queen. O, what a rash and bloody deed is this!
    Ham. A bloody deed! almost as bad, good mother,
as kill a king, and marry with his brother.
    Queen. As kill a king!
    Ham. Ay, lady, twas my word —
            [*Lifts up the arras and discovers* Polonius.
Thou wretched, rash-intruding fool, farewell!
I took thee for thy better: take thy fortune;
Thou find'st to be too busy is some danger —
Leave wringing of your hands: peace! sit you down
And let me wring your heart: for so I shall,
If it be made of penetrable stuff:
If damnèd custom have not cross'd it so,
That it is proof and bulwark against sense.
    Queen. What have I done, that thou darest wag thy
          tongue
In noise so rude against me?
    Ham.   Such an act
That blurs the grace and blush of modesty:
Calls virtue hypocrite; takes off the rose
From the fair forehead of an innocent love,
And sets a blister there; makes marriage vows
As false as dicers' oaths: O, such a deed

As from the body of contraction plucks
The very soul; and sweet religion makes
A rhapsody of words: Heaven's face doth glow;
Yea, this solidity and compound mass,
With tristful visage, as against the doom,
Is thought-sick at the act.
   Queen.   Ah me, what act,
That roars so loud and thunders in the index?
   Ham.   Look here upon this picture, and on this,
The counterfeit presentment of two brothers.
See what a grace was seated on this brow;
Hyperion's curls; the front of Jove himself;
An eye like Mars, to threaten and command;
A station like the herald Mercury
New-lighted on a heaven-kissing hill;
A combination and a form indeed,
Where every god did seem to set his seal,
To give the world assurance of a man:
This was your husband.   Look you now what follows:
Here is your husband; like a mildew'd ear,
Blasting his wholesome brother.   Have you eyes?
Could you on this fair mountain leave to feed,
And batten on this moor?   Ha! have you eyes?
You cannot call it love; for at your age
The heyday in the blood is tame, it's humble,
And waits upon the judgment: and what judgment
Would step from this to this?   Sense, sure you have,
Else could you not have motion; but sure that sense
Is apoplexed: for madness would not err,
Nor sense to ecstacy was ne'er so thrall'd,
But it reserved some quantity of choice,
To serve in such a difference.   What devil was't
That thus hath cozen'd you at hoodman blind?

Eyes without feeling, feeling without sight,
Ears without hands or eyes, smelling sans all,
Or but a sickly part of one true sense
Could not so mope.
O shame! where is thy blush?   Rebellious Hell,
If thou canst mutine in a matron's bones,
To flaming youth let virtue be as wax,
And melt in her own fire: proclaim no shame,
When the compulsive ardor gives the charge,
Since frost itself as actively doth burn,
And reason panders will.
  Queen.   O Hamlet, speak no more!
Thou turn'st mine eyes into my very soul;
And there I see such black and grainèd spots
As will not leave their tinct.
  Ham.   Nay, but to live
Stew'd in corruption —
  Queen.   O, speak to me no more!
These words like daggers enter in mine ears:
No more, sweet Hamlet!

  Ham.   A murderer and a villain;
A slave that is not twentieth part the tithe
Of your precedent lord; a Vice of kings!
A cutpurse of the empire and the rule,
That from a shelf the precious diadem stole,
And put it in his pocket!
  Queen.   No more!
  Ham. A king of shreds and patches—

Enter the Ghost.

Save me and hover o'er me with your wings,
You heavenly guards!— What would your gracious figure?
  Queen. Alas, he's mad!

Ham.   Do you not come your tardy son to chide,
That, lapsed in time and passion, lets go by
Th' important acting of your dread command?
O, say!

Ghost.   Do not forget.   This visitation
Is but to whet thy almost blunted purpose.
But, look, amazement on thy mother sits:
O, step between her and her fighting soul!
Conceit in weakest bodies strongest works.
Speak to her, Hamlet.

Ham.   How is't with you, lady?

Queen.   Alas, how is't with you,
That you do bend your eye on vacancy,
And with th' incorporal air do hold discourse?
Forth at your eyes your spirits wildly peep;
And, as the sleeping soldiers in th' alarm,
Your bedded hairs, like life in excrements,
Start up, and stand on end.   O gentle son,
Upon the heat and flame of thy distemper
Sprinkle cool patience.   Whereon do you look?

Ham.   On him, on him! Look you, how pale he glares,
His form and cause conjoin'd, preaching to stones,
Would make them capable. — Do not look upon me;
Lest with this piteous action you convert
My stern affects: — then what I have to do
Will want true color; tears, perchance, for blood.

Queen.   To whom do you speak this?

Ham.   Do you see nothing there?

Queen.   Nothing at all; yet all that is I see.

Ham.   Nor did you nothing hear?

Queen.   No, nothing but ourselves.

Ham. Why, look you there! look, how it steals away!
My father, in his habit as he lived !
Look, where he goes, even now, out at the portal!
[*Exit* Ghost.

Queen. This is the very coinage of your brain:
This bodiless creation ecstasy
Is very cunning in.
Ham. Ecstasy!
My pulse, as yours, doth temperately keep time,
And makes as healthful music: 'tis not madness
That I have uttered: bring me to the test,
And I the matter will re-word; which madness
Would gambol from. Mother, for love of grace,
Lay not that flattering unction to your soul,
That not your trespass but my madness speaks:
It will but skim and film the ulcerous place,
Whilst rank corruption, mining all within,
Infects unseen. Confess yourself to Heaven;
Repent what's past, avoid what is to come;
And do not spread the compost on the weeds,
To make them ranker. Forgive me this my virtue;
For in the fatness of these pursy times
Virtue itself of vice must pardon beg,
Yea, courb and woo for leave to do him good.
Queen. O Hamlet, thou hast cleft my heart in twain.
Ham. O, throw away the worser part of it
And live the purer with the other half.
Good night: but go not to my uncle's bed;
Assume a virtue, if you have it not.
That monster, custom, who all sense doth eat
Of habits evil, is angel yet in this,
That to the use of actions fair and good
He likewise gives a frock or livery,

  POETIC JEWELS

That aptly is put on.   Refrain to night,
And that shall lend a kind of easiness
To the next abstinence: the next more easy;
For use almost can change the stamp of nature,
And either shame the devil or throw him out
With wondrous potency.   Once more, good night:
And when you are desirous to be blest,
I'll blessing beg of you.   For this same lord,
                              [_Pointing to_ Polonius.
I do repent: but Heaven hath pleased it so,
To punish me with this and this with me,
That I must be their scourge and minister.
I will bestow him, and will answer well
The death I gave him.   So, again, good night.—
[_Aside._]   I must be cruel, only to be kind:
Thus bad begins, and worse remains behind.
                    William Shakespeare.

"'Twere pleasant, that in flowery June."

JUNE.

[Among the minor poems of Bryant, none has so much impressed me as the one which he entitles "June." The rhythmical flow here is even voluptuous — nothing could be more melodious. The poem has always affected me in a remarkable manner. The intense melancholy which seems to well up, per-force, to the surface of all the poet's cheerful sayings about his grave, we find thrilling us to the soul — while there is the truest poetic elevation in the thrill. The impression left is one of pleasurable sadness. *Edgar Allan Poe.*]

GAZED upon the glorious sky
   And the green mountains round;
And thought, that when I came to lie
   Within the silent ground,
'Twere pleasant, that in flowery June,
When brooks send up a cheerful tune,
   And groves a joyous sound,
The sexton's hand my grave to make,
The rich green mountain turf should break.

A cell within the frozen mold,
   A coffin borne through sleet,
And icy clods above it rolled,
   While fierce the tempests beat —
Away! I will not think of these —
Blue be the sky and soft the breeze,
   Earth green beneath the feet,
And be the damp mold gently pressed
Into my narrow place of rest.

There, through the long, long summer hours
   The golden light should lie,
And thick young herbs and groups of flowers
   Stand in their beauty by,
The oriole should build and tell
His love-tale close beside my cell;

The idle butterfly
Should rest him there, and there be heard
The housewife-bee and humming-bird.

And what if cheerful shouts, at noon,
  Come from the village sent,
Or songs of maids, beneath the moon,
  With fairy laughter blent?
And what if, in the evening light,
Betrothed lovers walk in sight
  Of my low monument?
I would the lovely scene around
Might know no sadder sight nor sound.

I know, I know I should not see
  The season's glorious show,
Nor would its brightness shine for me,
  Nor its wild music flow;
But if, around my place of sleep,
The friends I love should come to weep,
  They might not haste to go.
Soft airs, and song, and light, and bloom,
Should keep them lingering by my tomb.

These to their softened hearts should bear
  The thought of what has been,
And speak of one who cannot share
  The gladness of the scene;
Whose part, in all the pomp that fills
The circuit of the summer hills,
  Is — that his grave is green;
And deeply would their hearts rejoice
To hear, again, his living voice.

William Cullen Bryant.

"A GOOD, GREAT NAME."

FRANCES E. WILLARD.   CHAS. T. KIMBALL.

" A good, great name!" What millionaire
Has ever been remembered so?
What selfish life may ever share
The praise that makes these echoes flow?

" A good, great name! " it speaks to me
   Of love to God and love to men;
Those unities in which agree
   Both Now and Here, both There and Then.

" A good, great name!" the tuneful bells
   Ring on and on in their delight,
While my glad heart with purpose swells
   To serve my country with my might.

" A good, great name!" It is the goal
   Of all this splendid world can give;
Its conquest well may nerve the soul
   For man to die, for God to live.

" A good, great name!" Oh, Washington!
   We may not climb where thou hast stood,
Crowned with the people's loud " Well done!"
   A Pharos in time's rolling flood.

But to our measure's perfect height
   Let each climb on toward generous fame;
So may the future's bells delight
   To ring for us " A good, great name;"

Or sweet and low the human heart
   Shall gently chime our holier fame;
Beyond the magic of man's art
   It shall sing on, " A good, great name!"

THE FROST SPIRIT.

E comes — he comes — the Frost Spirit comes.
 You may trace his foot-steps now
On the naked woods, and the blasted fields, and the
 brown hill's withered brow.
He has smitten the leaves of the gray old trees where their
 pleasant green came forth,
And the winds, which follow wherever he goes, have
 shaken them down to earth.

He comes — he comes — the Frost Spirit comes! — from
 the frozen Labrador —
From the icy bridge of the northern seas, which the white
 bear wanders o'er —
Where the fisherman's sail is stiff with ice, and the luck-
 less forms below,
In the sunless cold of the lingering night, into marble
 statues grow!

He comes — he comes — the Frost Spirit comes! — on the
 rushing northern blast,
And the dark Norwegian pines have bowed as his fearful
 breath went past.
With an unscorched wing he has hurried on, where the
 fires of Hecla glow
On the darkly beautiful sky above, and the ancient ice
 below.

He comes — he comes — the Frost Spirit comes! — and
 the quiet lake shall feel
The torpid touch of his glazing breath, and ring to the
 skater's heel;

And the streams which danced on the broken rocks, or
    sang to the leaning grass,
Shall bow again to their winter chain, and in mournful
    silence pass.

He comes — he comes — the Frost Spirit comes! — let us
    meet him as we may,
And turn with the light of the parlor fire his evil power
    away;
And gather closer the circle round, when that firelight
    dances high,
And laugh at the shriek of the baffled Fiend as his sound-
    ing wing goes by!

John G. Whittier.

A PSALM OF LIFE.

WHAT THE HEART OF THE YOUNG MAN SAID TO THE PSALMIST.

TELL me not, in mournful numbers,
    " Life is but an empty dream!"
For the soul is dead that slumbers,
    And things are not what they seem.

Life is real! Life is earnest!
    And the grave is not its goal;
" Dust thou art, to dust returnest,"
    Was not spoken of the soul.

Not enjoyment, and not sorrow,
    Is our destined end or way;
But to act, that each to-morrow
    Find us farther than to-day.

Art is long, and Time is fleeting,
   And our hearts, though stout and brave,
Still, like muffled drums are beating
   Funeral marches to the grave.

In the world's broad field of battle,
   In the bivouac of life,
Be not like dumb, driven cattle!
   Be a hero in the strife!

Trust no future, howe'er pleasant!
   Let the dead Past bury its dead!
Act -act in the living Present!
   Heart within, and God o'erhead!

Lives of great men all remind us
   We can make our lives sublime,
And, departing, leave behind us
   Footprints on the sands of time; —

Footprints, that perhaps another,
   Sailing o'er life's solemn main,
A forlorn and shipwrecked brother,
   Seeing, shall take heart again.

Let us, then, be up and doing,
   With a heart for any fate;
Still achieving, still pursuing,
   Learn to labor and to wait.

Henry W. Longfellow.

THE RAVEN.

NCE upon a midnight dreary, while I pondered,
weak and weary,
Over many a quaint and curious volume of forgotten lore —
While I nodded, nearly napping, suddenly there came a
tapping,
As of some one gently rapping, rapping at my chamber
door.
" 'Tis some visitor," I muttered, " tapping at my chamber
door;
Only this, and nothing more."

Ah, distinctly I remember, it was in the bleak December,
And each separate, dying ember wrought its ghost upon
the floor.
Eagerly I wished the morrow; vainly I had sought to
borrow
From my books surcease of sorrow, sorrow for the lost
Lenore —
For the rare and radiant maiden, whom the angels name
Lenore,
Nameless here forevermore.

And the silken, sad, uncertain rustling of each purple
curtain
Thrilled me, filled me with fantastic terrors never felt
before;
So that now, to still the beating of my heart, I stood
repeating,
" 'Tis some visitor entreating entrance at my chamber
door,

Some late visitor entreating entrance at my chamber
    door;
        This it is, and nothing more."

Presently my soul grew stronger; hesitating then no longer,
" Sir," said I, " or madam, truly your forgiveness I implore;
But the fact is, I was napping, and so gently you came
    rapping,
And so faintly you came tapping, tapping at my chamber
    door,
That I scarce was sure I heard you."   Here I opened wide
    the door:—
        Darkness there, and nothing more.

Deep into that darkness peering, long I stood there, won-
    dering, fearing,
Doubting, dreaming dreams no mortals ever dared to dream
    before;
But the silence was unbroken, and the stillness gave no
    token,
And the only word there spoken was the whispered word,
    " Lenore; "
This I whispered, and an echo murmured back the word,
    " Lenore."
        Merely this, and nothing more.

Back into the chamber turning, all my soul within me
    burning,
Soon again I heard a tapping, something louder than
    before —
" Surely," said I, " surely, that is something at my window
    lattice;

Let me see, then, what thereat is, and this mystery explore,
Let my heart be still a moment, and this mystery explore;—
        'Tis the wind, and nothing more."

Open here I flung the shutter, when, with many a flirt and
        flutter,
In there stepped a stately raven, of the saintly days of
        yore —
Not the least obeisance made he; not a moment stopped or
        stayed he;
But, with mien of lord or lady, perched above my chamber
        door,
Perched upon the bust of Pallas, just above my chamber
        door;—
        Perched, and sat, and nothing more.

Then this ebon bird beguiling my sad fancy into smiling,
By the grave and stern decorum of the countenance it
        wore,
"Though thy crest be shorn and shaven, thou," I said,
        "art sure no craven,
Ghastly, grim, and ancient raven, wandering from the
        nightly shore,
Tell me what thy lordly name is on the night's Plutonian
        shore."
        Quoth the raven, " Nevermore."

Much I marveled this ungainly fowl to hear discourse so
        plainly,
Though its answer little meaning, little relevancy bore;
For we cannot help agreeing that no living human being
Ever yet was blessed with seeing bird above his chamber
        door,

Bird or beast upon the sculptured bust above his chamber
    door,
        With such name as " Nevermore."

But the raven, sitting lonely on that placid bust, spoke
    only
That one word, as if his soul in that one word _he_ did
    outpour.
Nothing further then he uttered; not a feather then he
    fluttered;
Till I scarcely more than muttered, " Other friends have
    flown before;
On the morrow *he* will leave me, as my hopes have flown
    before."
        Then the bird said, " Nevermore."

Startled at the stillness broken by reply so aptly spoken,
" Doubtless," said I, " what it utters is its only stock and
    store,
Caught from some unhappy master, whom unmerciful dis-
    aster
Followed fast and followed faster, till his songs one burden
    bore,
Till the dirges of his hope that melancholy burden bore,
        Of ' Never —nevermore!'"

But the raven still beguiling all my sad soul into smiling,
Straight I wheeled a cushioned seat in front of bird and
    bust and door;
Then upon the velvet sinking, I betook myself to linking
Fancy unto fancy, thinking what this ominous bird of yore,
What this grim, ungainly, ghastly, gaunt, and ominous
    bird of yore
        Meant in croaking, " Nevermore."

This I sat engaged in guessing, but no syllable expressing
To the fowl, whose fiery eyes now burned into my bosom's
    core;
This and more I sat divining, with my head in ease
    reclining
On the cushion's velvet lining that the lamplight gloated
    o'er,
But whose velvet violet lining with the lamplight gloating
    o'er,
        She shall press, ah, nevermore.

Then, methought, the air grew denser, perfumed from an
    unseen censer,
Swung by seraphim whose footfalls tinkled on the tufted
    floor,
" Wretch!" I cried, " thy God hath lent thee, by these
    angels he hath sent thee
Respite—respite and nepenthe from thy memories of
    Lenore!
Quaff, O quaff this kind nepenthe, and forget this lost
    Lenore! "
        Quoth the raven, " Nevermore. "

" Prophet," said I, " thing of evil! prophet still, if bird or
    devil!
Whether tempter sent, or tempest tossed thee here
    ashore
Desolate, yet all undaunted, on this desert land enchanted,
On this home by Horror haunted—tell me truly, I im-
    plore—   .
Is there—*is* there balm in Gilead? tell me, I implore!"
        Quoth the raven, " Nevermore,"

" Prophet!" said I, " thing of evil — prophet still, if bird
    or devil!
By that heaven that bends above us — by that God we
    both adore —
Tell this soul with sorrow laden, if, within the distant
    Aidenn,
It shall clasp a sainted maiden, whom the angels name
    Lenore —
Clasp a rare and radiant maiden, whom the angels name
    Lenore. "
        Quoth the raven, " Nevermore."

" Be that word our sign of parting, bird or fiend!" I shrieked,
    upstarting,
" Get thee back into the tempest and the night's Plutonian
    shore!
Leave no black plume as a token of that lie thy soul hath
    spoken!
Leave my loneliness unbroken — quit the bust above my
    door!
Take thy beak from out my heart, and take thy form from
    off my door!"
        Quoth the raven, " Nevermore."

And the raven, never flitting, still is sitting, still is sitting
On the pallid bust of Pallas, just above my chamber door,
And his eyes have all the seeming of a demon's that is
    dreaming;
And the lamplight o'er him streaming, throws his shadow
    on the floor;
And my soul from out that shadow that lies floating on
    the floor
        Shall be lifted — nevermore.
                Edgar Allan Poe.

A LEGEND OF TRANSMIGRATION.

KNOW a land where crafty priests
  Teach tenets strange, and still declare
That souls of men migrate to beasts,
  And expiate their sinnings there,
And live within another life,
  And in another being bear
The penalty of sin and strife —
  Desert for all their misdeeds here.

I know not if the creed be true —
  It passes all discreet belief ;—
And only seek to tell to you
  The story of a priestly chief,
A sad old man, whose tale was new —
  Albeit, neither sane nor brief.
And now I tell the story through
  He told me for his soul's relief.

His words were passionless and low,
  And trembled with the weight of years;
But in his face his thoughts would glow,
  And in his eyes the trembling tears
Would fain resist the overflow,
  As long remembered hopes and fears
Came back successive, sure and slow,
  And fell upon my listening ears.

It was a weird and weary tale,
  So passing strange and dreamy too,
That all its warmth would not avail
  To hide the mind's distempered view,

Which marked with madness all the trail,
  And tinctured all the story through.
And this, the old man's rapt detail
  As told to me I tell to you.

The hill-country hath many a worthy chief:
  Among the worthiest, my father wrought
To give his one besetting sin relief;
  And so, to elevate his soul, he sought
To consecrate his son in strong belief
  Of all our sacred oracles had taught
To lift the aspiring soul from sin and grief—
  And I was made a priest— alas!—for nought.

And I was learn'd in all our eastern lore—
  Alas for learning, when the soul is weak!—
And I did serve in sacred things before
  The holy altar; and 'twas mine to speak
The words of comfort at the temple door;
  To curb the proud and to console the weak;
To mark the votive gifts the people bore,
  And trim the lights which burned from week
      to week.

And all a faithful priest should be, still that was I;
  No less devout than constant was my prayer.
Or should a priest defend the faith and die,
  My life was ready for Gaudama there;
Or should a priest all carnal wants defy,
  And life to all created beings spare,
And all which ministers to self deny,
  That priest was I —'twas mine to bow and bear.

By holy vows a priestly celibate,
    I held my vows more sacred than my life!
In strong affection and emotion great,
    I loved all living, as should love a wife
Her lord and little ones.   O wondrous fate!—
    That love which hallows all things, should be rife
With evil too! I learned—but all too late—
    That love may wound the heart-strings like a
            knife.

In temporal as in all eternal things
    The priests of Buddha teach the people well—
I taught them as I loved them; and it brings
    My barren heart some slight relief to tell
How faithfully I loved and taught.   Nor kings,
    Nor princes, nor the opposing powers of hell,
Can spoil *that* solace; and if love hath stings,
    Love hath all power their poison to expel.

One day there came a maiden to be taught
    With other maidens dutiful as she;
And yet I looked into her face and caught
    An instant recognition—she with me
And I with her—as if one look had wrought
    Commingling love upon the heart's decree.
That blessed love it was which soon had brought
    My soul into a sin without a plea!

Her name is never more upon my tongue;
    And yet I would you saw her—as I see—
And hear her gentle voice, in words which hung
    For twoscore years of memory to me.

" And she was beautiful, and I was young."

And she was beautiful, and I was young,
  And both were human, and obeyed the plea
Of fatal love; and still together clung
  Till dungeons, doom and death had set us free.

Fate travels fast; we loved — were wedded —
  Sundered by avenging priests — denied
Defense — imprisoned in a dungeon bedded
  Deep within the temple's walls — decried
As impious — and, O fate most dreaded! —
  Met no more — my priestly vows defied,
My name cast out as vile, and I beheaded!
  Yet all were nothing had I only died.

You start — you stare. — Be still, and hear the whole.
  They say a demon racks my o'er-wrought brain:
Perhaps 'tis so; but not perverts my soul.
  These hands are not my hands; these throes of pain
Distort no limbs of mine to balk control;
  This tongue is not my tongue that speaks again;
My locks were glossy black — no grizzled poll!
  I loathe the flesh in which I still remain.

But you are Christian, and my creed despise;
  But I have been and am whereof I tell.
I died as every recreant priest that dies —
  To straight be born into a beast, or hell.
And e'en the base hyena, whose sharp cries
  Afflict the night with wailings fierce and fell,
Received my soul, and kept me from the skies!
  The priests pronounced their pitiless curses well.

For years my soul contended with the beast,
  And still the beast prevailed.   My will defied
By beastly appetites, had well nigh ceased
  To seek the higher life the beast denied.
One fatal night, as dawn stole up the East,
  The fierce hyena, darkly prowling, spied
And spoiled a tomb to make his hellish feast:—
  The sacred dead polluted was my bride!

My soul went out, and hell had done its worst.
  I knew myself a transmigrant once more;
But sought no murder, knew for blood no thirst,
  And gamboled playful on the grassy floor
Of flowery meads, by no fierce rage accurst.
  But still, a lamb is but a beast, though gore
Be not its nature: — I was still immersed
  Within a beastly body as before.

Whoso with his own suffering flesh relieves
  The hunger of a famished tiger, wins
Gaudama's high reward, and so receives
  The promise of Absorption, and begins
To enjoy the rapture which his soul conceives;
  I saw a tiger starving in the gins
Of tangled jungle—ran as one who leaves
  His life with joy, and perished for my sins!

Once more went out my sinful soul, that hour: —
  A beggar's body, waiting for the fire,
Received the lingering spirit as its dower,
  And I was born a beggar on the pyre.

The body rose alive, with pulse, and power,
   And consciousness; and hungry to respire
The breath of life, and feel the grateful shower,
   And be the slave of impulse and desire.

In this vile body I have dwelt and dwell;
   In this old ruin I remain, still young.
In these cold words in which I seek to tell
   My woful story, 'tis the beggar's tongue
That utters, all unmoved by passion's spell.
   Should I have poured my soul while you have hung
Upon the long recital, it were well
   Your ears were adder's ere the voice had rung.

I starve my beggar's body on a crust:
   I feast my 'prisoned soul with heavenly hope.
The body is all animal, and must
   Decline and perish; but the soul will grope
Its way from earth's gross darkness in the trust
   Of life eternal. Let the carcase mope,
And shrink, and shrivel in its mortal dust;
   The soul expands forever in its heavenly scope.

These glimmering orbs of sight that see, are blind:
   Yet I behold all things with spirit eyes.
I hear Gaudama in the changing wind,
   The gentle breeze, the storm which rends the skies;
And see him when the lightning flashes find
   All mortal eyes struck blind. The eagle flies
Invisible to mortal sight; the immortal mind
   Will still beyond the soaring eagle rise.

This loathsome flesh ere long will rot away;
  But I shall be absorbed into the eternal!
The earth will claim its lump of kindred clay,
  But I shall soar into the vast supernal.
The sin which marred the spirit's earthly stay,
  Will fall away to be with the infernal.
Even now my soul departs! O blessed day,
  Which bears me to a land forever vernal!

Edward R. Roe.

GENESIS.

THOU who didst beget the universe!
  Inspire with radiant truth my solemn theme.
  Exalt my tongue with praise while I rehearse
  Old Earth's mutations in the wondrous scheme.
Upon mine eyes let light supernal beam,
While I behold the wonders of Thy hand;
And let me catch the streaming rays which gleam
Like beacon-lights o'er all the varied land,
Guiding me on to Him who all these wonders planned.

Mountains that lift their hoary heads on high;
Oceans that dash their waves upon the shore;
Forests whose shade shuts out the sun and sky;
Torrents whose downward driven waters pour;
The lightning's living flash; the thunder's roar;
The prairie plains that spread themselves abroad,
Like seas of verdure filled with flowery store —
These are the laureate anthems which applaud
The King of Kings: these are the poetry of God!

But not alone in anthems deep and bold
The earth does homage to its Maker's skill —
The gentle flowers in lowly hymns unfold
The wonders of His all-creating will.
The waving boughs that rustle on the hill
In answering cadence to the wooing wind,
And all the lowlier, gentler hosts which fill
The teeming earth, though deaf, and dumb, and blind,
Bear witness to the wonders of the Eternal Mind.

Lo! every thing that liveth joins the song,
Touch Thou my wondering tongue, O God, with praise,
While I the ever-echoing hymn prolong.
I would the anthem of Creation raise —
The world pre-adamite, the ancient days,
And all the rocky records of old Time,
Filled with revealing witness of Thy ways.
So would I praise Thee in a theme sublime:
The story of old Earth when she was in her prime.

I.

Thou hast seen strange mutations, hoary Earth!
And man, the clay god, made of dust at first,
And unto dust returning — aftertype
Of thee and thine estate — has heard thy doom!
Thy birth was of the all-begetting fire:
And 'mid the all-destroying fire at last
Thou dying shalt return to elemental vapor.
Land and sea and sky shall pass away;
And like a wandering comet thou shalt cleave
The trackless void as thou of old didst cleave,
Ere sky, and sea, and land from chaos came,

Begotten of the fire, when Fire was king,
And ere the radiating rays had left
Repulsive atoms to the rule of powers
Attractive, reigned o'er all the world supreme.

In the beginning thus — At length the earth
Was left to other powers: to other laws
Obedient, atoms unto atoms cleaved,
And seething vapors veiled a molten world.
The glowing granite poured volcanic fire
In rolling floods from pole to pole abroad;
And mountains rose on mountains, down again
To sink into the fiery main below,
Dissolving in the flood; their towering peaks

Exploding in the murky air above,
Lighting the outer darkness as they burst.
The thunders, in amaze, deep silence kept,
And lightnings hid them in the outer air,
While thus volcanic tumult ruled the world
Darkness surrounded all : the steamy air
Shut out the upper light from earth below;
And while the molten granite hardened o'er,
As age by age went on, in torrents fell
Precipitate, until a boundless flood
Of seething brine prevailed from pole to pole.

At length the vapory air attenuate
Let in auroral light on all below.
The rolling ocean's lurid waters gleamed,
Reflecting back the twilight to the air;
The air diffused it o'er the sea again :
And all above — below — around — was day.

The chaotic age was ended —
Its wonders passed away;
The evening and the morning were
The first day.

Then spread the circling firmament on high;
Then howled the surges of the lower deep;
Then waked the tempests in the restless air,
And Storm usurped dominion from the fire.
And still the fire resisted, loath to lose
Its long supremacy.   The shoreless deep
Of rolling waters joined the rebel winds;
While elemental atoms infinite
Combined in firm revolt to stifle down
The struggling fire.   The rocky crystals shot
Their geometric angles as they cooled,
Granitic and perverse, but rigid still.
Beneath the flood upheaved, vast mountains rose,
Battling with waves as mountainous as they.
But still the sea prevailed — the constant sea!
Less changing than all nature's changing works —
The sea prevailed.   Its crushing waters rove
The rock-ribbed mountains, scattered them afar,
Grinding the rigid granite in the foam
And casting down the deep gneissoidal mass
Five thousand fathoms thick.
For ages thus:
No continents, no islands, and no shores —
An ocean everywhere.

But the age of waters ended —
Its wonders passed away;
Its evening and its morning were
The second day.

Thus lifeless lay the old azoic world,
Waiting the hour of change.   The moment came.
The pregnant waters brought forth things of life,
Both plants and animals; and creatures strange,
And marvelous to look upon, went forth
Amid the waves self-moving and alive!
The young Lingula in his tongue-shaped shell,
The quaint Obolus and Orbiculas,
The Trilobite, with eyes multangular,
And hosts of living things, aquatic all,
Came forth and lived.   The protozoic sea
Was moving with the mystery of life.

But over all the teeming waves still rolled
The murky air carbonic.   Life was in the sea.
Swift through the waves placoidal monsters moved,
The tyrants of the deep.   No love was there.
The strong, insatiate, still devoured the weak;
The weak devoured the weaker; all was strife.
The shark is not the monster of to-day: —
His ancestry, as bloody and as foul,
Spread havoc in the old Silurian sea.
The vengeful Gar there had his prototype;
And there — if deeds of rapine gild a line
Of long descent, and spread a halo round
Consanguine names in after ages — rose
The first illustrious lines!   Pterichthys and
Coccostius are names as noble then
As Macedonian Alexander's since.

> But the reign of fishes ended —
> Its wonders passed away;
> The evening and the morning were
> The third day.

Another day
Was dawning on the crude and nascent world.
Devonian tumult raged o'er all the sea:
The rocky bottom heaved in fiery throes,
Disrupted by the pent-up flames beneath.
Then mountains rose, and shores set boundaries
About the boundless sea, to sink no more.
And in the upper deep, darkness and light
Divided into night and day; and sun,
And moon, and stars shone out alternate on
The rolling world.

                    Thou flaming minister
Of God! mirror of past and future —Thou
Who broodest now on all this world of life,
As Thou of old didst brood on barren rocks
And oceans, leafless, pulseless, dumb and dead —
Thou shinest now as then; we look on Thee
Who didst look on a past eternity.
Ye retinue of Stars, and thou, bright Moon,
Their queen, first offspring of the quickening earth, —
Ye bind us to the past, of which ye are,
As of the present, part.   As now ye shine
So shone ye on the primal lands which rose
First fixed above the waters — on the mount
Of Sinai, sacred rendered since to God—
Upon the granite peaks uprising from
The old Devonian sea, where now extend
The clustered isles of Britain; and where'er
The syenitic monuments of time
Erected by the Eternal Architect,
Rise up amid the old Silurian rocks,
Distinct and unconformable.   How sink

The monuments of men since sculptur'd from
These same obdurate granites!   Where is now
Old Memnon's morning music?   Where the shaft
Of Roman Pompey?   Where the obelisk
Of Egypt's Cleopatra, and the host
Of rock mementos indurate as they?
Spoiled by the hand of time and ruder man.
And yet the fire-erected monuments remain
Still sacred to the silent power of God.
And so the fossil records of the past,
As written by His hand.   Go learn their lore,
Behold their marvels, wonder and adore.

As sunlight on the mountains now, so shone
The golden beams at dawn of that far day.
From out the deep the dripping lands uprose,
Their tepid waters gleaming in the day,
Reflecting honors to the lord of light.
And myriad plants of forms uncouth and strange,
Sprung up o'er all the dank and marshy plains,
And throve upon the hot carbonic air.
They throve, and grew, and died: and others sprung
In countless hosts from out the hot-bed heaps,
To thrive and fall in turn; till all the air
Was strained and purified above; and all
The coaly treasure stored for coming time,
Was fossilized below.

The age of plants was ended —
Its wonders passed away:
Its evening and its morning were
The fourth day.

Broad over all the basking continents,
And all the nameless isles, the brooding sun
Brought forth strange vegetation.   Giant ferns,
And mosses monstrous, conifers and palms,
And leafy hosts of wondrous forms uncouth,
Sprang up o'er all the moist and heated plains.
Along the breeze the venomed scorpion played,
And first of living things inspired the air.
Anon, amid the reeking fens went up,
In sounds lugubrious, the first acclaim
Of jubilant existence; life was in the air!
The Labyrinthodon croaked out his joy
In notes batrachian — most hideous he
Of all the denizens of that far day.
While on the plastic borders of the pools,
The Brontozoum, the Leviathan,
The Ornithopus, and a host of birds
As strange as they, impressed their tracks, in lines
Like epitaphs, upon the future rocks.
Then came the lizard fishes, ravenous,
Huge and unsightly, neither flesh nor fish.
O'er all the land and sea they reigned supreme;
While in the lazy air, with skinny wings,
The Pterodactyl flew, at home alike
In water, land or air, but hideous still.

The age wears on apace.   Vast rivers start,
And wind themselves amid the vernal plains.
Their ripples echo with the startled scream
Of creeping things gigantic.   Lakes and pools,
Wholesome and unsaline, distilled from out
The briny ocean, by the glowing sun,
Dot the umbrageous landscape round the world.

Earth, air and water; hills and boundless plains,
And forests intricate; the sea, the lake,
The bog, the wood, the world — was full of life!

    And the age of reptiles ended —
      Its wonders passed away.
    Its evening and its morning were
      The fifth day.

Another age came on: the world was ripe!
The yellow sunshine shone on gentle slopes,
And wooded hills, and verdure-covered plains;
And fruits and flowers their hues of beauty threw
Upon the gentle waters; and the song
Of birds went out upon the balmy air.
New forests sprung in keeping with the age,
New races roamed the earth, flew in the air,
Or sported in the waters — prototypes
Of these, coeval with the mastertype
To which all other types were tending, MAN!
Animals mammalian, nurturing
Their young from living fount lactiferous,
Roamed o'er the ripening world, and filled their times —
Alive without progenitors, or dead
Without descendants, as the eternal plan
Demanded — miracles alike, at once
Of life and death.   So died to live no more
The giant Mastodon, the Megathere,
The Mylodon, and hosts of giant forms
As huge as they, filling the eternal rocks
With strange, ossific records of their lives.

The early Eocene, the Miocene,
The Pliocene, successive came and went,

Marking the fullness of the times.   The Earth
Put on her rich adornments for her rest,
Decked in her beauty for a coming lord.
The Alps, the Andes, and the Apennines,
And mountain chains as nameless then as these,
Lifted their peaks still nearer to the sky,
To catch the crystal rain-drops as they passed.
The streamlets leaped along the grassy slopes;
Nomadic rivers wandered through the vales,
Seeking the distant sea, stretching afar
O'er isles or continents in gentle sweep,
Or eddying rapids; or in glorious plunge
Leaped loud Niagaras upon the plains.
The lily bathed her snowy petals in
The early dew beside the ruddy rose.
Beneath the golden sunshine luscious fruits

Their cooling juices ripened; while the field
Unfenced and free, waved in the gentle breeze
Their cereal grains nutritious, waiting yet
A little while the coming reaper's hook.
Upon the thousand hills and grassy plains
The lowing cattle grazed content —clean beasts,
That chew the cud, and part the hoof, and feed
Upon the grassy store, abhorring blood.

The world was waiting for its human lord.
He came —the obedient clay rose up alive,
And MAN walked upright in the image of
His God, a living soul.

The reign of Mammals ended —
Man rose unto his sway.
The evening and the morning were
The sixth day.

God of the rosy light—
  Lord of the earth and sea—
Spirit who maked'st all things bright—
  We utter our praise to Thee.
Morning and evening come—
  Darkness and light obey—
And all aloud their praise proclaim
      At the rise of the primal day.

God of the boundless sea—
  Lord of its finny brood—
We join its hosts in praise of Thee,
  Spirit of all things good.
Maker of beast and bird—
  Creator of all that live—
Thou who didst speak the creative word,
  And life to all things give!
God of the rosy light!
  Lord of the earth and sea!
Spirit of all things bright!
  Eternal praise to Thee!

Edward R. Roe.

POETRY OF ANCIENT BURIAL.

THEY buried the young in the olden time,
　In the morning twilight gray,
　　And a beautiful thought—
　　And a true, was it not?
That thought of the olden day.

They buried the young while the darkness hung
　Like a shroud on the earth below:
　　But a gladdening sight
　　Was the orient light,
As they gazed on its crimson glow.

The earth it was dark, but up-springing the lark,
　Her matins was singing on high;
　　It seemed as the birth
　　Of joy vanish'd from earth,
She taught them to seek in the sky.

And was there no reason for choosing this season
　The young in earth's bosom to lay,
　　Save the fanciful one,
　　That the bride of the sun,
Aurora, had stolen them away?

Yes! that thought it was given by a pitying Heaven,
　A foretaste of bliss to the blind,
　　A type and a warning
　　Of that glorious morning
That shall dawn upon all mankind.

John Lloyd.

HOW GOOD ARE THE POOR.

Translated from the French by Bishop Alexander.

'TIS night — within the close, stout cabin door,
  The room is wrapped in shade, save where there
    fall
  Some twilight rays that creep along the floor,
And show the fisher's nets upon the wall.

In the dim corner, from the oaken chest,
  A few white dishes glimmer; through the shade
Stands a tall bed with dusky curtains dressed,
  And a rough mattress at its side is laid.

Five children on the long, low mattress lie —
  A nest of little souls, it heaves with dreams;
In the high chimney the last embers die,
  And redden the dark gloom with crimson gleams.

The mother kneels and thinks, and, pale with fear,
  She prays alone, hearing the billows shout:
While to wild winds, to rocks, to midnight drear,
  The ominous old ocean sobs without.

Poor wives of fishers!   Ah! 'tis sad to say,
  Our sons, our husbands, all that we love best,
Our hearts, our souls, are on those waves away,
  Those ravening wolves that know not ruth nor rest.

Think how they sport with those beloved forms!
  And how the clarion-blowing wind unties
Above their heads the tresses of the storms;
  Perchance even now the child, the husband, dies.

For we can never tell where they may be,
   Who, to make head against the tide and gale,
Between them and the starless, soulless sea,
   Have but one bit of plank, with one poor sail.

Terrible fear! We seek the pebbly shore,
   Cry to the rising billows, " Bring them home."
Alas! what answer gives their troubled roar
   To the dark thought that haunts us as we roam.

Janet is sad; her husband is alone,
   Wrapped in the black shroud of this bitter night;
His children are so little, there is none
   To give him aid. " Were they but old they might."
Ah, mother! when they too are on the main,
How wilt thou weep: " Would they were young again."

She takes his lantern — 'tis his hour at last:
   She will go forth, and see if the day breaks,
And if his signal fire be at the mast;
   Ah, no — not yet — no breath of morning wakes.

No line of light o'er the dark water lies;
   It rains, it rains, how black is rain at morn:
The day comes trembling, and the young dawn cries —
   Cries like a baby fearing to be born.

Sudden her humane eyes that peer and watch
   Through the deep shade, a moldering dwelling find,
No light within — the thin door shakes — the thatch
   O'er the green walls is twisted of the wind,

Yellow and dirty as a swollen rill.
   " Ah, me," she saith, " here does that widow dwell;
Few days ago my good man left her ill:
   I will go in and see if all be well."

She strikes the door, she listens, none replies,
  And Janet shudders.   " Husbandless, alone,
And with two children —they have scant supplies.
  Good neighbor!   She sleeps heavy as a stone."

She calls again, she knocks, 'tis silence still;
  No sound, no answer — suddenly the door,
As if the senseless creature felt some thrill
  Of pity, turned — and open lay before.

She entered, and her lantern lighted all
  The house so still, but for the rude waves' din,
Through the thin roof the plashing raindrops fall,
  But something terrible is couched within.

    *   *   *   *   *   *

" So, for the kisses that delight the flesh,
  For mother's worship, and for children's bloom,
For song, for smile, for love so fair and fresh,
  For laugh, for dance, there is one goal — the tomb."

And why does Janet pass so fast away?
  What hath she done within that house of dread?
What folded she beneath her mantle gray?
  And hurries home, and hides it in her bed:
  With half-averted face, and nervous tread,
  What hath she stolen from the awful dead?

The dawn was whitening over the sea's verge,
  As she sat pensive, touching broken chords
Of half-remorseful thought, while the hoarse surge
  Howled a sad concert to her broken words.

" Ah, my poor husband! we had five before,
  Already so much care, so much to find,
For he must work for all.   I give him more.
  What was that noise?   His step!   Ah, no! the wind.

" That I should be afraid of him I love!
   I have done ill.   If he should beat me now,
I would not blame him.   Did not the door move?
   Not yet, poor man." She sits with careful brow
Wrapped in her inward grief ; nor hears the roar
   Of winds and waves that dash against his prow,
Nor the black cormorant shrieking on the shore.

Sudden the door flies open wide, and lets
   Noisily in the dawn-light scarcely clear,
And the good fisher, dragging his damp nets,
   Stands on the threshold, with a joyous cheer.

" 'Tis thou ! " she cries, and, eager as a lover,
   Leaps up and holds her husband to her breast;
Her greeting kisses all his vesture cover;
" 'Tis I, good wife ! " and his broad face expressed

How gay his heart that Janet's love made light.
   " What weather was it?" " Hard." " Your fishing?"
      " Bad."
The sea was like a nest of thieves to-night;
   But I embrace thee, and my heart is glad.

" There was a devil in the wind that blew;
   I tore my net, caught nothing, broke my line,
And once I thought the bark was broken, too;
   What did you all the night long, Janet mine?"

She, trembling in the darkness, answered, " I!
   Oh, naught — I sew'd, I watch'd, I was afraid,
The waves were loud as thunders from the sky;
   But it is over." Shyly then she said —

" Our neighbor died last night; it must have been
　　When you were gone.　She left two little ones,
So small, so frail—William and Madeline;
　　The one just lisps, the other scarcely runs. "

The man looked grave, and in the corner cast
　　His old fur bonnet, wet with rain and sea,
Muttered awhile, and scratched his head — at last:
　　" We have five children, this makes seven, " said he.

" Already in bad weather we must sleep
　　Sometimes without our supper.　Now! ah, well—
'Tis not my fault.　These accidents are deep;
　　It was the good God's will.　I cannot tell.

" Why did he take the mother from those scraps,
　　No bigger than my fist.　'Tis hard to read;
A learned man might understand, perhaps —
　　So little, they can neither work nor need.

" Go fetch them, wife; they will be frightened sore,
　　If with the dead alone they waken thus.
That was the mother knocking at our door,
　　And we must take the children home to us.

" Brother and sister shall they be to ours,
　　And they will learn to climb my knee at even;
When He shall see these strangers in our bowers,
　　More fish, more food, will give the God of Heaven.

" I will work harder; I will drink no wine—
　　Go fetch them.　Wherefore dost thou linger, dear?
Not thus were wont to move those feet of thine. "
　　She drew the curtain, saying, " They are here! "

Victor Hugo.

"And they will learn to climb my knee at even."

TRUTH AND FALSEHOOD.

A TALE.

ONCE on a time, in sunshine weather,
Falsehood and Truth walk'd out together
The neighboring woods and lawns to view,
As opposites will sometimes do.
Thro' many a blooming mead they pass'd,
And at a brook arriv'd at last.
The purling stream, the margin green,
With flowers bedeck'd, a vernal scene,
Invited each itinerant maid
To rest awhile beneath the shade.
Under a spreading beech they sat,
And pass'd the time with female chat;
Whilst each her character maintain'd,
One spoke her thoughts, the other feign'd.
At length, quoth Falsehood, " Sister Truth
(For so she called her from her youth),
What if, to shun yon sultry beam,
We bathe in this delightful stream;
The bottom smooth, the water clear,
And there's no prying shepherd near?"
" With all my heart," the nymph replied,
And threw her snowy robes aside,
Stript herself naked to the skin,
And with a spring leapt headlong in.
Falsehood more leisurely undrest,
And, laying by her tawdry vest,
Trick'd herself out in Truth's array,
And 'cross the meadows tript away.
From this curst hour the fraudful dame

Of sacred Truth usurps the name,
And, with a vile, perfidious mind,
Roams far and near, to cheat mankind;
False sighs suborns, and artful tears,
And starts with vain, pretended fears;
In visits still appears most wise,
And rolls at church her saint-like eyes;
Talks very much, plays vile tricks,
While rising stock* her conscience pricks;
When being, poor thing, extremely gravel'd,
The secrets op'd, and all unravel'd.
But on she will, and secrets tell
Of John and Joan, and Ned and Nell.

Matthew Prior.

———

THE DONCASTER ST. LEGER.

[This poem is intended to illustrate the spirit of Yorkshire racing, now
unhappily, or happily, as the case may be, on the decline.   The perfect acquaint-
ance of every peasant on the ground with the pedigrees, performances, and the
characters of the horses engaged — his genuine interest in the result — and the
mixture of hatred and contempt which he used to feel for the Newmarket
favorites, who came down to carry off the great national prize, must be well
known to all who have crossed the Trent in August or September: altogether it
constituted a peculiar modification of English feeling, which I thought deserved
to be recorded, and in default of a more accomplished Pindar, I have here
endeavored to do so. — *The Return of the Guards, and other Poems,* 1841.]

THE sun is bright, the sky is clear,
    Above the crowded course,
As the mighty moment draweth near
    Whose issue shows the horse.

The fairest of the land are here
To watch the struggle of the year,
The dew of beauty and of mirth

———

* South Sea, 1720.

Lies on the living flowers of earth,
And blushing cheek and kindling eye
Lend brightness to the sun on high;
And every corner of the north
Has poured her hardy yeomen forth;
The dweller by the glistening rills
That sound among the Craven hills;
The stalwart husbandman who holds
His plow upon the eastern wolds;
The sallow, shriveled artisan,
Twisted below the height of man,
Whose limbs and life have moldered down
Within some foul and clouded town,
Are gathered thickly on the lea,
Or streaming from far homes to see
If Yorkshire keeps her old renown;
Or if the dreaded Derby horse
Can sweep in triumph o'er her course;
With the same look in every face,
The same keen feeling they retrace
The legends of each ancient race;
Recalling Reveler in his pride.
Or Blacklock of the mighty stride,
Or listening to some gray-haired sage
Full of the dignity of age;
How neither pace nor length could tire,
Old Muley Moloch's speed and fire;
How Hambletonian beat of yore
Such racers as are seen no more;
How Yorkshire coursers, swift as they,
Would leave this southern horse half way,
But that the creatures of to-day

Are cast in quite a different mold
From what he recollects of old.
Clear peals the bell: at that known sound,
Like bees, the people cluster round;
On either side upstarting then,
One close dark wall of breathing men,
Far down as eye can stretch, are seen
Along yon vivid strip of green.
Where keenly watched by countless eyes,
'Mid hopes, and fears, and prophecies,
Now fast, now slow, now here, now there,
With hearts of fire, and limbs of air,
Snorting and prancing— sidling by
With arching necks, and glancing eye,
In every shape of strength and grace,
The horses gather for the race;
Soothed for a moment all, they stand
Together, like a sculptured band,
Each quivering eyelid flutters thick,
Each face is flushed, each heart beats quick;
    And all around dim murmurs pass,
Like low winds moaning on the grass.
Again — the thrilling signal sound —
And off at once, with one long bound,
Into the speed of thought they leap,
Like a proud ship rushing to the deep.
A start! a start! they're off, by heaven,
Like a single horse, though twenty-seven,
And 'mid the flash of silks we scan
A Yorkshire jacket in the van;
    Hurrah! for the bold bay mare!

I'll pawn my soul her place is there
  Unheaded to the last
For a thousand pounds, she wins unpast --
  Hurrah for the matchless mare!

A hundred yards have glided by
  And they settle to the race,
More keen becomes each straining eye,
  More terrible the pace.
Unbroken yet o'er the gravel road
Like maddening waves the troop has flowed,
  But the speed begins to tell;
And Yorkshire sees with eye of fear,
The Southron stealing from the rear.
    Ay! mark his action well!
Behind he is, but what repose!
How steadily and clean he goes!
What latent speed his limbs disclose!
What power in every stride he shows!
They see, they feel, from man to man
The shivering thrill of terror ran,
And every soul instinctive knew
It lay between the mighty two.
The world without, the sky above,
  Have glided from their straining eyes—
Future and past, and hate and love,
  The life that wanes, the friend that dies,
E'en grim remorse who sits behind
Each thought and motion of the mind,
These now are nothing, Time and Space
Lie in the rushing of the race;
As with keen shouts of hope and fear
They watch it in its wild career.

Still far ahead of the glittering throng,
Dashes the eager mare along,
And round the turn and past the hill,
Slides up the Derby winner still.
The twenty-five that lay between
Are blotted from the stirring scene,
And the wild cries which rang so loud,
Sink by degrees throughout the crowd,
To one deep humming, like the tremulous roar
Of seas remote along a northern shore.

In distance dwindling to the eye
Right opposite the stand they lie,
    And scarcely seem to stir;
Though an Arab sheik his wives would give
For a single steed, that with them could live
    Three hundred yards, without the spur,
But though so indistinct and small,
You hardly see them move at all,
There are not wanting signs which show
Defeat is busy as they go.
Look how the mass, which rushed away
As full of spirit as the day,
So close compacted for a while,
Is lengthening into single file.
Now inch by inch it breaks, and wide
And spreading gaps the line divide.
As forward still, and far away
Undulates on the tired array,
Gay colors, and momently less bright,
Fade flickering on the gazer's sight,
Till keenest eyes can scarcely trace
The homeward ripple of the race.

Care sits on every lip and brow.—
" Who leads? who fails? how goes it now? "
One shooting spark of life intense,
One throb of refluent suspense,
And a far rainbow-colored light
Trembles again upon the sight.
Look to your turn!   Already there
Gleams the pink and black of the fiery mare,
And through that, which but now was a gap,
Creeps on the terrible white cap.
Half-strangled in each throat, a shout
Wrung from their fevered spirits out,
Booms through the crowd like muffled drums,
" His jockey moves on him.   He comes! "
Then momently like gusts, you heard,
" He's sixth — he's fifth — he's fourth — he's third; "
And on, like some glancing meteor-flame,
The stride of the Derby winner came.

And during all that anxious time
(Sneer as it suits you at my rhyme),
The earnestness became sublime;
Common and trite as is the scene,
At once so thrilling, and so mean,
To him who tries his heart to scan,
And feels the brotherhood of man,
That needs must be a mighty minute,
When a crowd has but one soul within it.
As some bright ship with every sail
Obedient to the urging gale,
Darts by vext hulls, which side by side,
Dismasted on the raging tide,
Are struggling onward, wild and wide,

Thus, through the reeling field he flew,
And near, and yet more near he drew;
Each leap seems longer than the last,
Now — now — the second horse is past,
And the keen rider of the mare,
With haggard look of feverish care,
Hangs forward on the speechless air,
By steady stillness nursing in
The remnant of her speed to win.
One other bound — one more —'tis done;
Right up to her the horse has run,
And head to head, and stride for stride,
Newmarket's hope and Yorkshire's pride,
Like horses harnessed side by side,
    And struggling to the goal.
Ride! gallant son of Ebor, ride!
For the dear honor of the north,
Stretch every bursting sinew forth,
    Put out thy inmost soul —
And with knee, and thigh, and tightened rein,
Lift in the mare by might and main;
The feelings of the people reach,
What lies beyond the springs of speech,
So that there rises up no sound
From the wide human life around;
One spirit flashes from each eye,
One impulse lifts each heart throat-high,
One short and panting silence broods
O'er the wildly-working multitudes,
As on the struggling coursers press,
So deep the eager silentness,
That underneath their feet the turf

Seems shaken, like the eddying surf
　　When it tastes the rushing gale,
And the singing fall of the heavy whips,
Which tear the flesh away in strips,
　　As the tempest tears the sail,
On the throbbing heart and quivering ear,
Strike vividly distinct, and near.
But mark what an arrowy rush is there,
" He's beat! he's beat! by heaven!" the mare,
Just on the post, her spirit rare,
When Hope herself might well despair.

　　　　　　　Sir Francis Hastings Doyle.

MARCUS ANTONIUS.

'TIS vain, Fonteus!— As the half-tamed steed,
　Scenting the desert, lashes madly out,
　And strains and storms and struggles to be freed,
　Shaking his rattling harness all about —
So, fiercer for restraint, here in my breast
Hot passion rages, firing every thought;
For what is honor, prudence, interest
To the wild strength of love?　O best of life,
My joy, bliss, triumph, glory, my soul's wife,
My Cleopatra! I desire thee so
That all restraint to the wild winds I throw.
Come what come will, come life, come death, to me
'Tis equal, if again I look on thee.
Away, Fonteus! tell her that I rage
With madness for her.　Nothing can assuage
The strong desire, the torment, the fierce stress

That whirls my thoughts round, and inflames my brain,
But her great ardent eyes — dark eyes, that draw
My being to them with a subtle law
And an almost divine imperiousness.
Tell her I do not live until I feel
The thrill of her wild touch, that through each vein
Electric shoots its lightning; and again
Hear those low tones of hers, although they steal
As by some serpent-charm my will away;
And wreck my manhood.
                              Oh ! Octavia,
This lying galls me, and 'tis worse than vain!
Life is too short to waste in love's pretense,
In the bleak shadow of indifference.
And you — what are you but a galling chain!
I hate you that I cannot hate you more.
Even hate for you is only cold and dull —
Cold as your heart, and dull as is your sense.
Were you but savage, wicked to the core,
Less pious, prudish, prudent, made to rule,
I might have loved or hated more; but now
Nothing on earth seems half so deadly chill
As your insipid smile and placid brow,
Your glacial goodness and proprieties.
Tell my dear serpent I must see her — fill
My eyes with the glad light of her great eyes,
Though death, dishonor, anything you will,
Stand in the way!   Ah, by my soul! disgrace
Is better in the sun of Egypt's face
Than pomp or power in this detested place.
Oh! for the wine my queen alone can pour
From her rich nature!   Let me starve no more
On this weak, tepid drink that never warms

My life-blood : but away with shams and forms!
Away with Rome!   One hour in Egypt's eyes
Is worth a score of Roman centuries.
Away, Fonteus!   Tell her, till I see
Those eyes I do not live — that Rome to me
Is hateful.   Tell her — Oh! I know not what ! —
That every thought and feeling, space and spot,
Is like an ugly dream, where she is not ;
All persons plagues; all doings wearisome;
All talking empty; all these feasts and friends —
These slaves and courtiers, princes, palaces —
This Cæsar, with his selfish aims and ends,
His oily ways and sleek hypocrisies —
This Lepidus; and, worse than all by far,
This mawkish, pious, prude Octavia —
Are bonds and fetters, tedious as disease,
Not worth the parings of her finger-nails.
Oh for the breath of Egypt! —the soft nights
Of the voluptuous East — the dear delights
We tasted there — the lotus-perfumed gales
That dream along the low shores of the Nile,
And softly flutter in the languid sails!
Oh, for the queen of all ! —for the rich smile
That glows like autumn over her dark face
For her large nature — her enchanting grace —
Her arms, that are away so many a mile!
Away, Fonteus; — lose no hour — make sail —
Weigh anchor on the instant — woo a gale
To blow you to her.   Tell her I shall be
Close on your very heels across the sea,
Praying that Neptune send me storms as strong
As Passion is, to sweep me swift along,

Till the white spray sing whistling round my prow,
And the waves gurgle 'neath the keel's sharp plow.
Fly, fly, Fonteus! When I think of her
My soul within my body is astir!
My wild blood pulses, and my hot cheeks glow!
Love with its madness overwhelms me so
That I — Oh! go, I say! Fonteus, go! ——

W. W. Story.

THE UNIVERSAL PRAYER.

Translated from the French by Professor Henry Highton.

COME, child of prayer, the busy day is done,
     A golden star gleams through the dusk of night;
     The hills are trembling in the rising mist,
     The rumbling wain looms dim upon the sight;
All things wend home to rest; the roadside trees
Shake off their dust, stirred by the evening breeze.

The sparkling stars gush forth in sudden blaze,
     As twilight open flings the doors of night;
The fringe of carmine narrows in the west
     The rippling waves are tipped with silver light;
The bush, the path — all blend in one dull gray;
The doubtful traveler gropes his anxious way.

Oh, day! with toil, with wrong, with hatred rife;
     Oh, blessed night! with sober calmness sweet;
The sad winds moaning through the ruined tower,
     The age-worn hind, the sheep's sad broken bleat—
All nature groans opprest with toil and care,
And wearied craves for rest, and love, and prayer.

"Oh, happy worship! ever gay with smiles."

At eve the babes with angels converse hold,
    While we to our strange pleasures wend our way,
Each with its little face upraised to Heaven,
    With folded hands, barefoot kneels down to pray.
At self-same hour with self-same words they call
On God, the common Father of them all.

And then they sleep; and golden dreams anon,
    Born as the busy day's last murmurs die,
In swarms tumultuous flitting through the gloom,
    Their breathing lips and golden locks descry,
And as the bees o'er bright flowers joyous roam,
Around their curtained cradles clustering come.

Oh, prayer of childhood! simple, innocent;
    Oh, infant slumbers! peaceful, pure, and light;
Oh, happy worship! ever gay with smiles,
    Meet prelude to the harmonies of night;
As birds beneath the wing enfold their head,
Nestled in prayer the infant seeks its bed.

Victor Hugo.

THE YOUNG AVENGER.

THE warrior's strength is bowed by age, the warrior's step is slow,
And the beard upon his breast is white as is the winter's snow;
Yet his eye shines bright, as if not yet its last of fame were won;
Six sons stand ready in their arms to do as he has done.

" Now take your way, ye Laras bold, and to the battle ride;
For loud upon the Christian air are vaunts of Moorish pride:
Your six white steeds stand at the gate; go forth and let me see
Who will return the first and bring a Moslem head to me."

Forth they went, six gallant knights, all mail'd from head to heel;
Is it not death to him who first their fiery strength shall feel?
They spurr'd their steeds, and on they dash'd, as sweeps the midnight wind;
While their youngest brother stood and wept that he must stay behind.

" Come here, my child!" the father said, " and wherefore dost thou weep?
The time will come when from the fray nought shall my favorite keep;
When thou wilt be the first of all amid the hostile spears."
The boy shook back his raven hair, and laugh'd amid his tears.

The sun went down, but lance nor shield reflected back his
    light ;
The moon rose up, but not a sound broke on the rest of
    night.
The old man watched impatiently, till with morn o'er the
    plain
There came a sound of horses' feet, there came a martial
    train.

But gleamed not back the sunbeam glad from plume or
    helm of gold.
No, it shone upon the crimson vest, the turban's emerald
    fold.
A Moorish herald; six pale heads hung at his saddle-bow,
Gashed, changed, yet well the Father knew the lines of
    each fair brow.

" Oh ! did they fall by numbers, or did they basely
    yield? "
" Not so; beneath the same bold hand thy children press'd
    the field,
They died as Nourreddin would wish all foes of his should
    die;
Small honor does the conquest boast when won from those
    who fly.

" And thus he saith, ' This was the sword that swept down
    the brave band,
Find thou one who can draw it forth in all thy Christian
    land.'
If from a youth such sorrowing and scathe thou hast
    endured,
Dread thou to wait for vengeance till his summers are
    matured."

The aged chieftain took the sword, in vain his hand
    essay'd
To draw it from its scabbard forth, or poise the heavy
    blade;
He flung it to his only child, now sadly standing by,
" Now weep, for here is cause for tears; alas! mine own
    are dry."

Then answer'd proud the noble boy, " My tears last
    morning came
For weakness of my own right hand; to shed them now
    were shame;
I will not do my brothers' names such deep and deadly
    wrong;
Brave were they unto death, success can but to God
    belong."

And years have fled, that boy has sprung unto a goodly
    knight,
And fleet of foot and stout of arm in his old father's sight;
Yet breathed he never wish to take in glorious strife his
    part,
And shame and grief his backwardness was to that father's
    heart.

Cold, silent, stern, he let time pass, until he rush'd one
    day,
Where mourning o'er his waste of youth the weary chief-
    tain lay;
Unarm'd he was, but in his grasp he bore a heavy brand,
" My father, I can wield his sword; now, knighthood at
    thine hand!

" For years no hours of quiet sleep upon my eyelids came,
For Nourreddin had poison'd all my slumber with his
    fame.
I have waited for my vengeance; but now, alive or dead,
I swear to thee by my brothers' graves that thou shalt
    have his head!"

It was a glorious sight to see, when those two warriors
    met,
The one dark as a thunder-cloud, in strength and man·
    hood set;-
The other young and beautiful, with lithe and graceful
    form,
But terrible as is the flash that rushes through the storm.

And eye to eye, and hand to hand, in deadly strife they
    stood,
And smoked the ground whereon they fought, hot with
    their mingled blood;
Till dropped the valiant Infidel, fainter his blows and few,
While fiercer from the combat still the youthful Christian
    grew.

Nourreddin falls; his sever'd head, it is young Lara's prize:
But dizzily the field of death floats in the victor's eyes.
His cheek is as his foeman's pale, his white lips gasp for
    breath;
Ay, this was all he asked of Heaven, the victory and
    death.

He raised him on his arm, " My page, come thou and do
    my will;
Canst thou not see a turban'd band upon yon distant hill?

Now strip me of my armor, boy, by yonder river's side,
Place firm this head upon my breast, and fling me on the
    tide."

That river washed his natal halls, its waters bore him on,
Till the moonlight on the hero in his father's presence
    shone.
The old chief to the body drew, his gallant boy was dead,
But his vow of vengeance had been kept, he bore Nour-
    reddin's head.

                            L. E. L.

ANTONY IN ARMS.

O, we are side by side ! — One dark arm furls
  Around me like a serpent warm and bare;
The other, lifted 'mid a gleam of pearls,
  Holds a full golden goblet in the air:
Her face shining through her cloudy curls
  With light that makes me drunken unaware,
And with my chin upon my breast I smile
Upon her, darkening inward all the while.

And through the chamber curtains, backward roll'd
  By spicy winds that fan my fevered head,
I see a sandy, flat slope, yellow as gold,
  To the brown banks of Nilus wrinkling red
In the slow sunset ; and mine eyes behold
  The West, low down beyond the river's bed,
Grow sullen, ribbed with many a brazen bar,
Under the white smile of the Cyprian star.

A bitter Roman vision floateth black
  Before me, in my dizzy brain's despite;
The Roman armor brindles on my back,
  My swelling nostrils drink the fumes of fight:
But, then, she smiles upon me ! — and I lack
  The warrior will that frowns on lewd delight,
And passionately proud and desolate,
I smile to answer to the joy I hate.

Joy coming uninvoked, asleep, awake,
  Makes sunshine on the grave of buried powers;
Ofttimes I wholly loathe her for the sake
  Of manhood slipt away in easeful hours:
But from her lips mild words and kisses break,
  Till I am like a ruin mock'd with flowers;
I think of Honor's face — then turn to hers —
Dark, like the splendid shame that she confers.

Lo! how her dark arm holds me! — I am bound
  By the soft touch of fingers light as leaves:
I drag my face aside, but at the sound
  Of her low voice I turn — and she perceives
The cloud of Rome upon my face, and round
  My neck she twines her odorous arms and grieves,
Shedding upon a heart as soft as they,
Tears 'tis a hero's task to kiss away!

And then she loosens from me, trembling still,
  Like a bright, throbbing robe, and bids me " go! " —
When pearly tears her drooping eyelids fill,
  And lost to use of life and hope and will,
  I gaze upon her with a warrior's woe,
And turn, and watch her sidelong in annoy —
Then snatch her to me, flush'd with shame and joy!

Once more, O Rome! I would be son of thine —
  This constant prayer my chain'd soul ever saith —
I thirst for honorable end — I pine
  Not thus to kiss away my mortal breath.
But comfort such as this may not be mine —
  I cannot even die a Roman's death:
I seek a Roman's grave, a Roman's rest —
But, dying, I would die upon her breast!

Robert Buchanan.

THE IDEAL AND THE REAL.

MY passion days of poetry are o'er;
  And air, and earth, and teeming ocean wear
  Imagination's golden tint no more;
    No more can Fancy's scintillating glare
People the world with visions false as fair;
The day-dreams, full of ecstasy before,
  Which came into my thought and lingered there
Till all the earth a hue of beauty wore,
Are gone; I dream not now as I have dreamed of yore.

The eye hath bounds of vision o'er the deep,
  The thunder dies upon the distant ear,
And all the senses sink at last to sleep,
  Wearied and worn with that they witness here;
  But still untiring Fancy will appear
In search of all the beautiful and true;
  Bringing the distant glories ever near,
Clothing the old with vestments ever new,
And waking sounds and sights of multiplying hue.

Oh how the memory of those dream-lights rise
  Once more within my passionless survey!
I look again upon the sunny skies
  Peopled with all the vapory hosts of day,
  Reflecting back the sunlight in their play,
And seeming, in their far-off azure home,
  Like phantoms from the spirit-land away.—
The spell steals o'er me still; the visions come;
Out o'er the ideal world my raptured senses roam!

Oh, wondrous efflux from thy maker, God !
  Let me drink in thy glories once again.
As when the breath of morning is abroad,
  The level sun-ray shoots across the plain;
  The forest, dripping with the gentle rain,
Throws back the sunshine from its leafy gems;
  The rocks loom up from out the distant main —
Each like a monster sea-god, as it stems
The ocean surges with their spray-tipt diadems.

And all around is beautiful and bright;
  And all beneath, upon the valley's breast,
Is radiant with the rosy morning light;
  And all above, like mansions of the blest,
  The vapory world is moving to the west
In soft and silent grandeur through the sky.
  The song bird rises from his lowly nest
To meet the day-god with his cheerful cry.
And mounts away with grateful pinions upon high.

The fairy vision widens to my view,
  And all the earth a hue of beauty wears;
And still with magic changes ever new,
  The light of nature's necromancy bears;

I see the vivid lightning as it glares,
And hear the equatorial thunders roll;
    I watch the surges, startled from their lairs,
And driven before the tempest to the pole,
Like monster coursers to their far-off icy goal.

    The howling winds, the booming thunder's roar,
        The blinding lightning and the driving cloud,
    The bellowing waves that burst upon the shore,
        And all the conflict of the tempest loud,
        Still on the o'er wrought fancy crowd
    As scenes of beauty, stern, august, and deep!
        And even when Darkness wraps her nightly shroud
O'er earth, and sea, and storm, no dreamless sleep
Can banish vigils such as fancy still will keep.

    I read the lay of geologic lore;
        I count the finny dwellers of the sea;
    Survey the wonders of the shelly shore;
        Or in the forest measure every tree.
        I listen to the song of birds, or see
    The countless habitants of hill or plain,
        And all the hosts of nature, wild and free;
    And yet the crowning wonder will remain —
Man, the great Immortal, chief of all the train.

    Down in the rocky records of the earth
        Extends the epic of creative power.
    Before the seas were made or hills had birth,
        Before the hoary mountains learned to tower,
        Ere forest grew, or bloomed the primal flower,

Obedient atoms gathered into form,
 Chaotic Darkness wakened Morning's hour,
And all the elements of calm and storm
Obeyed the king of day with life and being warm.

Oh, these are poetry. — With solemn awe
 To watch the working of Almighty power,
And see the universe obedient to His law;
 Whether on earth expands the humblest flower,
 Forests extend, or hills and mountains tower;
Whether the heavens from star to star abroad,
 Proclaim the glory of the midnight hour —
My wrapt, adoring spirit still is awed
With that sublime, eternal poetry of God!

Edward R. Roe.

MAUD AND MADGE; OR, AFTER THE BALL.

THEY sat and combed their beautiful hair,
 Their long, bright tresses, one by one,
As they laughed and talked in the chamber there,
 After the revel was done.

Idly they talked of waltz and quadrille,
 Idly they laughed, like other girls,
Who, over the fire, when all is still,
 Comb out their braids and curls.

Robe of satin and Brussels lace,
 Knots of flowers, and ribbons, **too,**
Scattered about in every place,
 For the revel is through.

And Maud and Madge, in robes of white,
  The prettiest night-gowns under the sun,
Stockingless, slipperless, sit in the night,
  For the revel is done.—

Sit and comb their beautiful hair,
  Those wonderful waves of brown and gold,
Till the fire is out in the chamber there,
  And the little bare feet are cold.

Then out of the gathering winter chill,
  All out of the bitter St. Agnes weather,
While the fire is out and the house is still,
  Maud and Madge together,—

Maud and Madge in robes of white,
  The prettiest night-gowns under the sun,
Curtained away from the chilly night,
  After the revel is done,—

Float along in a splendid dream,
  To a golden gittern's tinkling tune,
While a thousand lusters shimmering stream,
  In a palace's grand saloon.

Flashing of jewels and flutter of laces,
  Tropical odors sweeter than musk,
Men and women with beautiful faces
  And eyes of tropical dusk, —

And one face shining out like a star,
  One face haunting the dreams of each,
And one voice, sweeter than others are,
  Breaking into silvery speech,—

Telling, through lips of bearded bloom,
  An old, old story over again,
As down the royal bannered room,
  To the golden gittern's strain,

Two and two, they dreamily walk,
  While an unseen spirit walks beside
And, all unheard in the lover's talk,
  He claimed the one for a bride.

Oh, Maud and Madge, dream on together,
  With never a pang of jealous fear —
For, ere the bitter Saint Agnes weather
  Shall whiten another year,

Robed for the bridal, and robed for the tomb,
  Braided brown hair, and golden tress,
There'll be only one of you left for the bloom
  Of the bearded lips to press, —

Only one for the bridal pearls,
  The robe of satin and Brussels lace, —
Only one to blush through her curls,
  At the sight of a lover's face.

Oh, beautiful Madge, in your bridal white,
  For you the revel has just begun ;
But for her who sleeps in your arms to-night
  The revel of Life is done !

But robed and crowned with your saintly bliss,
  Queen of heaven and bride of the sun,
Oh, beautiful Maud, you'll never miss
  The kisses another hath won !

Nora Perry.

ANNABEL LEE.

T was many and many a year ago,
  In a kingdom by the sea,
That a maiden there lived whom you may know
  By the name of Annabel Lee;
And this maiden lived with no other thought
  Than to love and be loved by me.

I was a child, and *she* was a child
  In this kingdom by the sea;
But we loved with a love that was more than love —
  I and my Annabel Lee;
With a love that the winged seraphs of Heaven
  Coveted her and me.

And this was the reason that, long ago,
  In this kingdom by the sea,
A wind blew out of a cloud, chilling
  My beautiful Annabel Lee;
So that her high-born kinsman came
  And bore her away from me,
To shut her up in a sepulcher
  In this kingdom by the sea.

The angels, not half so happy in Heaven,
  Went envying her and me —
Yes! — that was the reason (as all men know,
  In this kingdom by the sea)
That the wind came out of the cloud by night,
  Chilling and killing my Annabel Lee.

" *I* was a child. and *she* was a child."

But our love it was stronger by far than the love
  Of those who were older than we —
  Of many far wiser than we —·
And neither the angels in Heaven above,
  Nor the demons down under the sea,
Can ever dissever my soul from the soul
  Of the beautiful Annabel Lee:

For the moon never beams, without bringing me dreams
  Of the beautiful Annabel Lee;
And the stars never rise, but I feel the bright eyes
  Of the beautiful Annabel Lee;
And so, all the night-tide, I lie down by the side
Of my darling — my darling — my life and my bride,
  In the sepulcher there by the sea,
  In her tomb by the sounding sea.

E. A. Poe.

THY LOVE SHALL LEAD ME.

FAREWELL, sweet maiden, you I've loved so well —
Farewell, dear girl, I go where strangers dwell;
With thee will purest love and friendship rest,
Tho' far he goes that ever loved thee best.
No other life will ever seem so near,
No other name will ever be so dear.
Thy love shall lead me; tho' no little hand
In mine is placed to guide me in the land
I go to, still, unto my soul
Thy love will point the sought for goal.

E. T. R.

YOU KISSED ME.

[The following lines were written in 1867 by a lady under twenty years of age. James Redpath, the historian, thought so much of the poem that he had an edition printed on white satin. John G. Whittier, the Quaker poet, wrote of it and its young author that she had truly mastered the secret of English verse.]

YOU kissed me! My head
  Dropped low on your breast
With a feeling of shelter
  And infinite rest.
While the holy emotions
  My tongue dared not speak
Flashed up in a flame
  From my heart to my cheek.
Your arms held me fast:
  Oh! your arms were so bold;
Heart beat against heart
  In their passionate fold.
Your glances seemed drawing
  My soul through my eyes,
As the sun draws the mist
  From the sea to the skies.
Your lips clung to mine
  Till I prayed in my bliss
They might never unclasp
  From the rapturous kiss.
You kissed me! My heart.
  And my breath, and my will
In delirious joy
  For a moment stood still.
Life had for me then
  No temptations, no charms,
No visions of happiness

Outside of your arms.
And were I this instant
An angel possessed
Of the peace and the joy
That are given the blest,
I would fling my white robes
Unrepiningly down,
I would tear from my forehead
Its beautiful crown,
To nestle once more
In that haven of rest —
Your lips upon mine,
My head on your breast.
You kissed me!   My soul,
In a bliss so divine,
Reeled and swooned like a drunken man
Foolish with wine,
And I thought 'twere delicious
To die there if death
Would but come while my lips
Were yet moist with your breath:
'Twere delicious to die
If my heart might grow cold
While your arms clasped me round
In their passionate fold.
And these are the questions
I ask day and night:
Must lips taste no more
Such exquisite delight?
Would you care if your breast
Were my shelter as then,
And if you were here
Would you kiss me again?

" 'OSTLER JOE."

STOOD at eve, as the sun went down, by a grave
    where a woman lies,
Who lured men's souls to the shores of sin with the
    light of her wanton eyes;
Who sang the song that the siren sang on the treacherous
    Lurley height,
Whose face was as fair as a summer day, and whose heart
    was as black as night.

Yet a blossom I fain would pluck to-day from the garden
    above her dust —
Not the languorous lily of soulless sin, nor the blood-red
    rose of lust,
But a sweet white blossom of holy love that grew in the
    one green spot,
In the arid desert of Phryne's life where all was parched
    and hot.

In the summer, when the meadows were aglow with blue
    and red,
Joe, the 'ostler of the Magpie, and fair Annie Smith were
    wed.
Plump was Annie, plump and pretty, with a cheek as
    white as snow;
He was anything but handsome, was the Magpie's 'Ostler
    Joe.

But he won the winsome lassie. They'd a cottage and a
    cow,
And her matronhood sat lightly on the village beauty's
    brow;

Sped the months and came a baby—such a blue-eyed
    baby boy!
Joe was working in the stables when they told him of his
    joy,

He was rubbing down the horses, and he gave them then
    and there
All a special feed of clover, just in honor of the heir.
It had been his great ambition, and he told the horses so,
That the Fates would send a baby who might bear the
    name of Joe.

Little Joe the child was christened, and, like babies, grew
    apace;
He'd his mother's eyes of azure, and his father's honest
    face.
Swift the happy years went over, years of blue and cloud-
    less sky,
Love was lord of that small cottage, and the tempest
    passed them by.

Passed them by for years, then swiftly burst in fury o'er
    their home.
Down the lane by Annie's cottage chanced a gentleman to
    roam;
Thrice he came and saw her sitting by the window with
    her child,
And he nodded to the baby, and the baby laughed and
    smiled.

So at last it grew to know him—little Joe was nearly four;
He would call the " pretty gemplin " as he passed the
    open door;

And one day he ran and caught him, and in child's play
    pulled him in;
And the baby Joe had prayed for brought about the
    mother's sin.

'Twas the same old wretched story that for ages bards have
    sung —
'Twas a woman weak and wanton and a villain's tempting
    tongue;
'Twas a picture deftly painted for a silly creature's eyes
Of the Babylonian wonders and the joy that in them lies.

Annie listened and was tempted; she was tempted, and
    she fell,
As the angels fell from Heaven to the blackest depths of
    hell;
She was promised wealth and splendor, and a life of guilty
    sloth,
Yellow gold for child and husband, and the woman left
    them both.

Home one eve came Joe the 'Ostler with a cheery cry of
    " Wife! "—
Finding that which blurred forever all the story of his life.
She had left a silly letter — through the cruel scrawl he
    spelt;
Then he sought the lonely bedroom, joined his hands and
    knelt.

" Now, O Lord, O God, forgive her, for she ain't to blame, "
    he cried ;
" For I owt t' 'a seen her trouble, and 'a gone away and
    died.

Why, a wench like her — God bless her! — 'twasn't likely
    as her'd rest
With her bonny head forever on a 'ostler's ragged vest.

" It was kind o' her to bear me all this long and happy
    time;
So, for my sake please to bless her, though you count her
    deed a crime.
If so be I don't pray proper, Lord, forgive me; for, you
    see,
I can talk all right to 'osses, but I'm nervous like with
    Thee."

Never a line came to the cottage from the woman who had
    flown.
Joe, the baby, died that winter, and the man was left
    alone.
Ne'er a bitter word he uttered, but in silence kissed the
    rod,
Saving what he told the horses, saving what he told his
    God.

Far away, in mighty London, rose the woman into fame,
For her beauty won men's homage, and she prospered in
    her shame;
Quick from lord to lord she flitted, higher still each prize
    she won,
And her rival paled beside her, as the stars beside the
    sun.

Next she made the stage her market, and she dragged
    Art's temple down
To the level of a show-place for the outcasts of the town.

And the kisses she had given to poor 'Ostler Joe for nought,
With their gold and costly jewels rich and titled lovers
    bought.

Went the years with flying footsteps while the star was at
    its height;
Then the darkness came on swiftly, and the gloaming
    turned to night.
Shattered strength and faded beauty tore the laurels from
    her brow;
Of the thousands who had worshiped, never one came near
    her now.

Broken down in health and fortune, men forgot her very
    name,
'Till the news that she was dying woke the echoes of her
    fame;
And the papers, in their gossip, mentioned how an
    " actress " lay
Sick to death, in humble lodgings, growing weaker every
    day.

One there was who read the story in a far-off country
    place,
And that night the dying woman woke and looked upon
    his face;
Once again the strong arms clasped her that had clasped
    her long ago,
And the weary head lay pillowed on the breast of 'Ostler
    Joe.

All the past had he forgotten, all the sorrow and the
    shame;
He had found her sick and lonely, and his wife he now
    could claim.

Since the grand folks who had known her one and all had
    slunk away,
He could clasp his long-lost darling, and no man could
    say him nay.

In his arms death found her lying, in his arms her spirit
    fled;
And his tears came down in torrents as he knelt beside
    her dead.
Never once his love had faltered through her base, unhal-
    lowed life;
And the stone above her ashes bears the honored name
    of wife.

That's the blossom I fain would pluck to-day from the
    garden above her dust;
Not the languorous lily of soulless sin or the blood-red
    rose of lust;
But a sweet white blossom of holy love that grew in the
    one green spot
In the arid desert of Phryne's life where all was parched
    and hot.

George R. Sims.

THE CONFLAGRATION.

From Schiller's " Lay of the Bell."

HARK — a wail from the steeple! aloud
The bell shrills its voice to the crowd!
  Look — look — red as blood
      All on high!
It is not the daylight that fills with its flood
      The sky!
What a clamor awaking
  Roars up through the street,
What a hell vapor breaking
  Rolls on through the street,
And higher and higher
Aloft moves the column of fire!
Through the vistas and rows
Like a whirlwind it goes,
And the air like the steam from a furnace glows.
Beams are crackling — posts are shrinking —
Walls are sinking — windows clinking —
      Children crying —
      Mothers flying —
And the beast (the black ruin yet smoldering under)
Yells the howls of its pain and its ghastly wonder;

Hurry and skurry — away — away,
The face of the night is as clear as day!
      As the links in a chain,
      Again and again   .
Flies the bucket from hand to hand;
      High in arches up-rushing
      The engines are gushing,

And the flood, as a beast on the prey that it hounds,
With a roar on the breast of the element bounds,
  To the grain and the fruits,
  Through the rafters and beams,
Through the barns and the garners it crackles and streams!
As if they would rend up the earth from its roots,
  Rush the flames to the sky
  Giant high;
And at length,
Wearied out and despairing, man bows to their strength!
With an idle gaze sees their wrath consume,
And submits to his doom!
  Desolate
  The place, and dread,
  For storms the barren bed.
In the blank voids that cheerful casements were,
Comes to and fro the melancholy air
  And sits despair;
And through the ruin, blackening in its shroud,
Peers, as it flits, the melancholy cloud.

  One human glance of grief upon the grave
Of all that fortune gave
The loiterer takes; — then turns him to depart,
And grasps the wanderer's staff and mans his heart;
Whatever else the element bereaves,
One blessing more than all it reft — it leaves,
The faces that he loves! — He counts them o'er,
See — not one look is missing from that store!

"ONLY THE BRAKESMAN."

"ONLY the brakesman killed"—say, was that what they said?
The brakesman was our Joe; so, then—our Joe is dead!
Dead? Dead? Dead? — But I cannot think it's so;
It was some other brakesman; it cannot be our Joe.

Why, only this last evening I saw him riding past;
The trains don't stop here often — go rushing by as fast
As lightning — but Joe saw me, and waved his hand; he sat
On the very last old coal-car; how do you 'count for that —

That he was killed alone, and the others saved, when he
Was last inside the tunnel? Come, now, it couldn't be.
It's some mistake, of course; 'twas the fireman, you'll find:
The engine struck the rock, and he was just behind —

And the roof fell down on *him*, not on Joe, our Joe —I saw
That train myself, the engine had work enough to draw
The coal-cars full of coal that rattled, square and black,
By tens and twenties past our door, along that narrow track,

On into the dark mountains. I never see those peaks
'Thout hating them. For much *they* care whether the water leaks
Down their big sides, to wet the stones that arch the tunnels there,
So long — so black — they *all* may go, and much the mountains care!

I'm sorry for that fireman — What's that?   I don't pretend
To more than this: I saw that train, and Joe was at the
    end,
The very end, I tell you! Come, don't stand here and
    mock —
What! it was *there*, right at his end, the tunnel caved,
    the rock

Fell on him? But I don't believe a word — Yes, that's his
    chain,
And that's his poor old silver watch; he bought it —
    What's this stain
All over it? Why, it is red! — O Joe, my boy, O Joe,
Then it *was* you, and you are dead down in that tun-
    nel — Go

And bring my boy back! He was all the son I had;
    the girls
Are very well, but not like Joe. — Such pretty golden
    curls
Joe had until I cut them off at four years old; he ran
To meet me always at the gate, my bonny little man.

You don't remember him? But then you've only seen
    him when
He rides by on the coal-trains among the other men,
All of them black and grimed with coal, and circles round
    their eyes,
Whizzing along by day and night. — But you would feel
    surprise

To see how fair he is when clean on Sundays, and I know
You'd think him handsome then; I'll have — God! I for-
    got — O Joe,

My boy! my boy! and are you dead! So young — but
    twenty.— Dead
Down in that awful tunnel, with the mountain overhead!

They're bringing him? Oh, yes, I know; they'll bring
    him, and, what's more,
They'll do it free, the company! They'll leave him at my
    door
Just as he is, all grimed and black.— Jane, put the irons
    on,
And wash his shirt, his Sunday-shirt; it's white; he did
    have one

White shirt for best, and proud he wore it Sunday with
    a tie
Of blue — a new one. O my boy, how could they let you
    die
Crushed by those rocks! If I'd been there, I'd heaved
    them off — I know
They could have done it if they'd tried. They *let* you die
    — for, oh,

" Only the brakesman!" and his wage was small. The
    engineer
Must first be seen to there in front. — My God! it stands
    as clear
Before my eyes as though I'd seen it all — the dark — the
    crash —
The hissing steam — the wet stone sides — the arch above
    — the flash

Of lanterns coming — and my boy, poor boy, lying there,
Dying alone under the rocks — only his golden hair

To tell that it was Joe — a mass all grimed, that doesn't
    stir —
But mother'll know you, dear, 'twill make no difference to
    her

How black with coal-dust you may be, your poor, hard-
    working hands
All torn and crushed, perhaps; yes, yes — but no one
    understands
That, even though he's better off, poor lad, where he has
    gone,
I and the girls are left behind to stand it and live on

As best we can without him! — What? A wreath? A
    lady sent
Some flowers? Was passing through and heard — felt
    sorry — well, 'twas meant
Kindly, no doubt; but poor Joe'd been the very first to
    laugh
At white flowers round his blackened face. — You'll write
    his epitaph —

What's that? His name and age? Poor boy! — poor
    Joe! — his name has done
Its work in this life; for his age — he was not twenty-one,
Well grown but slender — far too young for such a place,
    but then
He wanted to " help mother," and to be among the men.

For he was always trying to be old — he carried wood
And built the fires for me before he hardly understood
What a fire was — my little boy — my darling baby Joe —
There's something snapped within my breast, I think; it
    hurts me so,

It must be something broken.   What is that ?   I felt the
    floor
Shake; there's some one on the step.— Go, Jennie, set the
    door
Wide open, for your brother Joe is coming home.   They
    said,
" Only the brakesman,"— but it is my only son that's
    dead!

Constance Fenimore Woolson.

BALAKLAVA.

THE charge at Balaklava!
  O that rash and fatal charge!
Never was a fiercer, braver,
Than that charge at Balaklava,
  On the battle's bloody marge!
All the day the Russian columns,
  Fortress huge, and blazing banks,
Poured their dread destructive volumes
  On the French and English ranks,
  On the gallant allied ranks!
Earth and sky seemed rent asunder
By the loud, incessant thunder!
When a strange but stern command
Needless, heedless, rash command —
Came to Lucan's little band —
Scarce six hundred men and horses
Of those vast contending forces:
" England's lost unless you save her!
Charge the pass at Balaklava!"
  O that rash and fatal charge,
  On the battle's bloody marge!

Far away the Russian Eagles
  Soar o'er smoky hill and dell,
And their hordes, like howling beagles
  Dense and countless, round them yell!
Thundering cannon, deadly mortar,
Sweep the field in every quarter!
Never, since the days of Jesus,
Trembled so the Chersonesus!
    Here behold the Gallic Lilies —
    Stout St. Louis' golden Lilies —
    Float as erst at old Ramillies!
    And beside them, lo! the Lion!
    With her trophied cross is flying!
Glorious standards! —shall they waver
On the field of Balaklava?
No, by Heavens! at that command —
Sudden, rash, but stern command —
Charges Lucan's little band!
    Brave six hundred! lo! they charge,
    On the battle's bloody marge!

Down yon deep and skirted valley,
  Where the crowded cannon play —
Where the Czar's fierce cohorts rally,
Cossack, Calmuck, savage Kalli —
  Down that gorge they swept away!
Down that new Thermopylæ.
Flashing swords and helmets see!
Underneath the iron shower,
  To the brazen cannon's jaws,
Heedless of their deadly power
    Press they without fear or pause —
    To the very cannon's jaws!

Gallant Nolan, brave as Roland
    At the field of Roncesvalles,
    Dashes down the fatal valley,
Dashes on the bolt of death,
Shouting with his latest breath,
" Charge, then, gallants! do not waver,
Charge the pass at Balaklava! "
    O that rash and fatal charge,
    On the battle's bloody marge!

Now the bolts of volleyed thunder
Rend that little band asunder,
Steed and rider wildly screaming,
    Screaming wildly, sink away;
Late so proudly, proudly gleaming,
    Now but lifeless clods of clay —
    Now but bleeding clods of clay!
Never, since the days of Jesus,
Saw such sight the Chersonesus!
Yet your remnant, brave six hundred,
Presses onward, onward, onward,
    Till they storm the bloody pass —
    Till, like brave Leonidas,
    They storm the deadly pass!
Sabring Cossack, Calmuck, Kalli,
In that wild, shot-rended valley —
Drenched with fire and blood, like lava,
Awful pass at Balaklava!
    O that rash and fatal charge,
    On that battle's bloody marge!

For now Russia's rallied forces
Swarming hordes of Cossack horses,
Trampling o'er the reeking corses,

Drive the thinned assailants back,
Drive the feeble remnant back,
O'er their late heroic track!
Vain, alas! now rent and sundered,
Vain your struggles, brave Two Hundred!
Twice your number lie asleep,
In that valley dark and deep,
Weak and wounded you retire
From that hurricane of fire —
That tempestuous storm of fire —
But no soldiers, firmer, braver,
   Ever trod the field of fame,
Than the knights of Balaklava —
   Honor to each hero's name!
Yet their country long shall mourn
For the rank so rashly shorn
So gallantly, but madly shorn,
   In that fierce and fatal charge,
   On the battle's bloody marge.

Alexander B. Meek.

A BALLAD OF ATHLONE;

OR, HOW THEY BROKE DOWN THE BRIDGE.

DOES any man dream that a Gael can fear? —
   Of a thousand deeds let him learn but one!
The Shannon swept onward, broad and clear,
   Between the leaguers and worn Athlone.

"Break down the bridge!" — Six warriors rushed
   Through the storm of shot and the storm of shell.
With late, but certain, victory flushed,
   The grim Dutch gunners eyed them well.

They wrenched at the planks 'mid a hail of fire;
  They fell in death, their work half done;
The bridge stood fast; and nigh and nigher
  The foe swarmed darkly, densely on.

" O who for Erin will strike a stroke?
  Who hurl yon planks where the waters roar? "
Six warriors forth from their comrades broke,
  And flung them upon that bridge once more.

Again at the rocking planks they dashed;
  And four dropped dead; and two remained:
The huge beams groaned, and the arch down-crashed;—
  Two stalwart swimmers the margin gained.

St. Ruth in his stirrups stood up, and cried,
  " I have seen no deed like that in France! "
With a toss of his head Sarsfield replied,
  " They had luck, the dogs ! 'Twas a merry chance!"

O many a year upon Shannon's side
  They sang upon moor and they sang upon heath
Of the twain that breasted that raging tide,
  And the ten that shook bloody hands with Death.

Aubrey De Vere.

WEARY.

[The following touching lines were found
under the pillow of a dead soldier at the hospital
at New Orleans during the war.]

I LAY me down to rest,
　　With little thought or care
Whether my waking find
　　Me here or there.

A bowed, bewildered head
　　That only asks to rest,
Unquestioning,
　　Upon the Saviour's breast.

I am not eager, bold, or strong,
　　All that is past;
I am ready not to do
　　At last! at last!

But grasp His banner still
　　Though its blue be dim;
These stripes no less than stars
　　Lead after Him.

THE DAYS THAT ARE NO MORE.

From "The Princess."

TEARS, idle tears, I know not what they mean,
   Tears from the depth of some divine despair
   Rise in the heart, and gather to the eyes,
   In looking on the happy Autumn fields,
And thinking of the days that are no more.

   Fresh as the first beam glittering on a sail,
That brings our friends up from the underworld,
Sad as the last which reddens over one
That sinks with all we love below the verge;
So sad, so fresh, the days that are no more.

   Ah, sad and strange as in dark summer dawns
The earliest pipe of half awakened birds
To dying ears, when unto dying eyes
The casement slowly grows a glimmering square;
So sad, so strange, the days that are no more.

   Dear as remembered kisses after death,
And sweet as those by hopeless fancy feigned
On lips that are for others; deep as love,
Deep as first love, and wild with all regret;
O Death in Life, the days that are no more.

Alfred Tennyson.

KUBLA KHAN; OR A VISION IN A DREAM.

A FRAGMENT.

[Algernon Charles Swinburne says of the following poem, " For absolute melody and splendor it were hardly rash to call it the first poem in the language."]

N Xanadu did Kubla Khan
A stately pleasure-dome decree,
Where Alph, the sacred river, ran
Through caverns measureless to man
Down to a sunless sea.
So twice five miles of fertile ground,
With walls and towers were girdled round;
And there were gardens bright with sinuous rills,
Where blossomed many an incense-bearing tree;
And here were forests ancient as the hills,
Enfolding sunny spots of greenery.

But oh! that deep romantic chasm which slanted
Down the green hill athwart a cedar cover!
A savage place! as holy and enchanted
As e'er beneath a waning moon was haunted
By woman wailing for her demon lover!
And from this chasm, with caseless turmoil seething,
As if this earth in fast thick pants were breathing,
A mighty fountain momently was forced.
Amid whose swift half intermitted burst
Huge fragments vaulted like rebounding hail,
Or chaffy grain beneath the thresher's flail;
And 'mid these dancing rocks at once and ever
It flung up momently the sacred river.
Five miles meandering with a mazy motion
Through wood and dale the sacred river ran,

Then reached the caverns measurless to man,
And sank in tumult to a lifeless ocean:
And 'mid this tumult Kubla heard from far
Ancestral voices prophesying war!

The shadow of the dome of pleasure
Floated midway on the waves;
Where was heard the mingled measure
From the fountain and the caves.
It was a miracle of rare device,
A sunny pleasure-dome with caves of ice!
A damsel with a dulcimer,
In a vision once I saw:
It was an Abyssinian maid,
And on her dulcimer she played,
Singing of Mount Abora.
Could I revive within me
Her symphony and song,
To such a deep delight 'twould win me,
That, with music loud and long,
I would build that dome in air,
That sunny dome! those caves of ice!
And all who heard should see them there,
And all should cry, Beware! Beware!
His flashing eyes, his floating hair!
Weave a circle round him thrice,
And close your eyes with holy dread,
For he on honey-dew hath fed,
And drunk the milk of Paradise.

Samuel Taylor Coleridge.

YOUNG MAN, BE WISE.

WOULDST thou reap life's golden treasure,
  Young man, be wise!
Cease to follow where light pleasure
  Cheats blinking eyes!
Let no flattering voices win thee,
Let no vauntful echoes din thee,
But the peace of God within thee
  Seek and be wise!

Where the fervid cup doth sparkle,
  Young man, be wise!
Where quick glances gleam and darkle,
  Danger surmise!
Where the rattling car is dashing,
Where the shallow wave is plashing,
Where the colored foam is flashing,
  Feast not thine eyes!

Rocking on a lazy billow
  With roaming eyes,
Cushioned on a dreary pillow,
  Thou art not wise;
Take the powers within thee sleeping,
Trim the plot that's in thy keeping;
Thou wilt bless the task when reaping
  Sweet labor's prize.

Since the green earth had beginning,
  Land, sea, and skies,
Toil their rounds with sleepless spinning,
  Suns sink and rise;

God, who with His image crown'd us,
Works within, above, around us;
Let us, where His will hath bound us,
    Work and be wise!

All the great that won before thee
    Stout labor's prize,
Wave their conquering banners o'er thee;
    Up and be wise!
Wilt thou from their sweat inherit
Fruits of peace and stars of merit,
While their sword, when thou shouldst wear it,
    Rust-eaten lies?

Work and wait, a sturdy liver;
    (Life fleetly flies!)
Work, and pray, and sing, and ever
    Lift hopeful eyes;
Let no blaring folly din thee!
Wisdom, when her charm may win thee,
Flows a well of life within thee;
    Young man, be wise!

                  John Stuart Blackie.

THE POOR AND HONEST SODGER.

WHEN wild war's deadly blast was blawn,
 And gentle peace returning,
Wi' mony a sweet babe fatherless,
 And mony a widow mourning;
I left the lines and tented field,
 Where lang I'd been a lodger,
My humble knapsack a' my wealth,
 A poor and honest sodger.

A leal light heart was in my breast,
 My hand unstained wi' plunder,
And for fair Scotia, hame again,
 I cheery on did wander.
I thought upon the banks o' Coil,
 I thought upon my Nancy,
I thought upon the witching smile
 That caught my youthful fancy.

At length I reached the bonny glen
 Where early life I sported;
I passed the mill, and trysting thorn,
 Where Nancy aft I courted:
Wha spied I but my ain dear maid,
 Down by her mother's dwelling!
And turned me round to hide the flood
 That in my een was swelling.

Wi' altered voice, quoth I, " Sweet lass,
 Sweet as yon hawthorn's blossom,
Oh! happy, happy may he be,
 That's dearest to thy bosom!

My purse is light, I've far to gang,
  And fain would be thy lodger;
I've served my king and country lang —
  Take pity on a sodger."

Sae wistfully she gazed on me,
  And lovelier was than ever;
Quo' she, " A sodger ance I lo'ed,
  Forget him shall I never:
Our humble cot, and hamely fare,
  Ye freely shall partake it,
That gallant badge — the dear cockade —
  Ye're welcome for the sake o't."

She gazed — she redden'd like a rose —
  Sayne[1] pale like any lily;
She sank within my arms, and cried,
  " Art thou my ain dear Willie?"
" By Him who made yon sun and sky,
  By whom true love's regarded,
I am the man; and thus may still
  True lovers be rewarded!

" The wars are o'er, and I'm come hame,
  And find thee still true-hearted;
Though poor in gear, we're rich in love,
  And mair, we'se ne'er be parted."
Quo' she, " My grandsire left me gowd,
  A mailen[2] plenished fairly,
And come, my faithful sodger lad,
  Thou'rt welcome to it dearly!"

---

1 Then.   2 Farm.

For gold the merchant plows the main,
 The farmer plows the manor;
But glory is the sodger's prize,
 The sodger's wealth is honor:
The brave poor sodger ne'er despise,
 Nor count him as a stranger;
Remember, he's his country's stay
 In day and hour of danger.

      Robert Burns.

FATHER'S GROWING OLD, JOHN!

OUR father's growing old, John!
 His eyes are growing dim,
And years are on his shoulders laid,
 A heavy weight for him.
And you and I are young and hale,
 And each a stalwart man,
And we must make his load as light
 And easy as we can.

He used to take the brunt, John!
 At cradle and the plow;
And earned our porridge by the sweat
 That trickled down his brow;
Yet never heard we him complain,
 Whate'er his toil might be,
Nor wanted e'er a welcome seat
 Upon his solid knee.

And when our boy-strength came, John!
  And sturdy grew each limb,
He brought us to the yellow field,
  To share the toil with him;
But he went foremost in the swath,
  Tossing aside the grain,
Just like the plow that heaves the soil,
  Or ships that sheer the main.

Now we must lead the van, John!
  Through weather foul and fair,
And let the old man read and doze,
  And tilt his easy-chair;
And he'll not mind it, John, you know,
  At eve to tell us o'er
Those brave old days of British times,
  Our grandsires and the war.

I heard you speak of ma'am, John!
  'Tis gospel what you say,
That caring for the like of us
  Has turned her head so gray!
Yes, John, I do remember well
  When neighbors called her vain,
And when her hair was long, and like
  A gleaming sheaf of grain.

Her lips were cherry red, John!
  Her cheeks were round and fair,
And like a ripened peach they swelled
  Against her wavy hair;

Her step fell lightly as the leaf
    From off the summer tree,
And all day busy at the wheel
    She sang to you and me.

She had a buxom arm, John!
    That wielded well the rod
Whene'er with willful step our feet
    The path forbidden trod;
But to the heaven of her eye
    We never looked in vain,
And evermore our yielding cry
    Brought down her tears like rain.

But this is long ago, John!
    And we are what we are,
And little heed we, day by day,
    Her fading cheek and hair;
And when beneath her faithful breast
    The tides no longer stir,
'Tis then, dear John, we most shall feel
    We had no friend like her!

Sure, there can be no harm, John!
    Thus speaking softly o'er
The blessed names of those, ere long,
  · Shall welcome us no more.
Nay, hide it not, for why shouldst thou
    An honest tear disown?
Thy heart will one day lighter be
    Remembering it has flown.

Yes, father's growing old, John!
  His eyes are getting dim,
And mother's treading softly down
  The deep descent with him.
And you and I are young and hale,
  And each a stalwart man,
And we must make their path as smooth
  And level as we can.

J. Q. A. Wood.

THE LOST AND FOUND.

SOME miners were sinking a shaft in Wales —
(I know not where — but the facts have fill'd
A chink in my brain, while other tales

Have been swept away, as when pearls are spill'd,
One pearl runs into a chink in the floor:) —
Somewhere, then, where God's light is kill'd,

And men tear in the dark at the earth's heart core,
These men were at work, when their axes knock'd
A hole in the passage closed years before.

A slip in the earth, I suppose, had block'd
This gallery suddenly up, with a heap
Of rubble, as safe as a chest is lock'd,

Till these men pick'd it! and 'gan to creep
In, on all fours.   Then a loud shout ran
Round the black roof — " Here's a man asleep!"

They all push'd forward, and scarce a span
From the mouth of the passage, in sooth, the lamp
Fell on the upturn'd face of a man.

No taint of death, no decaying damp
Had touch'd that fair young brow, whereon
Courage had set its glorious stamp.

Calm as a monarch upon his throne,
.Lips hard clench'd, no shadow of fear,
He sat there taking his rest, alone.

He must have been there for many a year;
The spirit had fled, but there was its shrine,
In clothes of a century old or near!

The dry and embalming air of the mine
Had arrested the natural hand of decay,
Nor faded the flesh, nor dimm'd a line.

Who was he, then?   No man could say
When the passage had suddenly fallen in —
Its memory, even, was passed away!

In their great rough arms, begrimed with coal,
They took him up, as a tender lass
Will carry a babe, from that darksome hole,

To the outer world of the short, warm grass;
Then up spoke one, " Let us send for Bess,
She is seventy-nine, come Martinmas;

" Older than any one here, I guess!
Belike, she may mind when the wall fell there,
And remember the chap by his comeliness! "

So they brought old Bess, with her silver hair,
To the side of the hill, where the dead man lay,
Ere the flesh had crumbled in outer air.

And the crowd around them all gave way,
As with tottering steps old Bess drew nigh,
And bent o'er the face of the unchanged clay.

Then suddenly rang a sharp, low cry!
Bess sank on her knees, and wildly toss'd
Her wither'd arms in the southern sky —

" O Willie! Willie! my lad! my lost!
The Lord be praised! after sixty years
I see you again! .   . .   The tears you cost,

" O Willie, darlin', were bitter tears!
They never looked for ye underground,
They told me a tale to mock my fears!

" They said ye were auver the sea — ye'd found
A lass ye loved better nor me — to explain
How ye'd a vanish'd fra sight and sound.

" O darlin', a long, long life o' pain
I ha' lived since then! . . . . And now I'm old,
'Seems a'most as if youth were come back again

" Seeing ye there wi' your locks o' gold,
And limbs as straight as ashen beams,
I a'most forget how the years ha' rolled

" Between us! . . . . O Willie! how strange it seems
To see ye here as I've seen ye oft,
Auver and auver again in dreams! "

In broken words like these, with soft,
Low wails she rock'd herself.   And none
Of the rough men around her scoff'd.

For surely a sight like this the sun
Had rarely looked upon.   Face to face,
The old dead love and the living one!

The dead, with its undimm'd fleshly grace,
At the end of threescore years; the quick,
Pucker'd and wither'd, without a trace

Of its warm girl-beauty!   A wizard's trick
Bringing the youth and the love that were
Back to the eyes of the old and sick!

Those bodies were just of one age; yet there
Death, clad in youth, had been standing still,
While Life had been fretting itself threadbare!

But the moment was come;—(as a moment will
To all who have loved, and have parted here,
And have toiled alone up the thorny hill ;

When, at the top, as their eyes see clear,
Over the mists in the vale below,
Mere specks their trials and toils appear,

Beside the eternal rest they know!)
Death came to old Bess that night, and gave
The welcome summons that she should go.

And now though the rains and the winds may rave,
Nothing can part them.   Deep and wide
The miners that evening dug one grave.

And there, while the summers and winters glide,
Old Bess and young Willie sleep side by side!

Hamilton Aide.

MASTER JOHNNY'S NEXT-DOOR NEIGHBOR.

"T was Spring the first time that I saw her, for her papa and mamma moved in
Next door, just as skating was over, and marbles about to begin;
For the fence in our back-yard was broken, and I saw as I peeped through the slat,
There were 'Johnny Jump-ups' all around her, and I knew it was Spring just by that.

"I never knew whether she saw me—for she didn't say nothing to me,
But 'Ma! here's a slat in the fence broke, and the boy that is next door can see.'
But the next day I climbed on our wood-shed, as, you know, mamma says I've a right,
And she calls out, 'Well, peekin' is manners!' and I answered her, 'Sass is perlite!'

"But I wasn't a bit mad, no, Papa, and to prove it, the very next day,
When she ran past our fence in the morning, I happened to get in her way,
For you know I am 'chunked' and clumsy, as she says are all boys of my size,
And she nearly upset me, she did, Pa, and laughed till tears came in her eyes.

"And then we were friends from that moment, for I know that she told Kitty Sage,
And she wasn't a girl that would flatter, 'that she thought I was tall for my age.'

And I gave her four apples that evening, and took her a
  ride on my sled,
And—'What am I telling you this for?' Why, Papa, my
  neighbor is *dead!*

" You don't hear one-half I am saying — I really do think
  It's too bad !
Why, you might have seen crape on her door-knob, and
  noticed to-day I've been sad.
And they've got her a coffin of rosewood, and they say
  they have dressed her in white,
And I've never once looked through the fence, Pa, since
  she died —- at eleven last night.

" And Ma says it's decent and proper, as I was her neighbor and friend,
That I should go there to the funeral, and she thinks that
  you ought to attend;
But I am so clumsy and awkward, I know I shall be in the
  way,
And suppose they should speak to me, Papa, I wouldn't
  know just what to say.

" So I think I will get up quite early, I know I sleep late,
  but I know
I'll be sure to wake up if our Bridget pulls the string that
  I'll tie to my toe,
And I'll crawl through the fence, and I'll gather the
  'Johnny Jump-ups' as they grew
Round her feet the first day that I saw her, and, Papa, I'll
  give them to you;

" For you're a big man, and you know, Pa, can come and
    go just where you choose;
And you'll take the flowers in to her, and surely they'll
    never refuse;
But, Papa, don't *say* they're from Johnny. *They* won't
    understand, don't you see —
But just lay them down on her bosom, and, Papa, *she'll*
    know they're from me."

Bret Harte.

ALONZO THE BRAVE AND THE FAIR IMOGENE.

WARRIOR bold, and a virgin so bright,
    Conversed as they sat on the green;
They gazed on each other with tender delight:
    Alonzo the Brave, was the name of the knight —
The maiden's, the Fair Imogene.

" And, oh," said the youth, " since to-morrow I go
    To fight in a far distant land,
Your tears for my absence soon ceasing to flow,
Some other will court you, and you will bestow
    On a wealthier suitor your hand! "

" Oh! hush these suspicions," Fair Imogene said,
    " Offensive to love and to me;
For, if you be living, or if you be dead,
I swear by the Virgin that none in your stead
    Shall husband of Imogene be.

" If e'er I by love or by wealth led aside,
    Forget my Alonzo the Brave,
God grant that, to punish my falsehood and pride,
Your ghost at the marriage may sit by my side,
May tax me with perjury, claim me as bride,
    And bear me away to the grave! "

To Palestine hastened the hero so bold,
    His love she lamented him sore;
But scarce had a twelvemonth elapsed, when, behold
A Baron, all covered with jewels and gold,
    Arrived at Fair Imogene's door.

His treasures, his presents, his spacious domain,
    Soon made her untrue to her vows;
He dazzled her eyes, he bewildered her brain;
He caught her affections, so light and so vain,
    And carried her home as his spouse.

And now had the marriage been blest by the priest;
    The revelry now was begun;
The tables they groaned with the weight of the feast,
Nor yet had the laughter and merriment ceased,
    When the bell at the castle tolled — one.

Then first with amazement Fair Imogene found
    A stranger was placed by her side:
His air was terrific; he uttered no sound —
He spoke not, he moved not, he looked not around —
    But earnestly gazed on the bride.

His vizor was closed, and gigantic his height,
    His armor was sable to view;
All pleasure and laughter was hushed at his sight;
The dogs, as they eyed him, drew back in affright ;
    The lights in the chamber burned blue!

His presence all bosoms appeared to dismay;
  The guests sat in silence and fear;
At length spoke the bride — while she trembled — " I pray,
Sir knight, that your helmet aside you would lay,
  And deign to partake of our cheer."

The lady is silent ; the stranger complies —
  His vizor he slowly unclosed;
Oh, God ! what a sight met Fair Imogene's eyes!
What words can express her dismay and surprise
  When a skeleton's head was exposed!

All present then uttered a terrified shout,
  All turned with disgust from the scene;
The worms they crept in, and the worms they crept out,
And sported his eyes and his temples about,
  While the specter addressed Imogene:

" Behold me, thou false one, behold me!" he cried.
  " Remember Alonzo the Brave!
God grants that, to punish thy falsehood and pride,
My ghost at thy marriage should sit by thy side;
Should tax thee with perjury, claim thee as bride,
  And bear thee away to the grave!"

Thus saying, his arms round the lady he wound,
  While loudly she shrieked in dismay;
Then sunk with his prey through the wide-yawning ground,
Nor ever again was Fair Imogene found,
  Or the specter that bore her away.

Not long lived the baron, and none since that time,
  To inhabit the castle presume;
For chronicles tell that, by order sublime,
There Imogene suffers the pain of her crime,
  And mourns her deplorable doom.

At midnight, four times in each year, does her sprite,
  When mortals in slumber are bound,
Arrayed in her bridal apparel of white,
Appear in the hall with her skeleton knight,
  And shriek as he whirls her around !

While they drink out of skulls newly torn from the grave,
  Dancing round them the specters are seen;
Their liquor is blood, and this horrible stave
They howl: " To the health of Alonzo the Brave,
  And his consort, the Fair Imogene!"

M. G. Lewis.

SONG OF THE MISER.

LINK, clink!
  There's a ray of light through the window
    chink,
  That comes to play with my gold, I think;
I must bar it out to-morrow.
I'll have no sun-rays counting my store:
They come from a world that's hungry for more,
That spieth my coffers and hateth me sore,
  That I know to my sorrow.

    Clink, clink!
How the golden eagles glow on the brink
Of the yellow pyramid, built, I think,
  From spoils of every people.
Say I frame me a miniature church the while,
Moidore and Sovereign will pave me the Aisle,
Doubloons and Ducats will wall it in style,
  And crowns run up to a steeple.

Clink, clink!
A beggar-girl stood on the parapet brink
Of the lonely bridge — quite crazy, I think,
    And I gazed on the moaning water.
She asked for a farthing; I gave her a curse;
She plunged and the city provided a hearse;
No matter — it might have been terribly worse;
    'Twas only a poor man's daughter.

Clink, clink!
A delicate eyelid flashed me a wink,
Yesterday — close by the park, I think;
    What widow was it, I wonder?
Who'll smile upon me, grim, ugly, and old;
If the forks of the lightning were woven with gold
They would lasso each flash with a veil's white fold,
    Despite the following thunder.

Clink, clink!
My beautiful gold, thy beams I drink;
Brighter, more nectrous than wine, I think:
    Thy glint like stars of even.
I love thee better than sun-brown hair,
Better than sick men June's warm air,
Better than angels the penitent prayer,
    Better, aye, better than Heaven.

Anonymous.

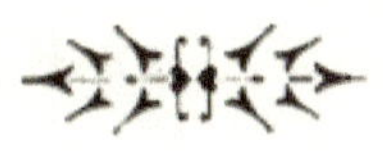

THE HARP OF FIONBELL.

["Feargus, called Fionbell, or 'The Sweet-Voiced,' was one of the most distinguished bards of Ancient Erin." An ode of his is said to have produced the effect mentioned in the following verses.]

FULL many triumphs hath music won, in cottage, and bower, and hall,
Since David harped in the days of old, to quiet the soul of Saul;
The evil spirit departed then, and the moody King " was well;"
And evil spirits were charmed to rest by the Harp of Fionbell!
    Who shall revive thy magic spell,
    O silent Harp of Fionbell?

Long time ago, when the ancient bards and wandering minstrels sang,
With lays of love and with martial strains their quivering harp-strings rang:
They soothed, or melted, or fired the soul, as the thrilling cadence fell —
The victor's pæan — the hymn of praise — the warrior's parting knell.
    But mightier was thy magic spell,
    O gentle Harp of Fionbell!

The voice of music hath roused the brave, and kindled the champion's zeal;
The voice of music hath softly lulled the sorrows it could not heal;

The voice of music hath roused to life fierce passions and
    purpose fell —
Of revels wild, and of festal mirth, the spirit of song can
    tell.
        But thine hath been a loftier spell,
        O silent Harp of Fionbell!

The power of music is imaged forth by the fabled
    Orpheus' lyre —
The voice of music hath skill to quell the glittering ser-
    pent's ire —
It wakes an echo in human hearts; from the organ's grand-
    est swell
To tiny sighings of prisoned airs that lurk in an ocean shell.
        But holier was thy magic spell,
        O gentle Harp of Fionbell!

Not only nerving the hero's arm, or vaunting the van-
    quished foe;
Or reaping laurels of smiles and tears, and conquests of
    joy and woe;
Not only breathing the notes of love, but pleading for
    war to cease,
In strain so dulcet that strife was stilled, and weapons
    were sheathed in peace!
        So rare — so sweet — thy magic spell,
        Long silent Harp of Fionbell!

Two hostile chiefs meet in armed array on the plains of
    Droom-Choll-Coil,*
In hot dispute to contest their claim of right to the battle-
    spoil;

---

* "Droom-Choll-Coil," the "Brow of a Hazel-Wood," was one of the
ancient names of Dublin.

And face to face with the marshaled foe, their valiant fol-
    lowers stand:
What turns the wrath from the angry brow? the axe from
    the lifted hand?
        Only a song of magic spell!
        Harped on the Harp of Fionbell!

The silvery tones have calmed the strife — the warrior
    feud is done —
The hostile chieftains are clasping hands, with a nobler
    battle won!
The battle over the *self within*, where deadliest foemen
    dwell;
With bloodshed stayed, and with friendship, sealed by the
    Harp of Fionbell.
        O to renew thy magic spell!
        Victorious Harp of Fionbell!

Where *now* would foemen forego their feuds, at the harp-
    ing of a bard?
Hath poet-genius no magic left? or are hero's hearts
    more hard?
Alas! alas! that the minstrel's art should triumph like
    this no more!
Alas! that never such " sweet-voiced " bard should waken
    on Erin's shore,
        To work again thy mighty spell,
        O glorious Harp of Fionbell.

                                    H. E. Hunter.

THE GREEN GNOME.

RING, sing! ring, sing! pleasant Sabbath bells!
Chime, rhyme! chime, rhyme! through dales and
    dells!
Rhyme, ring! chime, sing! pleasant Sabbath bells!
Chime, sing! rhyme, ring! over fields and fells!

And I gallop'd, and I gallop'd, on my palfry white as milk,
My robe was of the sea-green woof, my serk was of the
    silk;
My hair was golden yellow, and it floated to my shoe,
My eyes were like two harebells bathed in little drops of
    dew;
My palfrey, never stopping, made a music sweetly blent
With the leaves of autumn dropping all around me as I
    went;
And I heard the bells, grown fainter, far behind me peal
    and play,
Fainter, fainter, fainter, till they seemed to die away;
And beside a silver runnel, on a little heap of sand,
I saw the Green Gnome sitting, with his cheek upon his
    hand;
Then he started up to see me, and he ran with cry and
    bound,
And drew me from my palfrey white, and set me on the
    ground:
O crimson, crimson were his locks, his face was green to
    see,
But he cried, "O light-haired lassie, you are bound to
    marry me!"
He clasped me round the middle small, and kissed me on
    the cheek,

He kissed me once, he kissed me twice — I could not stir
    or speak;
He kissed me twice, he kissed me thrice — but when he
    kissed again,
I called aloud upon the name of him who died for men!

Ring, sing! ring, sing! pleasant Sabbath bells!
Chime, rhyme! chime, rhyme! through dales and dells!
Rhyme, ring! chime, sing! pleasant Sabbath bells!
Chime, sing! rhyme, ring! over fields and fells!

O faintly, faintly, faintly, calling men and maids to pray,
So faintly, faintly, faintly, rang the bells afar away;
And as I named the Blessed Name, as in our need we can,
The ugly green, green Gnome became a tall and comely
    man!
His hands were white, his beard was gold, his eyes were
    black as sloes,
His tunic was of scarlet woof, and silken were his hose;
A pensive light from Fairyland still lingered on his cheek,
His voice was like the running brook, when he began to
    speak:
" O you have cast away the charm my step-dame put on
    me,
Seven years I dwelt in Fairyland, and you have set me
    free!
O I will mount thy palfrey white, and ride to kirk with
    thee,
And by those little dewy eyes, we twain will wedded be!"
Back we gallop'd, never stopping, he before, and I behind,
And the autumn leaves were dropping, red and yellow, in
    the wind,

And the sun was shining clearer, and my heart was high
    and proud,
And nearer, nearer, nearer, rang the kirk-bells sweet and
    loud,
And we saw the kirk before us, as we trotted down the
    fells,
And nearer, clearer, o'er us, rang the welcome of the
    bells!

Ring, sing! ring, sing! pleasant Sabbath bells!
Chime, rhyme! chime, rhyme, through dales and dells!
Rhyme, ring! chime, sing! pleasant Sabbath bells!
Chime, sing! rhyme, ring! over fields and dells!

Robert Buchanan.

POVERTIE'S COUNSEL.

'IS a bitter spring, and everything
     Pineth for a sunny hour,
The bird on the tree, the honey-bee,
     And the early flower;
But the winds blow, and the wintry snow
     Falleth, shower on shower.

In a lodging bare, on an old fir chair,
     I sit by a gleamless hearth,
Dreaming alway of some by-gone day
     And its pleasant mirth;
And along with me, sitteth Povertie,
     Despised of all the earth.

Hours come and go, tides ebb and flow,
     And flow and ebb again—
But it seemeth no chance or circumstance
     Of time shall part us twain;
Fast bound unto me, seemeth Povertie,
     With an everlasting chain.

In the open street, old friends ne'er greet
     As they were wont of yore,
But hurry by, with averted eye,
     They can love me now no more,
For, arm-in-arm, with me walketh Povertie,
     And he scareth 'em by the score.

There and here ever, he leaveth me never,
     Though I've prayed 't might not be so,
And alack, I have sworn, and abused him sore,

Very oft that he might go;
But he still sat there, nor seemed to care,
    Answering me ever — " No. "

" Though all men hate and upbraid the fate,
    Makes them and me akin,
Yet better," he said, lifting his head,
    " Have me thine house within,
Much better have me," quoth Povertie,
    " Than either shame or sin."

'Tis a bitter spring, yet the birds will sing
    On the leafy boughs of each tree,
And flowers will blow, and green grass grow,
    And sunshine lure forth the bee,
And fortune may smile on thee, meanwhile
    Shake hands," quoth Povertie.

                                        W. S. Ridpath.

LANGLEY LANE.

A LOVE POEM.

N all the land, range up, range down,
    Is there ever a place so pleasant and sweet,
As Langley Lane in London town,
    Just out of the bustle of square and street?
Little white cottages all in a row,
Gardens where bachelors' buttons grow,
    Swallows' nests in roof and wall,
And up above the still blue sky
Where the woolly white clouds go sailing by —
    I seem to be able to see it all!

Fanny is sweet thirteen, and she
    Has fine black ringlets and dark eyes clear,
And I am older by summers three—
    Why should we hold one another so dear?
Because she cannot utter a word,
Nor hear the music of bee or bird,
    The water-cart's splash or the milkman's call!
Because I have never seen the sky,
Nor the little singers that hum and fly—
    Yet know she is gazing upon them all!

For the sun is shining, the swallows fly,
    The bees and the blue-flies murmur low,
And I hear the water-cart go by,
    With its cool splash-splash down the dusty row;
And the little one close at my side perceives
Mine eyes upraised to the cottage eaves,
    Where birds are chirping in summer shine,
And I hear, though I cannot look, and she,
Though she cannot hear, can the singers see—
    And the little soft fingers flutter in mine!

Hath not the dear little hand a tongue,
    When it stirs on my palm for the love of me?
Do I not know she is pretty and young?
    Hath not my soul an eye to see?—
'Tis pleasure to make one's bosom stir,
To wonder how things appear to her,
    That I only hear as they pass around;
And as long as we sit in the music and light,
She is happy to keep God's sight,
    And *I* am happy to keep God's sound.

For now, in summer, I take my chair,
    And sit outside in the sun, and hear
The distant murmur of street and square,
    And the swallows and sparrows chirping near;
And Fanny, who lives just over the way,
Comes running many a time each day
    With her little hand's touch so warm and kind,
And I smile and talk, with the sun on my cheek,
And the little live hand seems to stir and speak —
    For Fanny is dumb, and I am blind.

Why, I know her face, though I am blind —
    I made it of music long ago:
Strange large eyes, and dark hair twined
    Round the pensive light of a brow of snow;
And when I sit by my little one,
And hold her hand and talk in the sun,
    And hear the music that haunts the place,
I know she is raising her eyes to me,
And guessing how gentle my voice must be,
    And *seeing* the music on my face.

Though, if ever the Lord should grant me a prayer
    (I know the fancy is only vain),
I should pray; just once, when the weather is fair,
    To see little Fanny, and Langley Lane;
Though Fanny, perhaps, would pray to hear
The voice of the friend that she holds so dear,
    The song of the birds, the hum of the street —
It is better to be as we have been —
Each keeping up something, unheard, unseen,
    To make God's heaven more strange and sweet!

Ah! life is pleasant in Langley Lane!
　　There is always something sweet to hear!
Chirping of birds or patter of rain!
　　And Fanny, my little one, always near!
And though I am weakly and can't live long,
And Fanny my darling is far from strong,
　　And though we can never married be –
What then? – since we hold one another so dear,
For the sake of the pleasure one cannot hear,
　　And the pleasure that only one can see?

Robert Buchanan.

" The battle totters; now the wounds begin. "

THE BATTLE OF PELUSIUM.

ARM, arm, arm, arm! the scouts are all come in;
Keep your ranks close, and now your honors win.
Behold, from yonder hill the foe appears;
Bows, bills, glaves, arrows, shields, and spears!
Like a dark wood he comes, or tempest pausing;
Oh, view the wings of horse the meadows scouring.
The vanguard marches bravely.   Hark, the drums!
                    Dub, dub!

They meet, they meet, and now the battle comes:
            See how the arrows fly,
            That darken all the sky!
            Hark how the trumpets sound,
            Hark how the hills rebound.
                    Tara, tara, tara, tara, tara !

Hark how the horses charge! in, boys, boys, in!
The battle totters; now the wounds begin:
            Oh, how they cry!
            Oh, how they die!
Room for the valiant Memnon, armed with thunder!
See how he breaks the ranks asunder!
They fly! they fly! Eumenes has the chase,
And brave Polybius makes good his place.
            To the plains, to the woods,
            To the rocks, to the floods,
They fly for succor: Follow, follow, follow!
Hark how the soldiers holloa! *Hey, Hey!*
            Brave Diocles is dead,
            And all his soldiers fled;
            The battle's won, and lost,
            That many a life hath cost.
                    John Fletcher.

OFT, IN THE STILLY NIGHT.

SCOTCH AIR.

OFT, in the stilly night,
  Ere Slumber's chain has bound me,
Fond Memory brings the light
  Of other days around me;
    The smiles, the tears,
    Of boyhood's years,
  The words of love then spoken;
    The eyes that shone,
    Now dimm'd and gone,
  The cheerful hearts now broken!
Thus, in the stilly night,
  Ere Slumber's chain hath bound me,
Sad Memory brings the light
  Of other days around me.

When I remember all
  The friends, so link'd together,
I've seen around me fall,
  Like leaves in wintry weather;
    I feel like one
    Who treads alone
  Some banquet-hall deserted,
    Whose lights are fled,
    Whose garlands dead,
  And all but he departed!
Thus, in the stilly night,
  Ere Slumber's chain has bound me,
Sad Memory brings the light
  Of other days around me.

Moore.

THOSE EVENING BELLS.

AIR—THE BELLS OF ST. PETERSBURG.

THOSE evening bells! those evening bells!
  How many a tale their music tells,
Of youth, and home, and that sweet time,
When last I heard their soothing chime.

Those joyous hours are pass'd away;
And many a heart, that then was gay,
Within the tomb now darkly dwells,
And hears no more those evening bells.

And so 'twill be when I am gone;
That tuneful peal will still ring on,
While other bards shall walk these dells,
And sing your praise, sweet evening bells.

Moore.

A CANADIAN BOAT SONG.

WRITTEN ON THE RIVER ST. LAWRENCE.

Et remigem cantus hortatur.
Quintilian.

FAINTLY as tolls the evening chime,
  Our voices keep tune and our oars keep time,
Soon as the woods on shore look dim,
We'll sing at St. Ann's our parting hymn.
Row, brothers, row, the stream runs fast,
The Rapids are near and the daylight's past.

Why should we yet our sail unfurl?
There is not a breath the blue wave to curl;
But, when the wind blows off the shore,
Oh! sweetly we'll rest our weary oar.

Blow, breezes, blow, the stream runs fast,
The Rapids are near and the daylight's past.

Utawas' tide! this trembling moon
Shall see us float over thy surges soon.
Saint of this green isle! hear our prayers,
Oh, grant us cool heavens and favoring airs.
Blow, breezes, blow, the stream runs fast,
The Rapids are near and the daylight's past.

Moore.

THE IMMORTAL PANSIES.

[At an elegant lunch given by Mrs. Cleveland at the White House, in honor of Miss Hastings, the President's niece, sixty of the leading young ladies of Washington were present. At each plate was a corsage bouquet of pansies in all shades, from the most delicate lavender to the richest royal purple, interspersed with those of bright gold. The viands were of the richest, but no wine was offered, as Mrs. Cleveland does not drink it, nor will she offer it to her guests.]

BEAUTIFUL pansies, in royal robes
Of richest purple and brightest gold!
You could not smile on a lovelier scene,
Or grace the court of a fairer queen,
Than when you greeted this winsome band,
And by your fragrance the welcome told —
Told to each youthful guest, who joyed to come
To her gracious hostess' honored home.

No presence or breath of wine was there
To drown with its strength your rare perfume;
But fresh and pure from the hand which gives
The flowers, and their mission to bless our lives,
Your sweetness in praises was wafted wide,
And to you is given immortal bloom.
But the fairest flower of that radiant scene
Was our thoughtful pansy, our nation's queen.

Mrs. Marietta S. Case.